The Flower Show Murder

ALSO BY FAITH MARTIN

THE FLOWER SHOW MURDER

FAITH MARTIN

Revised edition 2024
Joffe Books, London
www.joffebooks.com

First published by Robert Hale in 2015
as *An Unholy Whiff of Death* by Joyce Cato

This paperback edition was first published
in Great Britain in 2024

Cover art by Nick Castle

ISBN: 978-1-83526-743-1

CHAPTER 1

Thunder was distinctly threatening to grace the sultry August afternoon with its noisy presence when Monica Noble prudently brought in the last of her washing from the line and entered her cheerful yellow kitchen.

Pushing the damp dark hair back off her forehead, she walked to the fridge and, pouring herself a long glass of deliciously cold lemonade, swallowed two-thirds of it thirstily before starting on the folding. She was just about finished when her husband, Graham Noble, walked in from his study and put the kettle on. He'd been the vicar of their small Cotswold village of Heyford Bassett for the past twenty years, but only a married man for nearly two of those years.

'Is Mrs Parsons all right?' Monica asked, knowing that he'd just had an appointment with one of the villagers, whose husband, due to a degenerative illness, would shortly be in need of a wheelchair.

'She's remarkably cheerful, all things considered,' he replied with a small sigh. 'I'm not sure that the reality of their situation has sunk in just yet. I'm getting on to social services first thing.' He poured hot water from the kettle into the teapot and said softly, 'You'll have a cup, won't you?'

Monica, putting the washing to one side, walked up behind him and slipped her arms around his waist, offering comfort and support. At thirty-six, she was fifteen years her husband's junior. Not that the age difference was particularly noticeable, since Graham looked a good decade younger than his fifty-one years. He was also one of those dark, lean, poetically good-looking men who seemed to have a magic formula against age, and who wore a handsome face with effortless ease and a complete lack of vanity.

No wonder the ladies of his parish had been rather put out to hear of his marriage to a widow from London, especially one with a rebellious teenage daughter.

Graham felt his wife's arms snake around his waist, and reached down to cover her hands with his. To say that Monica had come into his life and changed it as radically as a tornado was something of an understatement, and he was still saying thanks for her in his nightly prayers. And he expected he'd still be doing so when he was in his nineties.

'Oh, that's the afternoon post,' Monica said, hearing a distant rattle out in the hall. She moved off to collect the usual mixture of bills, circulars, and — at times — heartbreaking letters that came to the enormous vicarage.

The building itself was a 300-year-old edifice that had been converted into twelve flats not so long ago. An event that had not been entirely successful, since it had resulted in the murder of one of the tenants. Monica, however, was determined to put that terrible memory behind her, even though she herself had been instrumental in solving it. Besides, new people had since moved in, and with all the flats now full, the vicarage was once more a home, a place of noise and busy human interest. The Nobles inhabited flat 1, with its own private entrance on the ground floor and sweeping views of the huge communal gardens and the river beyond.

Monica was absently sifting through the post as she walked back to the kitchen, being careful to separate family mail from Graham's work-related correspondence.

Graham, in his habitual lightweight black trousers, blue-grey shirt, and pristine white dog collar, was sitting at the table sipping hot tea, apparently impervious to the enervating weather.

'Hello, there's something here from James,' Monica said, recognizing the handwriting of the Reverend James Davies, one of Graham's oldest friends, and the vicar of the large village of Caulcott Green, situated about six miles away. With a smile, she passed it across to her husband.

She then opened the telephone bill and blanched. Carol-Ann Clancy, Monica's daughter (who was sixteen going on thirty), hadn't been any too happy to leave the bustle of London behind along with her school and her vast network of friends for the peace and quiet of the rural Cotswolds. And because their change in lifestyle had been rather enormous, Monica had been prepared to be patient with her, and maybe just a bit too indulgent. But perhaps now, two years on, it was time that she started taking on a few more of the responsibilities of an adult.

Like paying her own telephone bill!

'What do you know about sweet peas, Mon?' Graham asked, making his wife blink at him blankly, and trawl her somewhat erratic memory for any horticultural data that may have come her way. Unfortunately, not a lot had, it seemed.

'Huh . . . they climb up sticks, they're pastel in colour, and they smell nice,' she said vaguely. 'Why?'

'Hmm, I doubt that'll be good enough, I'm afraid, so you might want to read up a bit on the subject. Apparently, you're judging them at this year's flower show at Caulcott Green,' he added casually, smiling across at her with just a little wicked twinkle in his dark eyes.

'Oh, that's nice,' Monica said weakly. 'James has been organizing again, has he?'

'James has,' Graham confirmed. His old friend was rather noted for it. 'And volunteering all and sundry for who knows what, it seems. We're probably getting off lightly, knowing James. I'm judging the lilies, apparently.'

'How nice of him to let us know,' Monica said, with a wicked twinkle of her own in her cornflower-blue eyes. This kind of by-your-leave bombshell was typical of Graham's friend.

Her husband laughed. 'I know, I know. But he always means well. Besides, the Caulcott Green annual flower show *is* quite an experience,' he assured her. 'It's been going on for donkey's years; the whole village is determined to keep it up and running on tried and true, good old-fashioned lines. *Tradition*, don't you know,' he said, mock gravely. 'Every year the same old die-hards set up the traditional stalls: white elephant, tombola, Aunt Sally, you name it. Everyone donates, everyone attends, everyone bakes cakes for the WI stall or whatever. I swear, between them, James, Wendy, Sir Hugh, and the countess are utterly determined to hold onto this one piece of medieval entertainment in defiance of any television sensation, pop culture or computer game.'

Monica, who'd been thinking how quaint it all sounded, and how comforting, in this day and age, to know that not all rural pastimes were disintegrating and disappearing, found her attention snared. 'The countess?' she echoed, questioningly, wondering what resident villager must have exhibited such excess signs of snobbery in order to be given such an unkind label. 'Not a real countess, presumably?'

'Oh, isn't she though?' Graham corrected her with a grin. 'But strictly of the impoverished and all-but-forgotten-and-extinct kind, mind you. Daphne Cadge-Hampton, Dowager Countess of Fulcome, to be exact. She lives in one of those big crumbling houses on the outskirts of the village,' Graham explained. 'Eighty if she's a day, and a character that would have made even Oscar Wilde think he was overdoing it if he'd put her in one of his plays. She's opening, of course.'

'Opening what?'

'The flower show. Do keep up,' he mock-admonished. Monica threw the dishcloth at him, which he ducked expertly. He continued to read his friend's letter. 'Sir Hugh

Featherstone is chairman of the flower show, by the way, and has his eye on the much coveted Cadge-Hampton Gladiolus Cup this year by the sounds of it.'

Monica's bright blue eyes, peering out from under her dark fringe, widened. 'Do I want to know about the Cadge-Hampton cup?' she asked cautiously.

Graham grinned. 'It's a monstrous piece of silver the late count forked out for back in the 1930s, and is the bee's knees.'

'Bee's knees?' her eyebrow elevated.

'Bee's knees,' Graham echoed firmly. 'It's only ever awarded for really grade-A gladioli, so it can go for whole decades without being given out at all. Sir Hugh covets it with a lust that is most unseemly.' He put on his pompous vicar voice, then spoiled it by grinning. 'The other hot area this year is the dahlias, apparently. The field's wide open for that one. Nobody much cares about the other categories, though, and it's generally accepted that old Sam Dix will always win the roses.'

'Poor us,' Monica said, reading over her husband's shoulder and grinning. 'I see James has nabbed the dahlias for himself.'

Graham laughed. 'Probably because that's the only way to stop World War Three from breaking out. Nobody is going to lay one on the vicar if he awards the top rosette to a hated rival. Though, come to think of it, I'm not so sure.' His eyes narrowed thoughtfully. 'Those dahlia-growers . . .' he lay his hand flat in the air and rocked it from side to side in a telling gesture, 'they're a dodgy lot.'

Monica laughed. 'Like that, is it? Oh well, so long as I don't get brained by a little old lady because I didn't appreciate her sweet peas, I suppose I'll survive.'

'Survive what?' asked a voice, proceeding from a blonde vision that had appeared in the doorway.

Monica observed her daughter with a fond eye as she sashayed across the kitchen, oozing near-fatal ennui as only a teenager can. 'Survive the Caulcott Green flower show,' she said, and waited for it.

She caught Graham's eye and found him also tensed for the attack, for Carol-Ann persisted in thinking that anything less grand than a first night at the opera was well below her attention. So it was hardly surprising that their jaws dropped with surprise when she swung around from the contents of the fridge that she'd been fussily contemplating with a smile on her face and her big blue eyes wide with interest.

'Really? When's this?'

'Er . . . a week next Saturday.' Monica, only by dint of having had more practice, recovered from the shock first.

'Great. Can I come?' Carol-Ann asked, oh so casually tossing her long, silk-straight blonde locks over one nicely tanned shoulder. She was wearing very short white shorts and a pink and white sleeveless top that didn't quite reach her navel. No doubt she felt she was overdressed.

'Of course you can,' Monica squeaked, foolishly hoping that, finally, her daughter was beginning to recover from her permanent countryside-blues sulk.

She really should have known better.

'OK. I'll have to buy a new outfit then,' Carol-Ann said sweetly.

Graham blinked. 'For a flower show?' he quavered. Even after two years of practice, he was nowhere close to playing in Carol-Ann's league yet.

Carol-Ann gave her stepfather an amused, reluctantly fond smile. 'Course,' she said scornfully. It was a constant source of annoyance to her that she found herself rather liking Graham Noble. When she'd told all her friends that her mother was marrying a vicar — a *vicar* of all people — she'd basked in all the horrified sympathy that had flooded her way, doomed as she was to suffer the slings and arrows of her stepfather's piety and tyranny.

So it was really jarring to her that she found Graham so likeable. Not to mention the fact that all her friends, both old and new, thought him 'hot.' Still, she was beginning to look on him not so much as a real dad, obviously, but as something akin to a favourite uncle, maybe.

'Er . . . OK then,' Graham agreed, forgivably losing his head. He reached for his wallet and extracted some ten pound notes.

'Thanks,' Carol-Ann said, graciously accepting the cash. 'I'll put the date in my diary.' They watched her saunter back out, as waif-like as she'd sauntered in, and looked at one another in blank amazement.

'Something's up,' Monica predicted gloomily.

'Has she got her exam results yet?' Graham asked cautiously, and their eyes met in mutually panicked understanding.

Carol-Ann wanted to be either a games designer or a supermodel. She hadn't yet made up her mind. And whilst she had the brains and ability to be a computer whizz-kid, she also had the face and physical wherewithal to at least think that she had a chance of being a model as well.

She'd inherited her natural father's blond hair and her mother's big blue eyes; she had an elfin face that was all her own, and a wispy, yet somehow quite substantial figure that had attracted boys like bees to honey pots ever since she'd hit puberty.

'No, I'm sure the exam results haven't been published yet,' Monica mused. And although prayer was usually her husband's department, she hadn't spared her own knees in getting down on them and asking the Almighty to make sure that Carol-Ann's grades were all straight As. Because Carol-Ann had stated that if they were, she was definitely going on to do A-levels and then, hopefully, to university to take a degree in computer science.

If not, she'd run away to London and become the next Kate Moss.

'Well, I suppose I'd better give James a ring and tell him that we accept his orders . . . sorry, I mean his gracious offer,' Graham corrected himself with a wicked little smile. 'He could have given us a bit more notice, though.'

Monica shrugged. 'I suppose he's had other things on his mind,' she said, her voice full of sudden sympathy.

Graham looked up and then went a little pale. 'Of course he has. I wasn't thinking.'

Six months ago, Wendy and James Davies had lost their eight-year-old son Tommy to that parental nightmare that was meningitis.

'He seems to be coping well,' Monica offered hopefully after a short, painful silence had fallen between them.

'Yes. Yes, I think so too — well, as well as can be expected. But Wendy definitely isn't. I saw her a few days ago in Cirencester; she looked like a ghost.'

Monica bit her lip. 'Well, it's bound to take time,' she said inadequately.

Also, it was always worse for a mother, she thought, but of course, wouldn't have dreamed of saying it out loud.

Graham sighed, then nodded and went to his study to telephone them. When he came back he looked a little more cheerful. 'Well, that's all arranged.'

'It's being held in the playing field, I take it?'

'Right,' Graham confirmed. 'With a bouncy castle, a vintage tractor display, and some sort of kiddies' roundabout. And the huge marquee, of course.' He sighed. 'I suppose the dreaded lab people will be there in force.'

Monica nodded. 'I daresay. Are they still being a thorn in the village's side?'

'Bound to be,' Graham said. 'But I would have hoped, by now at least, that the community leaders are beginning to accept them. James has been desperately building bridges between the two factions for months now.'

Monica didn't envy the vicar of Caulcott Green the task. Nearly a year ago, Franklyn House, a big old place with a plethora of outbuildings opposite Sir Hugh's own manor house, had been sold to Ross Ferris, a chemical manufacturer, who'd promptly converted the complex into a working research laboratory. And whilst it undoubtedly brought much-needed jobs to the area, the locals were hardly ecstatic about it. Complaints were constantly being made about the small incinerator, the potential, if unknown hazards to their health, and the unnecessary secrecy of what went on up there. The current rumour doing the rounds was that it was government funded, and that all sorts of bacteriological germ warfare nasties might accidentally be let loose. (Or maybe not even so accidentally, if you listened to some of the more vocal conspiracy nuts and anti-government enthusiasts.)

You name it, some villager suspected it.

To make matters worse, Ross Ferris was not the kind of man to win friends and influence people. A bombastic, self-satisfied, self-made millionaire, he seemed determined to railroad everyone to his way of thinking, which seemed to be that what was good for Ross Ferris was good for everyone. He'd recently shouldered his way onto the local council, and was fast becoming the most despised man for miles around.

Sir Hugh, for one, positively hated his guts.

'Things must have calmed down some since the last time we visited James and Wendy,' Monica offered hopefully.

Graham looked rather doubtful, but agreed obligingly, 'Yes. Perhaps.'

Monica rose and picked up the washing; a few days in the airing cupboard wouldn't hurt them. As she passed her husband, she blew him a kiss. 'You do take me to the nicest places,' she said cheekily.

* * *

Dr Gordon Trenning, one of Ferris Labs' top chemical and computer engineers, pulled his luxurious new BMW to a halt in a cul-de-sac of council houses and turned nervously towards the girl sitting beside him.

Linda Gregson was in her early twenties with a mass of reddish-brown hair, deep brown eyes, legs that never stopped, and a predatory sexual nature that both thrilled and alarmed Gordon's naturally cautious soul in equal measure.

'You coming in?' she asked nonchalantly, opening the door and swinging her legs out in a way that she'd once seen Beyoncé do in a pop video.

'Er, I'd better not,' Gordon said nervously. Linda's father didn't like him.

Like most unmarried women in Caulcott Green, Linda still lived with her parents. In the current financial market, it was hard for locals to afford a place of their own.

'Chicken,' she teased, but leaned back into the car and kissed him with some force, deliberately coating his thin mouth with 'blush of dawn' lipstick. 'See ya tomorrow, then?' she said, letting her hand linger suggestively against his thigh before getting out. Sometimes she found that his shyness and awkwardness around women brought out a spiteful streak in her nature.

Gordon gulped and nodded, then watched her short-skirted form walk around the front of his car and enter through her garden gate. The swish of a suspicious curtain from inside the house, however, had him quickly accelerating away.

At forty-two, Gordon was not an obvious ladies' man. His brown hair was thinning, his tall frame was lanky rather than lean, and his dress sense was not particularly notable. Back in London, he'd been eminently anonymous. But here in Caulcott Green, an unattached, highly educated professional male was a big catch. And the salary he earned at the lab was, by itself, enough to set many a fond mother's mouth a-watering and thrusting unmarried daughters his way.

Linda Gregson, however, was in the top running. She was wily and pretty, and had the instincts of an alley cat that had found a prime fishbone and wasn't about to give it up. And Gordon knew it. He just wasn't sure how to feel about it.

As he drove up to the front gate of the lab and nodded to the guard on duty there (a local lad who told everyone that he was 'in security'), he wiped a hand wearily over his forehead. Around him the air rumbled with ominous thunder, and fat raindrops began to bounce off his windshield.

He was not used to dealing with the likes of Linda, or the other young lady who was currently trying to wrest him so assiduously from Linda's ample bosom. In some ways he revelled in his new-found popularity and the suggestion of power it gave him. But an innately honest part of himself could never let him forget that it was all a sham, a misleading and potentially painful distortion of who he really was — a nondescript nobody. A failure. A nothing.

As the gates opened and the uniformed young man waved him in, Gordon had the grace to laugh at himself. If only his mother could see him now. She'd long despaired of ever getting him off her hands — quite rightly, as it had transpired, for he'd lived with her, in their neat little semi in Fulham, right up until her death. He'd been thirty-eight.

He'd always been a clever boy, a swot and a teacher's pet, a combination that had earned him a place at Oxford and his subsequent career, but he had few social skills and even fewer friends. And now even his professional life had become a mockery.

As he parked in his reserved space, he admitted to himself that Linda didn't love him. Indeed, for all he could tell, Linda might not even *like* him very much. It was a depressing thought, and coming, as it did, on top of a year of frustration and rage, it didn't help his frame of mind one little bit.

He nodded bleakly to a fellow chemist, who was just leaving for the day. 'Dave,' he said flatly.

'Gordon,' came the just as unenthusiastic response.

Feeling more and more depressed, he walked through a number of security devices and down antiseptic-smelling corridors, before using his keycard to open the electronic locking system to walk into his own tiny domain — the modern, clean, state-of-the-art laboratory that felt like home.

Whatever else that bastard Ross Ferris was, he was not a skinflint, Gordon admitted to himself sourly.

He walked to his locker, put on his white overcoat and went to a galvanized steel desk. There he very carefully unlocked the drawer and pulled out a small square tin. He couldn't help but look over his shoulder as he did so, even though he knew that no one would be able to get into his office unless they had a keycard like his own. Still, you never knew in this place when you were being watched.

And he wasn't being paranoid.

He slowly opened the tin and carefully placed the odd-looking pieces of scattered equipment onto a workspace. A clock ticked on the wall over the door. The air-conditioner hummed steadily.

In various other rooms just like this all around him, people as clever as him worked on all sorts of projects, from the new Frankenstein that was genetically modified foods, to old standbys like coming up with better, more environmentally friendly fertilizers and pesticides, to developing new uses for petroleum-based spin-offs.

Gordon's own area of expertise, however, was in miniaturized mechanics, which was proving especially useful when it came to keeping up with the ever-growing computer market. He also had a vast working knowledge of various gases and their properties and possibilities. And for years now, Gordon had been working, in his own time and with his own money, on the invention that would 'make' him.

It was not an uncommon dream for working scientists to have, of course. Actors dreamed of becoming the next Hollywood icon; artists of being the next Picasso (or Damien Hirst, at a pinch). Jobbing scientists dreamed of inventing the modern-day equivalent of cat's eyes, or television, or sliced bread. That one magical invention that took the world by storm and made its inventor both rich and famous, earning them a name that would go down in history.

And Gordon had done it. Or at least, sort of done it.

He hadn't come up with anything that the average man in the street would care about. But he *had* come up with something that had set those in the computer industry salivating.

He could still remember that day, nearly a year ago now, when he'd first realized the little gizmo he'd been working on was the real McCoy — a gadget that would revolutionize the computer world; something that was surely destined to be incorporated into every personal computer in the world. The royalties alone would have made him millions and millions and millions. At long last, his genius would have been recognized. He'd have been a man who could command and demand real respect.

Gordon nearly dropped the tiny glass capsule in his hand and he cursed himself bitterly. His hands were now shaking with rage, and he knew why. Like a sore tooth that he just had to probe with his tongue, he again went over that other fateful day in January.

And the visit from the lawyers.

For Ross Ferris, far from being in ignorance of what his employee had been up to, had been kept constantly informed of Gordon's progress on his revolutionary idea via a series of lab spies, illegal but effective bugging devices, and sheer instinctive canniness. And because he could afford it, he'd hired a bevy of lawyers who had successfully argued that because the gadget had been made using Ferris Labs' equipment, on Ferris Labs' time, and because Gordon was under contract to Ferris Labs, the invention belonged to his employer.

And although Gordon had tried to fight the lawsuit, putting up every penny of his own money to do so, he was defeated before he'd even started by what had happened with the patent.

He'd registered it under his own name, of course. But when his lawyers were preparing the case, the patent office informed them that the design had been registered under the name of Ferris Laboratories.

Gordon couldn't prove it, but he suspected that Ferris had either bribed someone in the patent office, or (far more likely) had paid a computer hacker to break into their system and substitute the names. For a man like Ferris, who had many contacts in the technological industry, it could easily have been done.

Naturally, Ferris had coolly threatened to sue Gordon for every penny he no longer had if he started voicing that theory in public.

And Gordon had very quickly learned that nothing was beyond his boss. The man was a monster. A liar, a cheat. He'd stolen his life's work and the kudos and respect that was due to him, and was now poised to reap the financial rewards that should also be his.

The scientist swallowed back the bile rising in his throat and wiped the sweat off his forehead with his sleeve. Although the labs were all carefully temperature controlled, he felt swelteringly hot.

Ross Ferris had even had the gall to demand that Gordon work out the rest of his three-year contract. To add insult to injury, the engineer still had to accept the man's pay cheque, to see his smug face every day, and work in his damned lab.

But no more! The worm was finally turning.

For long hours, Gordon continued to work frantically but with intense concentration on the tiny glass capsule that was being held suspended by two electronic pincers in front of him, all the time peering through a magnifying lens. Once he put on a mask as he produced a clear gas. Once he rushed to the sink to be sick.

But all the while as he worked on the tiny instrument of death, he kept telling himself over and over again that he *was* going to use it. That he *wasn't* going to wimp out. That this time, *this time*, he was going to come out on top, and damn the consequences.

He would, he promised himself, dance on Ross Ferris's grave. The trouble was, however, that Gordon knew, deep in his heart of hearts, that he couldn't dance.

He'd never learned how.

CHAPTER 2

London

Melissa Ferris slammed the cab door viciously behind her and thrust the fare into the taxi driver's hand. Away to the northwest somewhere, a thunderstorm was making its presence known, and she swore mightily when the first raindrops began to bombard her as she sprinted for the foyer of her home.

The Ferris London residence was a typically upmarket penthouse in a large converted Victorian mansion. As she walked through the small, fern-filled foyer to the stairs (she was trying to stay fit by shunning the lifts) she angrily pushed a tendril of long auburn hair off one damp cheek.

'Damned weather. I should be in Monaco,' she muttered grimly under her breath as she let herself into the two-bedroom, very artfully decorated apartment, and slung her Gucci handbag onto the nearest chair. Maria, the maid who came in when one of the couple was in residence, had been and gone, and Melissa gloomily put on the coffee percolator. She grimaced, feeling damp and thoroughly out of sorts, but then her visits to Hargrove, Gaines and Gaines always left her feeling like that.

'You'd think damned solicitors would actually do *something* to earn their money,' she snarled darkly to a stuffed tiger that perpetually lounged in an antique rocking chair. The coffee made, Melissa kicked off her Maud Frizon pumps (hopelessly rain-spotted) and tucked her long legs beneath her on the buttoned leather couch. Melissa had good legs. Long and shapely, they'd first attracted Ross Ferris's attention just over eight years ago. She'd been selling perfume at a counter in Debenhams then — their central London branch, naturally. Ross had been in to buy a tiny bottle of Joy for his latest mistress. And the fact that he'd just bought the most expensive perfume in the world had been enough for Melissa Bolan to give him a second look. And then a third.

At twenty-five, she'd been on the lookout for a man like Ross Ferris for years. The papers claimed that most women nowadays became rich by going into businesses for themselves, but Melissa knew that she had neither the brains nor the courage for such a career. Besides, she was lazy. And looking as good as she did, she had plenty of faith that the old-fashioned credo of sleeping your way to the top would suit her just fine.

The Ross–Melissa love affair had followed a fairly predictable path after that first, mutually flirtatious meeting. Dinners at expensive restaurants progressed to weekends in swanky country hotels. These were followed by days at Royal Ascot (showing off her new hat), punting at the Henley Royal Regatta, a thrilling balloon ride over Dorset at dawn, and partaking of strawberries and cream whilst watching the action on centre court at Wimbledon. All the things, in fact, that Melissa Bolan, daughter of a Hackney dustman, had always dreamed of.

She'd been very careful over sex, of course, letting him have just enough to whet his appetite, but always wanting to come back for more. Of course, Ross had not been fooled for one minute. Although she'd carefully erased the worst twangs of her cockney accent he had no illusions as to what was happening. But he had no objections either. He too had grown up poor in a big city (Birmingham, in his case) and thus felt no latent superiority over the grasping Melissa; indeed he under-stood her desperation to find something better only too well. In fact, he rather admired her gall. If a pretty gal didn't have enough gumption to try and better her life by fair means or foul, then she didn't have much going for her at all, in Ross's opinion. And since she knew how to dress and apply make-up properly and act like a lady around others, there was no worry that she'd be an embarrassment to him.

No, all in all, Ross hadn't minded being 'hooked.' He was at the age when he needed a wife if he wanted to have kids, and Melissa would certainly look and play the part of being a millionaire's wife very well.

And so, amid as much fanfare as they could manage between them, they were married. Ross had spared no expense, of course, and the press had been tipped off well in advance.

At first, it had all gone much as they'd both planned.

Melissa was no dummy and she was always careful to but-ter up her husband's business associates. She quickly learned the delicate art of hostessing, and for many years the Ferris marriage had if not love, then at least as much going for it as most marriages in modern-day Britain. But three years ago the cracks had begun to show.

The first major ruction was the issue of children. Ross, fast approaching the spectre of the dreaded middle age, wanted them immediately. Melissa didn't want them at all. She'd always had to fight a running battle with her weight, and she'd seen for herself the ravaging effects of child-bearing on some of her friends. She had a morbid fear of becoming fat and dowdy. Also, coming from a big family that had been packed into a tiny council house, just the thought of wailing babies sent her into a fit of the shudders. And then there was the thought of the pain of it all. All the sweating, scream-ing agony of childbirth. Who needed it? Besides, Melissa had never been good at pain.

So she'd kept putting him off, telling him that she was young yet, and that they had plenty of time to have fun and

17

see the world before babies irrevocably tied them down and drained all the fun and spontaneity out of life.

But Ross wasn't a patient man, and this, naturally, had led to resentment on both sides. Blazing rows had subsequently ensued.

But the final straw came when he'd bought a house in the middle of nowhere, and had it turned into a lab. Melissa had never before lived in the countryside, and she hated it. She hated Ross's obsession with his new business, and chose to ignore the fact that this latest addition to the Ferris empire was proving to be the best money-spinner of all.

Moreover, she found his determination to live close to his work somewhat bizarre. With the big house itself dedicated to offices and laboratories, he'd spent a fortune converting the old stable block into a luxurious bungalow for their private quarters. But although everyone else thought it a triumph, she'd always felt ridiculous living there. Bungalows were so . . . middle class. And she was a millionaire's wife. She felt cheated.

Unfortunately, so did Ross. He had finally realized that if he were ever to have heirs, it wouldn't be with Melissa. And so, one fine morning six months ago, Melissa found herself on the receiving end of divorce papers.

The trouble was, as Melissa quickly found out, she was now in an invidious position. Because he'd insisted on it, and because she'd been too afraid he'd slip the net if she refused, she'd signed a pre-nup agreement. At the time, its conditions had seemed marvellously generous. The maintenance payments had seemed huge to her then. Now, of course, when she finally realized how much it really cost to live as well as she did, she saw that the maintenance was peanuts compared with her average credit card spend.

But the pre-nup was airtight, as her lousy solicitors had just informed her.

The coffee finished, Melissa got up and moodily walked to the window, looking down at the rain-washed streets. Her solicitor was making hopeful noises that, to avoid a long, drawn-out and bitter court case, Ross might just be persuaded to throw in the London flat in the divorce settlement.

Melissa's lovely lips twisted into a snarling smile. Hah. And pigs might fly! She hadn't been married to the bastard for nearly seven years without learning a thing or two about him. And one of them was that Ross Ferris, when thwarted, was a spiteful, vindictive swine.

Her smile curved up into something more feline. Perhaps it wouldn't hurt to remind him just how *embarrassing* a bitter ex-wife could be . . .

Yes. For Melissa, who did indeed know her soon-to-be ex-husband very well indeed, knew too that if there was one thing Ross liked above all else, it was to be admired by his peers. Oh yes, that was definitely the way to go, Melissa thought, beginning to smile in earnest now.

It might well be a very good idea to remind him just how vulnerable to ridicule she could make him, if she felt like it. The secrets she could spill. And there was no time like the present, just before the divorce case came to court.

Melissa's chocolate-brown eyes crinkled at the corners as she laughed. Then she quickly walked to her laptop and opened up her diary. Her eyes scanned the data and narrowed thoughtfully on a date a little over a week away.

The Caulcott Green annual flower show. Hell, what a do that was going to be! The thought of all that rustic chi-chi made her want to throw up. But Ross was bound to have his finger stuck well and truly into that pie. Swanning around like Lord Muck! Since moving into the village, he seemed determined to make Caulcott Green his own private little fiefdom. Yes, he was bound to be present and playing to the crowd.

Melissa gave a satisfied smile as the thunderstorm broke in earnest over her head. Yes, the flower show would be ideal for what she had in mind.

* * *

19

Sean Gregson got off the bus at the main road turn-off to Caulcott Green and tramped the half a mile home. He worked as a mechanic at a garage in Cheltenham, which was ironic, since his own car had just given up the ghost and, unusually, with no spare scrapheaps back at work that he could borrow, he found himself temporarily carless.

Now, as he turned into a neat cul-de-sac of well-maintained council houses, he was half-heartedly whistling a vague rendition of 'Lady in Red.'

In the kitchen, his wife Belinda glanced out of the window and then checked on the progress of the chips frying away merrily in an ancient, blackened pan. Already at the table, Linda Gregson chewed gum and scrolled through her phone. 'Here's your dad,' Belinda said, unnecessarily.

Linda popped a gum bubble.

Sean eased off his work shoes by the back door and entered the kitchen like a returning soldier, sniffing the aroma of baking ham appreciatively.

'Did you see the rain this afternoon?' he asked, eyeing his wife fondly as she broke some eggs into a frying pan. 'And the lightning? I thought at one point it was going to short out the electric.' He sat down at the table, got told off by his wife, and promptly got up again to wash his filthy hands.

The food was served and duly eaten, and it wasn't until later, as the tea was poured out and the greasy dishes were soaking in the sink, that the trouble started.

'Fancy going out for a drink tonight, love?' Sean asked, looking across at Belinda, who sighed in response. Friday night at the local was darts night. It hardly offered a *Breakfast at Tiffany's* experience but it was better than staying in and watching the telly, she supposed.

'Yeah, might as well,' Belinda said indifferently. 'You coming, Lin?'

Linda shook her head, and helped herself to another spoonful of sugar in her tea. 'Nah. I'm going to Oxford. There's a new nightclub just opened.' She'd managed to persuade Gordon to take her there, even though he always looked like a fish out of water in such places, poor sod.

'Oh? Going with Jim?' Sean asked, his shaggy grey eyebrows going up questioningly as he looked across at her. He was a big man with the beginnings of a beer belly and the strong arms of a manual worker.

Linda sighed. 'No. I told you. Me and Jim don't go out no more.' When would the silly sod get it through his head? Jim Lavers was the son of Sean's best mate Colin, a fellow mechanic. Jim was looked on with approval by her parents because he had a good head on his shoulders and a steady job working on canal barges. At a nearby canal wharf, he and a team of electricians, plumbers, and carpenters converted the shells of old craft into the kind of boat that people liked to rent out for holidays.

'I thought I saw you with him the day before yesterday, down at the Arms,' Sean challenged, his stubble-shadowed jaw jutting out pugnaciously.

Linda sighed with the exaggerated patience of the put-upon. 'I went in for a drink. He was there. We said hello. Don't make nothing out of it, Dad. You know things are serious with Gordon and me. I'm gonna marry him — you'll see.'

'No you ain't!' Sean shot out, before he could stop himself.

'I dunno what you got against Gordon,' Linda said, flushing as her own volatile temper began to rise. 'He went to Oxford! He earns a fortune over at the lab, and he's unmarried and child-free — he's not even been divorced. Most dads would be pleased to see their daughters get a catch like him.' She shot her mum a look that appealed for support.

Belinda bit her lip and asked if anyone wanted pudding. There was a nice mint and chocolate-chip ice-cream bar in the freezer . . .

'For one thing, he's too old for you,' Sean snarled, leaning across the table aggressively. 'He's nearly the same age as me.'

'Nowadays that don't matter,' his daughter retorted stubbornly.

21

'And he's too damned slick. Talking down to you all the time.'

'He's just very clever. He's a scientist, for Pete's sake. What do you think he's going to talk about, Manchester bleeding United?'

By now, father and daughter were squared off across the table, eyes blazing, faces only inches apart.

'He's a twerp. He thinks just because he's got that fancy job he's better'n us. I tell you, my girl, you carry on with him and you're heading for a fall. Jim's the one you want to—'

'Oh, sod Jim,' Linda howled. 'I want to marry someone who's gonna take me outta this dump. Gordon says when his contract's through with Ferris Labs, he's gonna go to America. He says that's where—'

'America?' It was Belinda who howled now. 'But, love, that's so far away.'

'Hah, he won't take her to America, never you fear,' Sean snorted. 'He's just after one thing from her, and that ain't taking her to bloody America.'

'Sean!' Belinda wailed.

'You're so out of it, Dad,' Linda scorned. 'He's already "had it" from me, and he's still coming back for more. And he'll keep on coming back for more, and I'm going to—'

She shut up abruptly as Sean lunged to his feet, pushing his chair back and looking fit to burst. 'You think you're so damned clever, my girl, such a know-it-all. But your precious *doctor*, arty-farty scientist friend is two-timing you!'

Linda paled, but her eyes narrowed ominously. 'Who with?' If her terse response was somewhat more muted than the outraged, hurt reaction he'd been expecting, her father was too far gone to notice.

'Some woman who works in Cirencester. Burt told me he saw them checking into a hotel together. So what do you think of that?' he asked brutally, no doubt hoping that what she thought was that she should dump her unfaithful beau and go back to the stalwart Jim.

What Linda was actually thinking, however, was that she'd have to find out just who this interloper was and figure out a way to scupper her good and proper.

'I'm going to get ready,' she said abruptly and, turning on her heel, flounced out and headed for her bedroom. She had just the eye-popping outfit needed to make sure that Gordon forgot all about his hotel-loving little bit on the side.

The Gregsons watched their daughter go and sighed simultaneously.

'That bastard,' Sean said bitterly. 'The rotten, cradle-snatching, two-timing, arty-farty bastard.'

* * *

The church at Caulcott Green was nowhere near as ancient as that of Heyford Bassett, (as Graham Noble was always joshing his friend James Davies) but it did the village very well nonetheless. Pushing open the rusty gate that always seemed to squeak no matter how often James oiled it, Wendy Davies walked up the weed-strewn path, following it around to the back of the church, where the latest graves were located.

The thunderstorm had passed, leaving the air fresh and the grass wet, and the birds singing in the trees. In one hand she carried a brightly coloured mixed bunch of asters and in the other a bottle full of water. In the long shadow of the church, she set off across the drenched grass, unaware that her shoes had a hole in them and that her feet were getting wet.

The last gravestone in the ongoing line looked shockingly white and new against the moss- and lichen-bedecked Victorian stones set at the front of the church. As she approached it, her knees got that old weak feeling, her body cooled down to a shivering mass of pain, and her mind, as usual, made itself quickly blank.

It was a pity that it didn't help numb the raw ache in her chest.

At thirty-five, Wendy's curly blonde hair was already turning silver. She'd always been plump, but the ravages of grief in recent months had resulted in lost pounds that now made her look positively haggard.

As she crouched beside her son's grave, over against the drystone wall, Lady Daphne Cadge-Hampton was putting a vase of chrysanthemums on her husband's much grander stone sarcophagus. She was dressed in old riding jodhpurs caked with mud, a man's lavishly embroidered waistcoat, and a long cardigan with more holes in it than Swiss cheese.

People tended to put her bizarre dress sense down to senility (she was over eighty) or eccentricity, but the simple fact was that she hadn't bought herself any new clothes since 1951. She couldn't afford to. All the money there was left in the Cadge-Hampton estate (and there wasn't a fat lot to begin with) had gone to her son when he'd inherited the title. Hence, she'd long since been reduced to raiding her husband's old wardrobe as well as the trunks stored in the attic for something to wear.

It was better than going about buck-naked, the countess had always thought, philosophically.

'There you go, old boy,' she said fondly, depositing the flowers and then standing back and rubbing her arthritic bones with a wince. 'Don't say I never give you anything.'

She turned, and was about to tramp back to her dower house with its precarious wiring, damp rooms, and one grumbling retainer (who was nearly as old as she was) when she spotted the vicar's wife.

Daphne's face took on a grim, unhappy look. A bad business, losing an only child like that, and a son to boot. Young Tommy Davies had been such a scamp, too. A face full of freckles and a mouthful of cheek, there had been no real harm in the lad; she'd caught him scrumping her apples only last year, and had chased him out of the garden, an experience they'd both thoroughly enjoyed.

And then a cough, a rise in temperature, a bit of a rash, and he was gone. In one night. Just like that.

Careful of the uneven ground, the old woman made her way towards the younger, and stood watching as Wendy arranged the flowers. Daphne raised a hand to scratch an itchy wart on her chin. As she did so Wendy caught the impression of movement in her peripheral vision, and her hands trembled wildly.

She turned to see one of her husband's most illustrious parishioners, and smiled. 'Oh, good evening, Your Ladyship,' she said respectfully.

In this modern age, cash-poor families with obscure titles were an anachronism that most people thought should be allowed to die out with dignity. But Wendy was rather fond of the old lady, who was nothing if not a character; and besides, Daphne was always going to be someone who commanded respect.

'Evenin',' Daphne said. 'Nice asters you've got there. You entering some for the flower show?' she demanded in that gruff way she had of barking out questions.

'Oh no, I'm judging them this year,' Wendy said, hastily getting to her knees and ignoring the damp patches left on her skirt. She was too afraid to turn her head for a quick look at the flowers. If she did so, she might just catch a glimpse of those stark black letters on the headstone, and read her son's name, and know . . .

'Er, what are you judging this year, Your Ladyship?' she asked desperately.

Daphne gave her a quick, gimlet-eyed look as if to say, what an extraordinary question! 'The gladioli, same as always.'

Wendy felt herself flush. How stupid could she get? Everyone knew that the countess always judged the gladioli, but she was very reluctant, James said, to actually award anyone the ultimate prize and part with that big silver cup of hers.

James had a sneaking feeling that the old girl really wanted to melt it down or sell it, but didn't quite dare.

'Well, I mustn't dawdle,' Wendy said, her smile as brittle as a cracked vase. 'Got things to be getting on with.'

Daphne smiled. 'The lot of a vicar's wife is not a happy one, eh?' she said, and chuckled robustly. But something in her voice made Wendy shoot her a quick look.

'Oh, I mustn't complain,' she said, and, giving the imperious old woman a quick bob of the head, turned and hurried away.

The Dowager Countess of Fulcome watched her go, a distinctly worried look on her lined, ancient face. Then she turned and looked sadly down at the headstone.

'Your mother, Tommy-me-lad, is cracking up,' she said pityingly. 'Yerse, definitely cracking up. And that's not good . . .'

CHAPTER 3

The early evening sun shone warmly through the big French windows, highlighting the dust motes dancing in the air. Sir Hugh Featherstone climbed carefully back down a nine-teenth-century oak library ladder that creaked a little alarmingly under his weight, a book clutched triumphantly in one hand.

He knew it had been up there somewhere.

He took the book, an 1894 dissertation on gladiolus growing by an eminent Victorian luminary on the subject, to a padded window seat covered in badly faded chintz, and sat down to read.

The man himself looked as if he were an intrinsic part of the furniture, which was not surprising, since he'd been born in the house of well-to-do parents and had grown up as a typical country squire. He'd gone to a good (but nothing fancy) public school as a boarder, earned a BA at Durham (squeaking by with a Third) and had then gone on to enjoy a career in the army, following in his father's, grandfather's, and great-grandfather's footsteps. Long since retired, he was now at home seeing out his golden years.

Unfortunately, the Featherstone family fortunes had not survived the twentieth century very well, and Sir Hugh

27

had to make do with one live-in housekeeper and old Malvin Cook in the garden. What's more, and much as he'd bitterly hated to do so, he'd been forced to sell off the part of his family estate that had included the mill house and its grounds. Although the milling part of the operation had, of course, long since ceased to function as a business, the house was still a prime property, and no doubt the capital from it would see him out nicely.

Sir Hugh slowly lowered the book in his hand, gladioli temporarily forgotten.

At almost seventy-two, he was still a distinguished-looking man, having retained the upright bearing of a soldier and a fine head of silver hair, although at the moment his face was angrily reddening in colour. It was something that tended to happen to him whenever he thought about Ross Ferris.

Nowadays he seldom thought of anything else.

When he'd sold the mill, the buyer, a charming Irishman, had assured him that he wanted it only for a country residence for himself and his growing family. A big wheel in the horse-racing fraternity and celebrity trainer, he'd seemed just the sort you wanted in Caulcott Green, and Sir Hugh, all things considered, couldn't have been happier.

Unfortunately, his best horses and the bookies' hot favourites began, unaccountably, to finish last, which had led to some very nasty rumours flying around at the jockey club, which in turn resulted in the trainer's rather hasty 'retirement' back to Ireland. This had seen the mill house once more come onto the market.

Unfortunately, this time Sir Hugh had no say in the purchaser and the Irishman, curse him, had only been interested in a quick sale at the right price. And thus, Caulcott Green had become home to that one-man plague, otherwise known as Ross Ferris.

With a snort, Sir Hugh thrust the book to one side and stood up. He had the look of a man still active and alert and his face, after his many years spent outdoors in various climes, had a leathery look to it that was not unattractive. His clothes — old but good tweeds — completed the picture of a perfect English squire. Not that Sir Hugh would ever have paused to consider the impression he presented.

Now he walked to the French windows and glanced out across the lawns and rhododendron bushes before going over to his desk. There he pulled out the latest correspondence from his solicitors concerning their long-running battle against Ferris Labs and reread it, a ferocious scowl drawing his thick white eyebrows together.

When the racing chap had still been in residence, Sir Hugh had decided that just living off the money from the sale of the mill house was wanton laziness. A man had an obligation to make money work for itself, after all, and so he'd cast around for a scheme to suit him, but it had been an old friend of his who'd finally suggested trout fishing.

Sir Hugh's family had owned the fishing rights to a long and clean stretch of a trout stream for centuries. His friend, a decent chap even if he was a civil servant, had bought him magazines dedicated to game fishing, and the prices charged for a single day's fishing had made Sir Hugh's eyes bulge. As his friend had pointed out, nothing could be simpler, easier, and as hassle-free than to get into something like this. All he had to do was acquire the necessary licences, then advertise in all the right magazines – *Country Life*, *Angling Times* — that type of thing, and then just sit back and rake in the dough.

It had seemed ideal.

And for the first three years, so it had proved. Sir Hugh's stretch of river was only an hour or so from London, after all, and could almost guarantee you a catch of some description. Also, since the proprietor of the country residence in question was the real McCoy and gentry from centuries back (which pleased the snobs) it was hardly surprising that it had caught on.

And then disaster had struck.

The first problem came when he met the new owner of the mill house, Ross Ferris. A big personality with a correspondingly big head, he'd riled Sir Hugh in a way that few men had ever done before. The old soldier had sensed something sneering and grasping about the man right from the beginning, and his hackles had been duly raised. But there had been very little that he could actually do about the Ferris blight. The luckless horse trainer had already sold up to the man, not even telling Sir Hugh about the change of ownership until it was a fait accompli.

And then, six months later, the first rumours began to circulate.

Ross Ferris was becoming a very prominent figure in the village by then, and was making noises about running for the local council. Also, so it was said, he had plans for the mill house itself. Big plans. The very whisper was enough to make Sir Hugh's blood pressure soar with a sort of atavistic foreboding that soon became all too real when the bombshell struck. Ferris really did have plans for the mill house that were far worse than merely turning it into a hotel (which had been the most favoured rumour).

No. The man was turning it into a research complex, complete with labs, full-on security, and its own independent hydroelectric power source. No doubt the big rooms, easy access and millrace were ideal for the job.

'But how did the clever bastard ever get planning permission, eh?' Sir Hugh heard himself speak aloud, then flushed, fighting back the instinctive urge to look around to make sure that no one had overheard him, knowing that he was quite alone in the room.

Damn it, he was even beginning to talk to himself now! Gruffly, he rattled the letter from his solicitors, making a half-hearted attempt to read it again, but he couldn't bring himself to concentrate, even though the case was due to come to court next month. Slowly he leaned back in his chair, and tiredly rubbed his forehead. He was getting a headache, something he'd rarely ever suffered from until Ferris had come on the scene.

He put the letter to one side and wondered again how Ferris had ever got permission to turn the mill house into a working laboratory. The conversion of the outbuildings he could perhaps understand, but the main house itself? True, it wasn't a listed building, nor yet of any particular historical interest. And true again, Ferris hadn't changed the *outside* of the building one iota. No, all the radical changes had gone on inside, or so he'd heard. The locals who worked there said that it was like NASA inside the complex itself — all computer equipment, and fancy labs, and high-tech security.

Apart from all the hush-hush projects and brainwork that went on in the inner sanctum, the facility also produced experimental fertilizers and other less glamorous things that were shipped out regularly for testing. And that meant lorries. Lots of them.

True, the mill had its own access road, but even so.

'He bribed somebody on that board, I'd bet money on it!' Sir Hugh, once again, found himself speaking out loud and walked restlessly back to the French windows.

His gaze moved further across the gardens and through one of the side gates where he could just see glimpses of the water meadows that lay beyond. Every spring they came up in a profusion of colour: poppies, daisies, pink campions, forget-me-nots, buttercups, and cornflowers. It was a sight that had prompted many a trout fisher to bring a camera with them the next time they came.

But this year, there'd been no fishermen.

Last winter, Sir Hugh had been appalled to find his fish going belly-up all over the place. And not just his precious trout, either. The river's other inhabitants — fish like perch, roach, dace, and rudd — were also floating to the surface. It had been a stunning ecological disaster, and had killed Sir Hugh's business stone dead.

There had then started months of wrangling. He'd had the Environmental Agency out at once, of course, with their sample bottles and meters. They'd mentioned all sorts of things as possible sources of contamination; farmers, apparently, were responsible for more river pollution than anyone else. But as Sir Hugh told them (or rather, shouted at them), they'd find out that it was that damned lab that was to blame.

And so it had turned out.

The chemical that had devastated the life in the river *had* definitely been traced back to Ferris Labs. An accident, they said. A new employee had failed to observe protocols. Some kind of agent had been emptied into the usual sinks, not the lab's own private system. This had led to it finding its way through the local sewer and drainage system and thus into the river.

Unlike Melissa Ferris's legal team down in London, however, Sir Hugh's lawyers were much more optimistic about his chances of winning his case. In fact, they were almost guaranteeing it, so strong was the evidence. Typically, Ferris had tried to deny personal responsibility and had promptly hired a team of lawyers in a clear and blatant attempt to drag it out for years, hoping that Sir Hugh would either lose heart, die of old age, or eventually run out of money for legal fees.

But there, and for once, Sir Hugh had the edge over him. He knew the local magistrate, the local MP, and many more people of influence besides who owed him favours. And this time, Ross Ferris didn't find it so easy to get his own way.

Not that it was all plain sailing for Sir Hugh either. With the loss of his revenue, things were tight. Lawyers cost money. And if he wanted to restock, once the river was finally declared safe again, he'd need capital. No, for all the promise of compensation in the future, right now Sir Hugh was on the verge of bankruptcy and he knew it. He only hoped that Ferris didn't know it too. He wouldn't put it past him to try and pull some kind of a fast one, even now.

'Ah, but I've got a little something in the works that'll spike you, Ferris,' Sir Hugh muttered, his voice rich with satisfaction. And this time, he didn't feel one whit ridiculous to find himself speaking the words out loud.

As he thought of the upcoming flower show and all the rewards that he hoped it would bring him, he began to smile.

Oh yes, he was looking forward to this particular fete and flower show more than he had any other.

And not only because, at long last, he and Malvin had come up with the gladioli that would finally make old Daphne part with that cup of hers. Oh no.

Sir Hugh had hopes of something even better. If it all went to plan, that is.

* * *

As Sir Hugh alternately gloated, fretted, scowled, and talked to himself in the library, outside in the garden, Malvin Cook checked on the cucumbers under the glass frames.

Someone had sent him some apple cucumber seeds from Australia and he was growing them for the first time this year. They looked fat enough, but distressingly pale. Still, perhaps they were supposed to be that colour. He scratched his head and regarded the cucumbers with a slow, thoughtful, countryman's patience.

The same age as his employer, Malvin was barely five feet four in height, and was getting a pronounced stoop. His hands were gnarled and darkened from years of working the earth, and he wore filthy trousers and a loose, once white shirt. His salt-and-pepper hair stood up on his head in surprised spikes, and his eyes were so deeply set and lost in folds of leathery skin that they were almost invisible, but glimpses showed them to be a fierce electric blue.

He'd worked as one of the gardeners for Sir Hugh's family man and boy, but now had the grounds to himself. He still did the work of five, even at his age. Retirement, long since a dream of his wife, Phyllis, wasn't something that either Malvin or Sir Hugh had ever even contemplated. So, although it was fast approaching half past seven at night, and he'd been there since six that morning, Malvin was only just now thinking of going home.

He lived but three minutes' walk away in a nice little cottage that went with the job, so he always went home for his main cooked meal at midday, but he looked forward to his supper best. Cheese and pickle. A bit of chicken and ham pie. Whatever his Phyllis had made, it always went down well with Malvin.

But recently, there was no pleasure to be had in going home. No pleasure in good food. No pleasure in Phyllis's welcoming smile. The snuffle of his dog's nose in fond greeting. Since his Stephen had been killed, there was no pleasure in anything any more.

And the life had gone out of Phyllis too, Malvin knew. Everyone had remarked on it. He sighed heavily.

A lot of folk had laughed at his Stephen, still living at home with his old mum and dad when he was already well into his forties and still unmarried. But it had suited the Cooks. They'd only been able to have the one child, and Stephen had always been precious. And it had been a good life, just the three of them together. Stephen was a big shambling lad, not at all like his father, but the apple of his eye, nonetheless. And Malvin knew that Phyllis had always had it in the back of her mind that, if her husband went first, she'd still have Stephen around, so there'd be no lonely old age for her.

And then . . .

Malvin sighed, bending down to poke one of the apple cucumbers. Should he cut some? As one of the perks, he always got to try out the first of the fruit and veg, just to make sure that everything was ripe and ready for harvesting. It was a running joke here at the manor.

Back in the early fifties, his job had been a godsend. Then, the odd leek, a few potatoes, a handful of tomatoes out of the greenhouse, had all added up to a genuine and welcome supplement to the family diet. Now, of course, he didn't need to 'secretly' raid the kitchen garden. In point of fact, because of what had happened to his Stephen, he now had more money in the bank than Sir Hugh. A lot more money, in fact.

It was something that both men would have found deeply ironic, if either of them had ever stopped to think about it seriously.

But neither did.

Now the old gardener carefully replaced the glass panes, did a final check to make sure that all the tools were put away clean in the sheds, and that no mess was visible. He'd been weeding the herbaceous borders that afternoon, and he deposited the last load on the compost heap. Then he wheeled his barrow into what had once been the old pigsty, shut the crudely made gate behind him, and looked up at the sky. It was going to be a lovely sunset again.

He couldn't resist a last check on the gladioli. They'd worked for years to grow enough prize-winning blooms to win the cup, and this year Sir Hugh was confident that they'd finally cracked it.

Malvin, for the first time in a long time, smiled with real pleasure as he contemplated the tall spiky flowers and quickly counted off the days. Yes, he too was confident that they'd have a display to be proud of come the flower show. If these beauties didn't persuade the old gal to part with the cup for a year then Malvin didn't know what would. He was confident that they'd walk away with the prizes for the sweet peas and the lilies too. The asters, however . . . well, they were a bit on the straggly side.

As he passed the French windows leading into the library, he saw a movement out of the corner of his eye, and turned. Inside, Sir Hugh, standing in front of the window, raised a hand in farewell and Malvin nodded back.

As he watched his gardener shuffle off, Sir Hugh shook his head. 'Now there's someone who has even more reason to hate Ross Ferris than I do,' he muttered grimly.

And wondered.

CHAPTER 4

The John Radcliffe Hospital in Oxford sits atop Headington Hill like a modern-day castle, a big, sprawling white building, a landmark visible for miles around. In one of life's little quirks, a big cemetery borders one side of it, no doubt providing some of its patients with a thought-provoking view.

The Reverend James Davies parked his twenty-year-old car in the car park, gave a brief prayer of thanks that he'd been able to find a parking space so easily (a minor miracle in itself) and tried not to begrudge paying the parking fees. Reminding himself to render under Caesar the things that were Caesar's, as the Good Book advised him, he climbed out of the small hatchback rather clumsily and sighed wearily.

At fifty-two, James was gaining a heavy, if rather teddy bear-like appearance that he found just a shade embarrassing. He'd always thought that there was something incongruous about a man of God looking like he should be advertising children's toys on a television shopping channel, and he thought enviously of his friend, Graham Noble, with his lean height and angelic good looks.

'Evening, Vicar,' someone called, bringing his head around as he bent over to lock the car. Although why he bothered with such precautions, he wasn't entirely sure, since no self-respecting car thief would ever dream of stealing the old rust-bucket.

'Sister,' he said amiably, recognizing the nurse's uniform rather than the woman in it. The John Radcliffe was a huge place, and James visited it often. Not surprisingly, his was a known face around the busy wards, but his own memory for faces was rather poor.

The streetlights were coming on, and in one of the trees in the small park opposite a song thrush gave out a tuneful melody. James took a deep, wistful breath. Then he was stepping through the automatic doors into the lobby area, and it was a different world altogether. No matter how many times he visited, it always took him by surprise.

Here, nature had been kept strictly at bay with scrubbed floor tiles, air conditioning, and that all-pervading smell that was utterly hospital: a strange mixture of antiseptic, flowers, polish, sickness and quiet. Death walks here, James thought, and into his mind leapt that night, not so long ago, when he'd lost his son.

With a little shiver and a determined effort to shake off his demons, he walked briskly along the ground floor, passing the small newspaper store and heading for the lifts. He'd come to visit Mrs Jarvis, who was on the fifth floor, recovering from a gallstone operation. A regular of his Sunday morning services, he'd also been preaching to her for years the rather more worldly message of the benefits of a low-fat diet, but alas to no avail. He had in his hand a bag of peaches that he'd picked up earlier in the day, although he had no idea whether she'd be allowed to eat them yet. He suspected not. During his long working life as a vicar of various parishes, he'd become a bit of an expert on post-operative recovery. Oh well. They were a little hard, so by the time she was allowed solid food, they'd probably have ripened off just nicely.

The nurse on duty at the desk smiled and pointed him in the right direction for Mrs Jarvis, who was, she said jovially, a bit of a duck.

There were three women in the ward and (very rare indeed) an empty bed. He nodded amiably at the younger woman, who was obviously not at all interested, and smiled at the older woman, whose eyes lit up briefly as she spied his dog collar. He made a mental note to have a few words with her after visiting Gladys Jarvis.

'Hello, Vicar,' Gladys said cheerfully, looking remarkably well for a woman who'd just undergone surgery. But then Gladys was one of those robust ladies who always seemed to have roses in her cheeks and an indomitable outlook on life, no matter what it threw at her. A dying breed, the Gladyses of the world, James thought sadly.

'Hello, Gladys, I brought you some of your favourites,' he said, holding aloft the brown bag. And then felt a momentary pang of doubt. Was it peaches or plums she was so fond of?

'Peaches!' Gladys said, her whole face beaming, and James breathed a sigh of relief that he'd got it right. He rattled the bag playfully before putting it down on her small bedside locker.

'But no munching before the doctor says so.' He wagged a finger at her in warning.

'Oh, don't you worry about that,' Gladys said comfortably. 'Now then, how are you?'

The question was typical of Gladys. *She* was the one in hospital, and no doubt worrying about how her husband was coping with the housework on his own, and yet her first thought was to ask after his health and well-being.

'I'm fine, Gladys, thank you,' James said humbly.

Gladys looked at her vicar with a thoughtful eye. 'And Mrs Vicar?' she added sharply.

James smiled. 'Wendy's fine too.'

Huh, Gladys thought. That's not what I've heard. Or seen for myself. But she smiled obligingly. 'You ought to take her away on one of them foreign holidays, Vicar,' she said. 'My Jim and Shirley went on one last year. To Benidorm,' she added proudly. 'I'll bet Mrs Vicar would like that. Some sun and sea, like.'

James grinned, trying to picture Wendy in Benidorm and failing miserably. Somewhere in Italy, perhaps. Lake Garda, maybe? It had been years since they'd taken a proper holiday, but Wendy understood how it was. A vicar's pay was not much, and with all his commitments, he just never seemed to be able to arrange the time off.

'I'll put it to her when I get home,' James lied, hardly aware of committing the sin, let alone considering the fact that, as a man of the cloth, he shouldn't have been doing it at all.

'Now, what do the doctors say about when you can go home?' he asked brightly.

'Three days, they reckon,' Gladys said smugly.

'Do you have transport? I can come and pick you up in my car if you like.'

'Bless you, Vicar, that's nice, but Brenda says she'll pick me up. She's passed her test now, you know.'

Since the Jarvis family was huge, and he wasn't sure whether Brenda was a daughter or a daughter-in-law, he merely nodded wisely and patted her hand. 'Good, good. And you're feeling all right? Apart from being sore, of course.'

'Oh yes,' Gladys said dismissively. Then she leaned forward, wincing at the pull on her stitches, and whispered, 'You see that poor old thing over there?'

James managed to stop himself from looking over. 'Yes.'

'She's not at all well,' Gladys whispered, and inclined her head meaningfully.

James nodded. 'I'll be sure to go and see her before I leave,' he whispered back.

Gladys leaned back on her pillows, nodding her head in satisfaction, her good deed done for the day.

The next twenty minutes passed pleasantly in idle chit-chat about the village, especially the upcoming fete and flower show. Gladys was particularly interested to hear that he was judging the dahlias, and managed to slip it in that her own husband (more of a regular at the Cadge-Hampton Arms than the church) was entering some dahlias of his own that she was sure were of exceptional quality.

James, of course, was not to be swayed.

Gladys accepted it like the trooper that she was, and the talk went on to more general gossip. As usual, the Ferris lab came in for more than its fair share of pot shots, since, because none of her brood had managed to obtain work there, Gladys was dead against it.

As the vicar finally made getting-ready-to-leave noises, Gladys thanked him for the peaches. 'And I'm glad to see you looking so well,' she added impulsively. 'What with your Tommy and all.'

Although the boy had been gone for some months now, she didn't like to speak about it. But tonight the vicar had seemed so much like his old self that she felt the time had come to let him know that she was still thinking about him. That the whole village was. 'We all know that that there lab isn't a healthy thing to have around. Stands to reason, don't it? All them chemicals in the air and whatnot. They ought to shut it down, so they should, before any other kiddies get ill.'

'Thank you, Gladys,' James said, his voice thickening just a little, and hastening to cut off her diatribe. 'But it *was* meningitis, you know — nothing to do with the lab. The coroner made that very clear.'

'Ah, yes, so it was. You was out the night it happened, I remember,' she said with real sympathy, tutting and shaking her head. 'That must be real hard on a soul.'

James nodded, tears coming to his eyes and making his vision blur as he remembered back to that awful night.

Tommy had come home from school complaining of a headache. Snow had been on the ground for nearly a week and more snow was forecast that day, so it was hardly surprising that there was a flu bug going around; a lot of people had come down with the sniffles. Naturally, neither he nor Wendy had been unduly concerned about him running the expected high temperature, and had packed him off to bed with some Calpol and a mug of cocoa.

James had then taken the car through the snow-clogged roads to one of the more remote villages to visit a parishioner who was nearly crippled with chilblains. Finding her fire nearly out and nothing cooked, he'd stayed far longer than he'd intended, doing much-needed jobs for her about the house and calling the local Age Concern centre to arrange for somebody to visit more often.

By the time he'd set off for home, the expected fresh snow had arrived and he'd had to dig the car out of several snowdrifts. He'd finally arrived home very late to find that a worried Wendy had already called in the local doctor. A terse note left on the kitchen table had informed him that Tommy had been rushed into hospital.

He'd driven straight there, of course, where he and Wendy had spent the night in the intensive care unit, each of them holding one of Tommy's little hands in one of theirs. The doctors did everything that they could, but by the time it was light, Tommy was dead.

James could still clearly remember walking down to the non-denominational chapel and praying. Wendy, unusually, had refused to come with him, and had instead sat, stiff-backed and dry-eyed, in one of those hard plastic chairs that filled the public spaces in such places. He'd put that down to shock, of course, and hadn't left her alone for long.

But those few minutes he spent in the small, quiet room had been like a balm to his shattered soul.

Afterwards, once the initial numbness had worn off, he'd been desperately angry, but then, needing the release that he knew it would bring, he slowly came to accept that it was God's will. This had enabled him to pass through the next few weeks — the funeral and all its attendant duties — with a stoical acceptance that was remarked on by more than one.

But the pain, of course, never left him. He simply became more and more used to it.

'Well,' he said softly, bringing himself back to the present, and the bird-like but not unkind curiosity of Gladys Jarvis, 'he's with the Lord now, and I daresay it's a far better place than this.'

'And that's a fact,' Gladys agreed, heaving a sigh. 'A wicked world, this is,' she added judiciously. 'I often say my generation has seen the best of this world. Second World War or no Second World War.' And with that pronouncement, she thanked him again for the peaches and watched him walk over to the patient in the bed opposite.

Gladys didn't reckon the old woman was long for this world, and it warmed her heart to see her face light up when James sat down beside her. Caulcott Green was lucky when it came to their vicar, Gladys reckoned. He'd been there nearly twenty years now, and was the best the village had ever had. Even old Mrs Basted, ninety-five and still going strong, said so. And she should know. She'd lived through the reign of no less than twelve vicars.

Pity about young Tommy being taken like that, Gladys mused. It fair turned your stomach to think a vicar's kid could be taken. She'd lost none of her own, thank the Lord. But, she supposed, it just goes to show . . .

As Gladys began to nod off, she thought how hard it must all be on poor Mrs Vicar. Her husband was a good man, one of the best, but Gladys often thought it must be hard to be married to him. He was so busy, he could hardly ever be home. And she never saw them out together, not even at the pub for a meal. And losing her only babe like that . . .

No doubt about it, Mrs Vicar was but a shadow of her former self. She'd lost so much weight, too. Luckily for her, her husband was coping much better. A pillar of strength he must be, and she, poor lady, needed someone to lean on.

* * *

In the converted stables at the old mill house, Ross Ferris poured himself a large cognac. It was good stuff — old, mellowed, and expensive. The glasses were from a set that his wife had chosen, and were of the finest cut crystal.

The new cook he'd hired seemed to be working out, and as he thought about the dinner he'd just enjoyed — scallops, followed by lamb and one of those fancy foreign desserts covered in alcohol and set alight — he felt good.

The interior designer he'd hired to transform the single-storey building had kept to an original rustic theme, and had been careful to preserve the exposed old beams and the white-plastered walls. He'd gone wild with brasses, and throw rugs were definitely the order of the day. The result was rustic chic on a grand scale. Ross quite liked it. It suited the image he had of himself as the new squire. Once Sir Hugh finally kicked the bucket, there'd certainly be no other contender to the throne, and Ross was quite looking forward to getting his knighthood.

He had no doubts that, sooner or later, a New Year's honours list would find his name mentioned. He sure as hell gave enough to charity, and when that new computer gizmo of Gordon Trenning's finally hit the market, he would be a bona fide captain of industry.

And wouldn't it just make Melissa choke, he thought with a gust of savage laughter, to miss out on being Lady Melissa. He laughed so hard imagining the chagrin on her pretty little face that he had to wipe away a tear or two.

His lawyers had told him only that morning that she was cutting up rough, angling, no doubt, to keep the flat in Notting Hill. He grunted at her gall and took his cognac to the armchair in front of the inglenook fireplace, which was unlit on this warm August evening. He stretched his rather short legs out in front of him, and contemplated the grate.

He was forty-two, a squat, heavy man with a mop of blond hair and rather striking grey eyes. He was attractive in an unusual sort of way, and was rather vain about it. He wore, even at home alone, a Versace jacket and Italian-made loafers.

He supposed, in the long run, it would probably be worth letting Melissa keep the flat just to be rid of her. The trouble was it grated; letting go of anything that was his rubbed him up the wrong way. And it was almost a physical pain for him to see money leaving his coffers.

And last year he'd already come such a cropper over that Cook business. That had cost him plenty. Or rather, it had cost his insurance company plenty, but since they'd promptly hiked up his contribution payments, it amounted to the same thing.

One of the men working in the loading area at the labs had been killed by falling containers. The health and safety people had swooped like bloody vultures, of course, and had found that the forklift truck involved in the accident had been 'improperly maintained,' and was directly responsible for the fatality. They'd also criticized the training system in place for the drivers.

Ross's insurance company had fought it, but in the end had had no choice but to pay out compensation, and pay out *big*. It had been just his luck that the man killed had been a lifelong inhabitant of Caulcott Green, which had put the villagers up in arms. And, would you believe it, the dead man had been no less than the son of Sir Hugh's gardener!

Ross grunted as he remembered the flack he'd taken over that, and tossed back the last of his brandy angrily. The negative publicity had been a nightmare and he was still dogged by bad feeling from some of the villagers wherever he went.

To make matters even worse it now looked as if this damned lawsuit with Featherstone was going to go against him as well. Another big compensation payout was going to see his insurance company getting very nasty indeed.

Next time, Ross was damned well going to go with another company for all his business enterprises. See how they liked them apples!

He got up and refilled his glass, pouring an overly generous measure and walking with it to one of the windows. Through the screen of weeping willows, he could just make out the big manor house beyond. Sourly, he wondered what Sir Hugh was doing right now.

Gloating, he'd be bound.

'Oh, screw it,' Ross growled, and walked to the telephone. Although it was long past office hours, he had no compunction in ringing up his divorce lawyer at his home and telling him that Melissa would get the flat in Notting Hill only over his dead body.

He was in no mood to be generous today. No mood at all.

* * *

Over the coming week, the village of Caulcott Green began to gird its collective loins and gear itself up for the spectacle that was the annual Caulcott Green fete and flower show. Over at Miss Simpkins' house on Thursday night, the WI ladies gathered to organize their baking schedules. There was a bit of a tiff over who got to do the flapjacks, with both Vera Gant and Mrs Toynbee insisting that they each had the best recipe, but Miss Simpkins refereed brilliantly like the old hand that she was.

At the Cadge-Hampton Arms, the landlord opened up his big storage shed where the stalls and other paraphernalia were always kept, and Ernie Gant and other long-time stall-holders busily checked the equipment for any necessary repairs that might be needed.

Friday saw old men out and about measuring marrows, pulling up onions, and polishing shallots. Mrs Collins stitched the old effigy of Aunt Sally where the stuffing was coming out, sneezing copiously as she did so. The musty, smelly, rotten old thing! Still, it *was* ancient, and it was a tradition that it be set up beside the skittles to oversee fair play.

Over in the converted vicarage at Heyford Bassett, Carol-Ann Clancy finally decided on what she was going to wear then studied the picture of the famous photographer who lived in Caulcott Green, just so that she'd be sure to know him when she saw him at the fair. She'd got one of his later, more arty books out of the Cheltenham library and wondered if the photograph on the back had been touched up, maybe by himself, to give him a younger-looking vibe. As a wannabe model, she was wise to all the tricks of the trade. But she'd know him when she saw him, which was all that mattered.

* * *

Ross Ferris slept like a baby.

Gordon Trenning slept not at all, but lay staring up at the ceiling, listening to Linda Gregson snoring beside him and telling himself over and over again that tomorrow, tomorrow, he was going to *do it*. He was. *He was*. Linda stirred, flinging an arm across his chest and muttering in her sleep, and he felt abruptly irritated. They'd taken a room at the Windsheaf Inn in a nearby town, but he still had no idea why Linda had insisted on it.

James Davies was called out to the old woman in the John Radcliffe Hospital, who was dying and asking for him.

Wendy Davies got up and made herself a cup of tea.

In London, Melissa Ferris got very drunk and took a bank manager home to bed with her. Unfortunately, she was too drunk to realize he didn't even work at her particular bank.

Monica and Graham Noble made gentle love and fell asleep early, entwined in each other's arms.

Malvin Cook sat up all night guarding the gladioli. He didn't think anyone would sabotage them, but it was a fine night and the moon was full, and nowadays he didn't seem to need to sleep so much anyway. Besides, he was as anxious as Sir Hugh to win the Gladiola Cup that year. It had become something of an obsession by now for both of them.

Sir Hugh himself slept the sleep of the just.

And it was just as well that none of these people had the gift of prophecy. Because tomorrow, before the day was out, two of them would be dead, murdered in ways both fantastic and crude.

CHAPTER 5

The day of the annual Caulcott Green flower show dawned as bright as a new penny. By ten o'clock it was already blazingly hot, and as the playing field became gradually more and more crowded with busily working people, tempers frayed, were repaired, and then frayed again.

In the tea tent, Vera Gant surveyed the rows of rather mismatched cups and saucers, the packets of as-yet-unopened biscuits and bottles of squash with a gloomy eye. 'We're gonna need more squash, Ernie,' she yelled over to her spouse, who was the show's unofficial odd-job man. But he only grunted vaguely and carried on industriously hammering in tent pegs, his brawny, hairy arms glistening with sweat.

Around the outskirts of the playing field, stalls were being erected at a cracking pace, and the WI ladies, worried about the heat, fretted about the best time to bring out their cakes from Miss Simpkins' huge fridge. There was a brief break at lunchtime, when several of the lesser minded skived off to the pub for a cold pint. But by two o'clock, everyone was back at their posts, and the gates were being duly guarded by the two dragons who wouldn't have let in their own grandmothers unless they paid the fifty pence entrance fee.

Monica and Graham arrived more or less on time, but already the field was full.

'The usual scrum around the jumble sale, I see,' Graham whispered in his wife's ear, as she forked over their money. 'If you were thinking of getting a bargain, for— Ooof,' he grunted, as her well-placed but not quite fatal elbow caught him nicely in the ribs.

Carol-Ann shot one of the dragons a bedazzling smile, partly for the hell of it, but also because she knew her mother would appreciate her making the effort. Nevertheless she felt their eyes boring into her back all the way through the rusty gates. It was not, in truth, all that surprising, since Carol-Ann was wearing a bright white mini skirt that really was true to its name, coupled with a pair of high-heeled white sandals that showed off her long, tanned legs to perfection. Over this she had donned a floaty chiffon blouse in a white and mint green floral pattern, which was only just on the respectable side of translucent. Her long, silky blonde hair had been left free to cascade around her face and shoulders and her face was artfully applied with make-up stolen from her mother's more expensive bag of tricks.

She wondered if the photographer she'd come to solicit liked the windblown look. If not, she had pins and combs in her shoulder bag and could quickly pin her tresses up into a chignon, if asked. She'd been practising the art for days.

Already she could see herself on the cover of *Vogue*. Well, maybe one of the lesser known mags to start off with, she corrected herself a little guiltily, remembering one of her step-father's more recent sermons on vanity.

'They've certainly attracted a good crowd,' Monica mused thoughtfully, looking around. There were indeed plenty of stalls, from the modern to the more arcane. She spotted the 'Bowling for a Pig' stall, and her eyes widened in alarm. If there was a live pig involved . . .

'Relax,' Graham said, catching her appalled expression and grinning widely. 'The pig is already in nice packs of cutlets and bacon at the butcher's in town. Whoever wins has to go in and collect it, all hygienically sealed in polythene bags.'

'Ugh, yuck,' Carol-Ann said, wrinkling her nose. 'Oh by the way, did I tell you that I was thinking of becoming a vegetarian?' she added loftily.

Monica gulped slightly, then consoled herself with the thought that Carol-Ann's fads never lasted long. She might pile her plate with veggies for a while, and sniff disdainfully at the rest of them eating roast beef, but after a week or so, the lure of a bacon sandwich would be bound to bring her to her senses.

Now Monica watched suspiciously as her daughter craned her neck around, ogling the crowd intently. Very sweetly, she said, 'Looking for someone in particular, Carol-Ann?'

'Huh? Oh yes, Marc Linacre,' she said, as nonchalantly as only a found-out teenager can.

'Who's Marc Linacre?' Monica demanded archly, fearing the worst.

As befits a vicar's wife, it went without saying that she was dressed far more modestly than her daughter, in a pretty calf-length dress of off-white, patterned with tiny sprigs of scarlet poppies and blue cornflowers. Nevertheless, it hugged her trim figure and showed off her slender waist. When she'd bought it, it had come with a floppy hat to match, but she hadn't quite dared to wear it. She wasn't totally sure that she could carry it off. Like her daughter, she too was wearing white sandals, but her heels were wedged and modest, making walking over the grass a much easier proposition.

'Oh, just a photographer,' Carol-Ann said in answer to her mother's shrewd questioning, and airily shrugged a shoulder in dismissal.

'Carol-Ann . . .' Monica strung out her name in a telling tone. 'If you've come here just to pester Mr Linacre into taking pictures of you, I'll—'

Graham, sensing ructions, coughed gently. 'Oh, he's not that kind of photographer, Mon,' he said quickly. 'He's won loads of awards for black-and-white pictures of old garages and rundown industrial estates. That sort of thing.'

Carol-Ann hid a smile. All that Graham had just said was true, but he'd missed out the most important bit. Before becoming so arty he'd been a fashion photographer, and in the nineties had 'invented' the supermodel Olivia Gee. Linacre had been her manager as well as her favourite photographer, making her one of the most photographed women on the planet. And what he'd done once, Carol-Ann thought hopefully, he could do again!

She shot Graham a grateful smile for coming to her defence, and then spotted the ice-cream van. Surely she wouldn't put on a pound just by licking a lolly, would she?

Monica sighed as she watched her daughter saunter off. No wonder she was dressed like something out of a schoolboy's fantasy.

Just then, a piercing shriek like an animal in agony carried across the field, paralyzing everyone who hadn't been quick enough to slap their hands over their ears. Ernie Gant quickly adjusted the microphone, giving it a hefty thump, and the noise mercifully abated. 'Testing, like, one two . . .' *Screech!*

'I thought they was gonna get that damned thing fixed?' someone near the Aunt Sally stall muttered darkly.

'Costs money,' his companion muttered back, which explained everything, since several of those overhearing this exchange nodded their heads in sympathy.

A WI luminary approached the podium and gingerly took over. She cleared her throat nervously. 'Er . . . ladies and gentlemen . . .' Everyone paused, expecting the screech. It never came. She let out a very audible sigh of relief. 'Thank you for coming to our sixty-fifth annual flower show. Now, to open for us, I'd like you to . . .' *Screech!* '. . . put your hands together for Her Ladyship the . . .' *Screech!* '. . . Dowager Countess of Fulcome.'

And so saying, she stepped with some alacrity away from the microphone and a vision straight out of a gothic horror

50

film stepped up. Until then, the dowager had been hidden by the crowds, and this first glimpse of her had Monica's jaw dropping.

The woman, who began to confidently make the opening speech, apparently unaware of the microphone's discordant interruptions, was dressed in an original tea gown that must have been all the rage in, say, 1890. A full-blown silk gown in bronze, the thing fluffed around her like a hideous tea cosy. But it had competition. A chunky necklace that looked like . . .

'Good grief, are those *real*?' Monica gasped, staring at the huge yellow diamonds that were draped around the wrinkled throat.

'Oh I wouldn't think so,' Graham said carelessly. 'They were probably sold off and replaced with glass long before the war. The First World War, I mean. And even if her disreputable ancestors managed to keep their grasping hands off them and they're still the real McCoy, she still won't be able to sell them. They're bound to be entailed and will have to go to the next generation when she dies.'

'So her daughter-in-law will get them?'

'That's right. And if they are the real thing, I bet that thought drives the old girl wild,' her husband added with a somewhat less than Christian twinkle in his eye. It was well known that Her Ladyship didn't see eye to eye with her eldest son's wife.

'And so, without further ado,' Daphne Cadge-Hampton continued, 'I announce . . .' *Screech!* '. . . this flower . . .' *Screech!* '. . . show open. She literally gabbled out the last two words, before the next ear-splitter could pierce the air, and then, picking up a dangling pair of opera glasses from her bosom, looked out over the crowd.

Monica grinned. 'Graham, she's absolutely wonderful,' she whispered.

'I know. Magnificent, isn't she?' her husband whispered back in agreement. 'And she's got the personality to match the trappings, believe me. You'll have to speak to her sometime this afternoon.'

Monica doubted that she'd have the nerve.

There then followed a concerted rush to a big tent right at the back of the field, which turned out to be the tea tent. There were two other tents, Monica noticed. The biggest of the two belonged to the flower show competition itself, of course; the other, smaller tent belonged to Madame Zorgo, who apparently 'saw all.' Except, it seemed, for the fact that the weather was going to be so hot that the inside of her tent would turn into a veritable furnace, and that she'd have been far better off outside. Still, perhaps the Oracle didn't do weather forecasts.

Monica wondered vaguely if crystal balls could still do the job if they were fogged up with condensation.

'Fancy your chances on the coconut shy?' Graham asked, interrupting her whimsical musings as they passed the stall. Monica glanced at them all lined up, and whispered, 'Do you think they're nailed on?'

'Oh, bound to be, I should think,' her husband whispered back. For as long as he could remember, nobody had ever succeeded in dislodging one of them.

'Go on, then. I don't like coconuts, but if there's no chance of actually winning one . . .' Monica said, stifling a giggle.

They spent a good ten minutes, and a fair amount of money, chucking balls at coconuts and getting cheered on by a pair of late-returning boozers from the pub. Graham actually hit one of the coconuts with a hefty wallop at one point, but the article itself remained suspiciously unmoved. The stall-holder, noting Graham's dog collar, had the grace to blush.

Over in the flower tent, the serious gardeners and the merely curious sneaked in for a quick pre-judging peek. Children ran and squealed underfoot, getting in everyone's way. The five-a-side football teams changed in the new pavilion and trudged out onto the pitch in bright colours to meet either cheers or boos, depending on allegiances. The WI ladies

did a cracking trade, even if their Victoria sponges were wilting a little in the fierce sunlight.

The flower show was underway.

* * *

Melissa Ferris, well aware that she was the closest that Caulcott
Green would ever come to harbouring a femme fatale at its
bosom (and determined to uphold her reputation), made an
entrance that would have done a Hollywood starlet proud.

First, she arrived in a big, chauffeur-driven car (hired for
the day) and wafted through the gates (not without paying
her fifty pence, mind) like Scarlett O'Hara might have wafted
into the halls of Tara in search of Rhett. She was wearing a fig-
ure-hugging ice-blue dress with silver threads; sleeveless, back-
less, and almost frontless as well. With it she wore three-inch
high heels and a domed hat with a huge rim. Her lips were as
scarlet as the poppies growing in the surrounding cornfields
and huge dark sunglasses shaded her eyes.

Whispers followed her passing. She wasn't quite sure
where her husband was in the crowd, but she was certain that
news of her unexpected appearance would soon find its way
to his less than shell-like ears. She smiled at the WI ladies'
stall, but didn't pause. She graciously bought a glass of lemon
squash from the tea tent, and took it to stand in the shade
of the pavilion and watch the footballers. Number eight had
really good legs.

* * *

Over on his tombola stall, Sean Gregson was on his fourth
bottle of beer. Ernie Gant always bought a few crates in and
sold them on the quiet to his cronies. Like Melissa, he was
also looking out for one man in the crowd, but in his case, it
wasn't Ross Ferris.

* * *

Carol-Ann Clancy finally spotted a possible contender for the Cotswolds' most famous photographer, and eyed the woman by his side warily. She looked like trouble. Probably the wife. 'Damn,' Carol-Ann muttered. 'Why couldn't he have been gay?'

* * *

Wendy Davies was in the tea tent, listening to Vera Gant's woes (which consisted of varicose veins, a rent man who didn't understand her, and a grandson who kept growing out of his shoes), and served her eighteenth cup of tea and biscuits to her husband. James then informed her that he was off to the flower show tent for the start of the judging.

* * *

From two different directions, Ross Ferris and Gordon Trenning were also making their way to the tea tent, but Gordon spotted his hated nemesis first and slowed cautiously, watching him go inside before turning away to pace and wait.

Gordon didn't look well. Despite the heat he was wearing dark trousers, a long-sleeved white shirt, and — unbelievably — a jacket. Not surprisingly, he was sweating profusely. Every now and then his tongue would slip out over his lips in a nervous habit that made many people look at him queerly. He jumped when a sinuous arm slipped through his, and he whipped his head around wildly. What he saw made his face fall comically.

Melissa laughed. 'Oh, Gordon, that's not very flattering. Most men are pleased to see me. And you are now a veritable ladies' man, or so I hear.' She found it rather amusing that Gordon, *Gordon* of all people, should be considered such a catch by the local female residents. It just goes to show what a silly backwater this really is, she thought sourly.

Gordon managed a rather sickly smile. 'Mel— Mrs Ferris, I didn't know you were going to be here today,' he gulped miserably.

'Melissa, please, Gordon,' she purred, and laughed. 'And I hope that *nobody* expected me to be here today. Least of all my ever-loving husband.'

At the mention of that man, Gordon winced, and automatically his hand went to his inside jacket pocket. He felt the tiny hard capsule in there with reassurance tinged with a nauseating kind of panic, and he swallowed back something nasty in his throat. He wanted to throw up.

Melissa's dark eyes flashed curiously at his expression, her gaze following the movement of his hand, and she smiled sardonically. 'You don't have to guard your wallet, you know, Gordon,' she laughed. 'There's no chance you'll get pickpocketed here,' she scoffed, waving a hand around. 'I doubt the locals even know what it means. Or are you guarding something even more precious?'

Gordon saw something suddenly flash in her eyes that went beyond mere curiosity, and he felt a lurch of sheer panic. He'd always been scared of this woman. The habit she had of always getting her own way chilled his blood. 'Well, I think I'll go and . . . er . . . buy a cake,' he said desperately, his eyes happening to fall on the WI stall.

Melissa blinked, her eyes narrowing suspiciously as he moved away. She'd heard the rumours about his abortive attempt to sue Ross over something or other that he'd created, and wondered how much the scientist really resented his boss. She was beginning to think that he resented him quite a lot. And that could prove useful — very useful indeed.

Melissa resolved to keep a close eye on Gordon Trenning for the rest of the afternoon. And, if possible, find out exactly what it was that he had in that jacket pocket of his that was causing him so much stress.

* * *

In the flower show tent, Sir Hugh checked his notes for the rallying little pep talk that he always gave his fellow judges before the serious business of awarding the rosettes began.

This year it gave old Daphne a little nudge and a broad hint about parting with that cup of hers.

His eyes looked to the small top table, where the various rosettes and other more modest cups were placed, ready to be awarded. Dwarfing them all was the Cadge-Hampton Gladiola Cup — a real silver monstrosity with carved ivory handles.

He spied Malvin Cook, casting his experienced eye over the onions and slowly wandering down the rows of vegetables. His gardener, Sir Hugh noticed with a slight start of surprise, looked very tired indeed.

* * *

Sean Gregson was on his sixth bottle of beer when he finally saw his quarry wandering around looking like he was going to a bank manager's meeting.

'Git,' Sean snarled, startling the timid Mrs Weston, who was buying some raffle tickets from him. She hastily handed over her precious pennies and hurried away, hoping that she won the bottle of sherry. She was rather fond of sherry.

Sean spotted Ernie Gant helping someone with a recalcitrant trestle table, and wandered over. 'Hey, Ernie, watch me stall for a minute, will ya?' he asked, and without waiting for a response set off through the crowd.

Monica and Graham were exploring the jumble sale items when they heard the first ructions.

'But, Mr Gregson, I assure you . . .' a worried voice floated past two ladies haggling over who had seen a beaded handbag first.

'Assure me nothing, you poncy git,' a voice growled back in response. 'You ain't talking to one of your arty-farty friends now.'

'Mr Gregson, please.'

Graham, sensing trouble, politely smiled at the ladies, who each had a firm grip on the handbag, and sidestepped around them, Monica hot on his heels.

'You gonna leave my Linda alone or what?'

A small gap had opened up between the interested observers forming around the two men, one of whom was now aggressively leaning against the other, chin thrust forward.

'But Linda wants—' the suited man began, but wasn't allowed to get any further. Sean lunged, grabbing his lapels and somewhat comically pulling him up onto tiptoe.

The other man squeaked something very odd, given the circumstances. 'Watch my pocket, you fool!' he yelled, panic evident in his voice, silencing the crowd within a ten-yard radius.

Sean Gregson sneered. 'Worried about the cut of your suit, are yer?' he snarled, himself a little surprised by the sudden and out-of-proportion terror on the other man's face. He almost let him go, such was his disdain. 'Now you listen here — you think I don't know that you've been two-timing my Linda, but I does, see?' Sean thrust his face further towards Gordon's white-lipped one. 'So you leave her alone, or one of these dark nights . . .' The threat hung heavy in the air, but Gordon didn't seem to hear it. Instead his hand went over Sean Gregson's right hand, feeling around it, trying to find out . . .

'Here, leave off,' Sean said in some alarm, snatching his hand away. Instantly, Gordon's hand shot inside his jacket pocket. He seemed to wilt with relief.

'I think that'll do, don't you?' a voice said mildly, breaking into the strained atmosphere.

Sean turned abruptly, intent on giving a snarling rejoinder that the interloper should mind his own bloody business. Just in time he noticed the tall, dark, handsome man's dog collar and the words were hastily swallowed back. Sean, like most villagers born and bred in the countryside, still retained, even in this day and age, an almost automatic respect for the clergy. Even if it wasn't his own vicar doing the interfering.

'Oh, yeah, right,' Sean muttered, belatedly removing his other hand from Gordon's jacket, as if he'd just touched something unmentionable. 'Sorry . . . er . . . Reverend.' He vaguely recognized the other man now. He was local somewhere, one of the vicar's pals. 'Bit of a misunderstanding,' he added, blushing a little under Graham's steady gaze. 'On account of someone,' and here he glowered at the pale-faced Gordon, 'messing me daughter about, two-timing her and such.'

This time Graham turned to look at Gordon, who also promptly flushed. He opened his mouth to say something hotly, then seemed to think better of it.

Monica bit her lip.

The poor little man didn't look like anybody's idea of a Lothario, and she couldn't be the only one to hear the little titters and the beginnings of avid whispers going around the crowd. She felt quite sorry for him, in fact.

Gordon muttered something that might have been an apology, and then plunged off through the crowd. Sean, family honour restored, gave himself a mental pat on the back and wandered back to his stall. The entertainment over, the decibel level rose once more.

Graham turned to Monica, who grinned up at him. 'The scourge of ruffians everywhere, aren't you?' she said softly, and fluttered her eyelashes. 'My hero.'

Graham gave her a flat stare. 'Just call me Dirty Harry.' Monica burst into laughter.

She didn't know it, but it was to be her last carefree moment of the afternoon.

CHAPTER 6

In the tea tent, the two lady volunteers were wilting. Vera Gant wiped a dark lock off her wet forehead and said gruffly to Wendy, 'Right, that's it. I've had enough of this,' and marched out firmly in search of her husband. She found him behind the pavilion, drinking with his mates, and succinctly told him what she thought of husbands sitting in the shade and getting drunk whilst their suffering wives baked.

Grumbling guiltily, Ernie followed her into the tent, taking a quick gasp as the hot moist air hit him. Monica Noble, who'd popped in for a squash, smiled at him knowingly.

'Blimey, love, you're right,' he said to his wife. 'It's sweltering in here. What you need is to get a bit of a breeze blowing through. Hold on and I'll open up some flaps at the back for you. That should do the trick.'

'See that you do,' Vera said grimly. 'And be careful which flaps you open. The chemical loos have been put around the back there too somewhere, and on a hot day like this . . .' she trailed off meaningfully.

Ernie blanched. 'Righto, love,' he mumbled.

He walked to the back of the huge tent, where interior canvas walls tapered to a dog-legged narrow canvas corridor.

On his left, a flap led off into a separate area that read 'Gents,' and on his right were the 'Ladies.' Going on further — and as far as he could possibly get from the conveniences — he quickly knelt down at the back of the tent and began untying strategically placed strings. Within ten minutes he had the back middle flap loose, allowing in some fresher air, and he looked back thoughtfully into the interior of the tent. The positioning of the toilets made the open egress invisible to those inside, and he only hoped that the breeze would be able to make its way back into the main area. To be sure, he stepped outside, almost cannoning into the chain-link fence that backed onto the next field. Containing newly cut barley, the field had wicked-looking stubble. The gap between the fence and the tent was just enough for one man to be able to walk through, and Ernie quickly set about folding the flap back and making it bigger. Then he walked all the way around the left-hand side of the tent, nodding a pleasant greeting to a thin man dressed in a suit, who was hovering around the main front entrance as he passed. But Ernie couldn't find any more suitable or potential openings. The tent was very well made.

He came in through the front again, and to his relief felt a definite breeze blowing in from the back.

'Oh, Ernie, thank you, that's at least a little bit better,' Wendy Davies said gratefully as she served Ross Ferris with a glass of squash.

'That's all right, missus,' he mumbled. 'I'll just go have a look on the other side and see if I can't find another flap to open.'

James Davies, having been waylaid on his way to the flower tent by a parishioner, watched from a short distance away as Ernie began to loosen one of the tent flaps at the bottom and then raise it up with a few stakes.

Gordon Trenning, unnerved by the big odd-job man stalking the tent, was still hovering just outside and waiting for Ross Ferris to leave. Monica Noble looked at him curiously as she exited with her much-needed glass of squash.

Gordon was growing increasingly light-headed, and if he didn't have something cold to drink soon, he feared he might even pass out. Besides, there was someone inside he wanted to talk to. Unfortunately, he'd arrived just too late to see James Davies walk away.

* * *

Inside, Ross Ferris looked scornfully down into the lemon squash that he'd just bought and wondered why he bothered. There wasn't even any ice in it.

'Thank you, Mrs Davies,' he smiled across at Wendy, noticing that she'd lost weight recently. In the heat, all her blonde curls had straightened out into damp strings, and her hands had had a small but obvious tremor when handing over his plastic glass of squash. He was vaguely aware that there'd been some sort of a tragedy in the Davies household, but now he couldn't quite remember what. 'So, are you judging anything this year?' he asked politely.

'Yes, the asters,' Wendy responded listlessly.

'Ah, lovely flowers,' he muttered, thinking nothing of the sort. Vera Gant, who had a nose for hypocrisy, shot him a dirty look.

'Do you think so?' Wendy asked limply, obviously not at all interested but trying to make conversation with this most contentious of her husband's flock.

'Oh yes. I told my gardener, we must have asters. I'm judging the roses myself this year,' he added smugly.

Vera snorted. Oh yes, he was judging the roses this year all right, and didn't the whole village know it? For the last twenty odd years or so, Millie Fletcher had always judged the roses and was an acknowledged expert on the subject, albeit in an amateurish sort of way. And then, suddenly, Ross Ferris had nosed his way in. Vera had heard that Sir Hugh had put up a good fight for Millie, but in vain. Especially when Ross had cunningly introduced to the village committee the possibility of donating a Ferris Rose Cup in the future. Gold, he said he was going to make it, or so they said. The big show-off.

'Ah well, that'll be easy,' Vera sniffed, hijacking the conversation. She'd never been able to avoid making mischief when the chance arose. 'Sam Dix's entry is bound to win. Everyone's saying so, so you won't have much work to do, Ross.'

She saw him wince, and smiled happily. Not only did she refuse to call him Mr Ferris, she also knew that she was getting at him, even if he wasn't quite sure how himself.

'Oh well, we'll see.' Ross forced a laugh. 'After all, I'm the judge, so I get the final say.'

Vera felt a sudden twinge of misgiving as she realized that she'd probably just done Sam out of his first-prize rosette. She could easily imagine Ross Ferris giving it to another entry just to spite her and declare his independence against the prevailing consensus of opinion.

'It's my James who's got the biggest problem, I'm thinking,' Wendy Davies put in quickly, sensing the antagonism arising between them. 'He's judging the dahlias this year. There are so many entries and all of them so good. Everyone's buzzing to see who wins.'

Ross turned to her, his eyes suddenly sharpening. 'Really?' Uh-oh, thought Vera. That's torn it.

'Oh yes. But James is always scrupulously fair.' The vicar's wife gave a slight laugh. 'Even though the bribes have been coming in thick and fast.'

Ross blinked in astonishment. 'Bribes?' he asked, his eyes avid.

Wendy smiled. 'Well, Robbie Broadbent suddenly offered us the best of his cowslip wine the other day. And Mrs Watkins came over with some early apples. Her tree always does fruit first. Then there was Jack Rapton's offer to fix that broken pew in the church. He's a marvellous carpenter, you know, and his pom-pom entry really is a contender . . .'

Even the innocent and naive Wendy began to sense that something was wrong and slowly her voice trailed off. She shot the grim-faced Vera a questioning look.

'So, dahlias are where the action is this year?' Ross mused, and quickly glanced around. 'And where is the vicar, Mrs Davies? I thought he was in here a moment ago.'

Wendy, suddenly cottoning on, looked alarmed. 'Oh, he's already gone to the flower tent, I think,' she said, then added quickly, 'but Sir Hugh doesn't like judges swapping classes right at the last minute.' But she had to call the last few words to his already retreating back. She bit her lip. 'Oh dear. Poor James.'

'What's up?' Monica Noble asked, having come back into the tent and caught Wendy's lament. Carol-Ann, having spotted her mother with refreshments, had waylaid her and nabbed the booty, hence her return for more liquid sustenance. 'Is James having difficulties?'

'Oh no, it's nothing,' Wendy said vaguely, rearranging the cups.

'That man's a menace,' Vera said grimly, and explained what had happened to Monica, who did her best to pour oil onto troubled waters.

Wendy sighed and felt her head swim. It was so *hot*. And she'd had a headache all day. She really wanted to go home. She didn't need these petty upsets and all these stupid people. But of course, she couldn't go home. Even now, another customer was walking in.

A strange fellow, in a suit of all things.

* * *

James Davies had just managed to disentangle himself from the clutches of his needy parishioner when once again he found himself being hailed. He'd just gone past the second-hand bookstall when Ross Ferris caught up with him.

'Ah, Vicar, there you are. I was just wondering if I might have a quick word.'

James looked around for escape, but for once there was no one within earshot who might come to his rescue. He took a fortifying breath.

'Mr Ferris,' James beamed, turning head on to face him. 'What can I do for you?'

* * *

In the flower show tent, Sir Hugh glanced around the small group of wandering spectators, and once again checked his watch. Damn it, where was everybody? The judging was due to start soon and he liked to keep to the schedule. The children's races were due to start promptly at 3:45 p.m. and he was scheduled to award the egg-and-spoon prize.

He'd have to slip out now if he hoped to catch Gordon Trenning. Damn the man, why hadn't he sought him out before this? The scientist must have guessed where he'd be. As chairman of the flower show he wasn't likely to be anywhere else but in this tent.

Sir Hugh, always punctual and strictly a to-the-letter man, didn't care for this modern, casual way of doing things. If a man said he'd meet you, he should keep his word. Besides, he was itching with impatience to see what Trenning had for him. He'd sounded quite excited over the phone the other night.

Sir Hugh heaved a sigh. Well, if the mountain wouldn't come to Mohammed . . .

* * *

Over by the gladiolus displays, Malvin Cook made sure that the last finishing touches to their entry had been completed. At the last minute, he'd lightly sprayed their lovely Green Woodpecker exhibit with water, pleased at their lime-green and red patterns. They were lovely, and the spray perked them up just right.

He went on past the other gladiolus displays, smiling at the small blooms, the less intense colours, and then stopped dead in front of a display of pure white blooms. They were beauties. Real beauties. A look of sudden and intense hatred

64

shot across Malvin's normally placid face as he spied the name affixed to them. It would have shocked any of his friends who might have seen it, but luckily — or unluckily, depending on your viewpoint — Malvin was alone.

He stood staring at the flowers for a long, long time.

* * *

Carol-Ann Clancy had managed to find out quite a lot about her quarry in the last half an hour or so.

By judicious questioning of the teenage boys who were hanging about, she'd discovered that Marc Linacre lived in a big farmhouse a mile from the village and had arrived in a nifty red sports car with his second wife. His first wife, she knew, had divorced him after his scandalous affair with Olivia Gee and, as a result of this, his second wife now kept him on a very tight leash indeed. She'd also discovered that he was going down to London next week to a gallery opening of his own works. So he was still 'in' and hopefully in the mood to discover another model to capture the spirit of today's youth. She could see her name up in lights now.

All things considered, Carol-Ann was feeling optimistic.

* * *

In the tea tent, Gordon Trenning gratefully accepted a glass of squash, and gulped it down in one go. Vera Gant watched him, half-amused, half-maternal, and said flatly, 'You should take that silly jacket off, you know. No wonder you're gasping for a drink. Here, have another one.'

Gordon, a touch wild-eyed, took a step back, as if afraid the big, cheerful woman would try to physically divest him of his garment, but gratefully accepted the second glass that she had made him.

'Er, thanks,' he mumbled.

Monica, sipping her own squash, watched him with open concern.

'You know, you don't look at all well,' Wendy's gentle voice chipped in, and Gordon glanced across at the local vicar's wife in surprise. If she'd been a bit fatter and a bit older, she'd have reminded him quite forcefully of his own mother. As it was, she had the same kind of quiet, dulcet tone of voice that his mother had always possessed. Unexpectedly, he felt a lump jump into his throat, and he quickly blinked back tears.

Good grief, he thought with sudden, bitter self-disgust. I'm coming apart at the seams. Just because of this damned thing in my pocket. Oh why oh why did I ever make it? Let alone bring it here.

'Mrs Davies,' he said, something in his voice making all three women in the tent look at him sharply. 'Is your husband here?'

Vera felt herself bristle with sudden interest. Here was human drama and no mistake. She sidled just a bit closer, her avid ears flapping, whilst Monica felt her sympathies go out to Wendy. As a fellow vicar's wife, she knew just how much pressure ordinary people could put on you without even trying.

From outside, Daphne Cadge-Hampton's eccentric and bizarre figure half-stepped into the doorway. Her quick and sharp eyes went over the scene like twin lasers.

'No, I'm afraid James has already gone to the judging tent,' Wendy said, biting her lip at the sudden desperation in the younger man's face. She felt herself crumbling. This was all she needed. Monica, sensing it, took a half-step towards her, to see if Wendy might pass the problem over to her.

But Wendy, who would forever know her duty, said gently, 'Do you want me to go and get him, Dr . . . er . . . ?'

'Trenning,' Gordon said, not surprised that she didn't know his name. 'I don't know. Really, I'm not sure what to do,' he added, looking at her with the kind of appeal some stray dogs had when you were eating a particularly tasty meat-filled sandwich.

Wendy felt herself surrendering. Yet again, someone in need, she thought despairingly. Always someone else in need.

'Why don't we just step outside for a moment?' she asked softly, coming from around the table with its cheerful teacups and packets of biscuits and gently reaching for him. 'It'll be cooler outside.' She took him firmly by the arm and led him outside, but the hand she put on his arm was not quite steady itself.

Gordon nodded and allowed himself to be led, relieved to have someone else making the decisions for him. He'd been such a damned fool. But here was hope that he could still sort it out.

They sidestepped the countess, who watched them walk away thoughtfully, and instinctively headed towards the now temporarily deserted second-hand bookstall. It was just the sort of place that they could talk without interruption.

Daphne watched them go, and sighed. 'Damn, where's the vicar when you need him?' the old aristocrat mumbled to herself, loudly enough to be overheard.

Monica, who'd been the one to inadvertently do the over-hearing, was thinking much the same thing as she once again left the tent and set off to find her own husband. She'd have to have a long talk with Graham about persuading James to take Wendy away for a nice long holiday one day soon.

* * *

A quarter of an hour later, at three o'clock, the loud speakers suddenly squawked to attention, and Sir Hugh's ponderous, never-to-be-mistaken voice called for all flower show judges to make their way to the tent. The judging was to begin.

And in more ways than one.

CHAPTER 7

Carol-Ann heard the announcement over the loudspeaker just as she was loosening her diaphanous blouse in order to tie it into a knot at her midriff, thus emphasizing her slender waist. Naturally, she made sure that the resultant knot was strategically placed to draw attention to her attractive shape and for this procedure she had, perhaps not unsurprisingly, earned herself a small but dedicated audience consisting mostly, but not entirely, of teenage boys.

'Sir Hugh's got his finger on the pulse, I see,' a beer-bellied man, stretched out on the grass and turning lobster pink in the sun, said sarcastically to his friend, who was stretched out beside him, and likewise changing colour. Both men's eyes were fixed firmly on Carol-Ann.

'Don't he always? Still thinks he's in the flaming army,' his companion responded morosely.

Carol-Ann, now showing even more flesh than she had been before (and secretly feeling just a little bit nervous about it), set off determinedly to the sidelines of the football field. She knew her mother would not approve of the new-look blouse, and hoped she'd never have to find out about it, but you couldn't afford not to use every trick in the book if you wanted to get ahead. Or so she'd read.

Marc Linacre was obviously something of a football fan, she mused, since he'd been watching the games in progress ever since the first two teams had started playing.

She carefully sidled up to the lone man. It was no coincidence that she'd waited until his wife had gone off to the tea tent for refreshments. She wasn't sure that the wife would understand that, for her, it was strictly business, and that she had absolutely no designs on her husband.

Hearing a repeated call for the attendance of the judges over the loudhailer, Carol-Ann glanced casually across at the flower tent, seeing the tall, erect, military-looking figure standing in the entrance. Not so long ago, she'd noticed him at the tea tent, not going in, but instead slipping around the side and disappearing behind the back. And when, almost straight after, a man in a suit had done exactly the same thing, she was sure that they must both be using that area to have a crafty pee. Talk about gross.

Unless, of course, they were having a secret assignation, she thought, the idea of a clandestine tryst perking her up somewhat. Not that the old man looked the type. Still, Carol-Ann thought judiciously, you never can tell.

But other people's peccadilloes, interesting though they might be, were not her top priority just then, and she quickly snapped her mind back to the project in hand. Marc Linacre had *noticed* her. Finally!

The celebrity photographer was in his fifties, she gauged astutely, but careful grooming had made him look much younger. Which was not surprising — a man such as this must know all the tricks of the trade when it came to making the human form look good.

She was careful to look surprised, as if only just now noticing his presence, then she tossed her head, making sure that her long blonde hair fell around her shoulders, before turning slightly away. Playing hard to get was still the best way to get a man's attention, wasn't it? she wondered uneasily. Or was that so yesterday now? She cast him a quick look out of the corner of her eye to see how well the ploy had worked.

Damn, he was watching the football again!

Carol-Ann sidled a few steps closer and said casually, 'Who's winning?'

Marc Linacre shot her a startled look and automatically looked over his shoulder. But for once his wife's inimical glare was nowhere to be seen. 'Er, the home team,' he said.

She took yet another tiny crab-like step closer, trying to feel confident and at ease. Instead, she was uncomfortably aware that she was beginning to perspire, just a little bit. She tried to push aside her sudden attack of nerves. 'Do I know you?' she blurted out, then felt herself flush. How trite was that? She forced a laugh. 'I mean, your face is kinda familiar. Are you an actor or something?' she tried again.

Far from looking flattered, his eyes took on that particularly haunted look of a man who knew when he was in trouble. 'No, no, nothing like that,' he said hastily.

Snapping her fingers — hoping she wasn't overdoing it — Carol-Ann grinned broadly. 'I've got it. You're that famous photographer. I read an interview you did once for . . . now what was it. *Cosmopolitan*?'

Marc shrugged. 'Maybe,' he said, and suddenly bellowed at a nearby striker to pass the damned ball to his unmarked friend.

Carol-Ann hid a groan. This was obviously not going to be as easy a nut to crack as she'd thought. Behind her, unobserved, Angela Linacre emerged from the tent, two cups of tea in her hand.

'I read a lot of magazines, of course,' Carol-Ann continued blithely. 'Well, when you're a model, you have to. You know, to keep up to date with everything.'

'Hmm.'

'You used to be somebody big in the fashion world, didn't you?' she added, figuring that a bit of reverse psychology couldn't hurt. Perhaps she could sting his vanity and make him admit to his past greatness?

'Hmm. I used to be,' he gritted, feeling himself break out into a fine sweat. His wife had a very sharp tongue when it came to expressing her opinions about the nubile young women that haunted the fashion industry.

'So do you think photographers nowadays would be able to spot another Olivia Gee in the crowd?' she asked, making it clear with a faultlessly worshipping look that she considered that only he, the great Marc Linacre, had the ability to spot such winners.

Men could never resist flattery, Carol-Ann knew. Even her mother said so.

A lock of long blonde hair fell over her arm. Carelessly, she lifted a hand to toss it back.

Marc Linacre gulped.

'My husband doesn't do models,' an icy voice suddenly cut across the grunting and yelling of the male voices on the pitch, and Carol-Ann spun around. The woman in front of her was dressed in a cream blouse and a long scarlet skirt. Dark hair going grey at the temples matched the dark brown eyes that glared at her like two currants in a suet pudding.

Carol-Ann did a gulp of her own. 'Oh, hello,' she managed weakly.

'Darling, your tea,' Angela said, handing over a cup to her bemused husband, who was doing his best to look as innocent as he actually was.

Which was never a good idea.

Angela cast a 'get lost' look at the beautiful teenager that not even Carol-Ann could ignore, and with a blush that she forced into a sniff and a flounce, Carol-Ann walked off, head held high. But definitely defeated.

Only for now, though, she thought, her face flaming. She wasn't giving up just yet.

* * *

On the other side of the field, her mother and stepfather, in a state of blissful ignorance as to their daughter's endeavours, entered the flower show tent with twin smiles of delight.

Here every other flap was turned back, and a large gap was missing in the roof, allowing a pleasantly cooling breeze to circulate inside. The rows and rows of colourful flowers, some giving off a sweet scent, made the scene pretty enough to paint.

The tent was divided into two sections, with the fruit and veg at the back, and the jams, preserves, pickles and other old country-recipe baked goods flanking them on either side. The flowers took pride of place in the front.

'Ah, here I am,' Graham said, eyeing the lily table with a faintly worried look. He wished now that he'd paid more attention to the flower books that Monica had got out of the library for him.

'I like those pink ones,' Monica said promptly.

'Hey, no getting to the judge,' Graham objected. 'Can you see the sweet peas?'

It took only a minute to find Monica's own table, and she eyed the expanse of pastel-coloured sweetly smelling blooms with just a little trepidation. 'Graham, they all look the same to me,' she said in mild panic.

'Don't worry. Just sniff them, hold them up to the light, check the stems and pretend you know what you're doing. No one will know the difference. At least, that's what I always do and I seem to get away with it,' he advised her with a somewhat shocking, cavalier insouciance.

'Oh, thanks a bunch,' Monica said sourly, not so sure by any means that she'd be able to get away with such a bluff as easily as a man wearing a dog collar, but she shot him a grateful grin nevertheless. 'Let's have a look at these famous roses then,' she said, for even in Heyford Bassett they'd heard the rumours that Sam Dix had come up with a cracker of a display of his favourite Peace rose.

It wasn't hard to find, and looking at the huge, pretty heads of pink, cream, and yellow, Monica couldn't resist lowering her dark head for a crafty sniff.

'Hmm, wonderful,' she said softly.

'Quick, Sir Hugh's coming,' Graham hissed at her, and Monica shot back upright to guilty attention. It would definitely blot her copybook to have the chairman catch her out poaching on a fellow judge's terrain.

'Ah, Mrs Noble,' Sir Hugh said jovially in passing, pretending — like the gentleman that he was — not to have noticed her lapse in etiquette. For although it was undoubtedly very bad form for judges to inspect other judges' tables like that, he was rather fond of Peace, and had been longing to have a sniff himself. In fact, it was no secret that it was his absolute favourite, and once the judging was over he'd probably have a proper look-see.

Malvin Cook, oblivious to protocol, was still wandering around the fruit and veg section, admiring an entry of carrots.

Sir Hugh, wondering why there were always stragglers, glanced impatiently at his watch. They were still short of several judges, including Lady Daphne herself. He smiled indulgently at the thought of her, as always. A law unto herself was Her Ladyship — she always had been, and no doubt always would be.

With time on his hands, and happy about the little item now safely tucked away in his inside pocket, he wandered around the stalls, winding up at the gladiolus table. His own Woodpecker entry was especially fine, although he had entered others, of course; but he suspected the Woodpecker would clinch it for him.

He continued on slowly down the table, his knowledgeable eyes going ahead to scrutinize the others as he did so, and suddenly he stiffened. At the very end of the table were four entries, but it was the pure white blooms that immediately caught his eye. Slowly, feeling his pulse quicken in dread, he walked up to them, giving himself time to take in their form. Yes, as he'd suspected, they were perfect. Damn! A challenger.

Although he knew Daphne liked colour and drama, like Woodpecker, she also had the true aristo's liking for purity and simplicity of form.

Quickly his eye fell to the name on the little plaque in front of the display, and his eyes bulged. He went so red he looked as if he was about to have a fit of apoplexy. Sir Hugh saw his gardener and, most unusually, imperiously beckoned him over.

'Uh-oh,' said Graham, who'd been one of the few to notice Sir Hugh's sudden ire. 'It looks as if poor old Malvin's done something to get himself into the dog house. Sir Hugh looks madder than a wet hen.'

'Who?' Monica said.

Quickly her husband explained to her the history of Sir Hugh and Malvin, and their mutual obsession with getting Sir Hugh's name on the Cadge-Hampton cup.

'You think he's spotted some hitch in the plan, then?' Monica smiled, unable to take it at all seriously.

Graham, a little more experienced when it came to the passions and obsessions of men, deemed it wise to slowly meander over and see if he could head off any unpleasantness.

'Look at that!' he heard Sir Hugh hiss in his gardener's gnome-like ear. 'He didn't even grow them himself. I heard he'd hired some damn fancy gardener from the parks service!'

Graham hid a smile. Strictly speaking, Sir Hugh hadn't grown his own flowers either — Malvin had. But this hardly seemed the time to point it out. He glanced at the flowers in question. They were certainly lovely examples. He also had excellent vision and was just able to make out the name on the rival entry. And his heart sank: Ross Ferris.

'Arrr, I knows,' Malvin said, his rolling Cotswolds accent even thicker than usual. His accent always became more noticeable the more excited or angry he got. 'I noticed 'em afore.'

'Well, what do you think?' Sir Hugh spluttered, still red-faced and incensed.

Malvin looked troubled. 'Thems good 'uns,' he muttered reluctantly.

James Davies, looking over the roses, also sensed the strain and tension emanating from the small group of men and, curious, started to come over.

'They'd better not win,' Sir Hugh growled. To have the Ross Ferris name on his cup . . . it wasn't even to be thought about! 'If they do, mind you, Cook,' Sir Hugh hissed, 'you're fired!'

Beside her husband, Monica, who'd just joined him, gasped in genuine distress. 'Oh no,' she whispered, clutching his arm. 'That poor old man!'

But Graham merely patted her hand mildly, and smiled comfortingly. 'No, it's all right. He threatens to fire Malvin at least once a month, or so I've heard. Neither of them takes the threats seriously,' he whispered back. Then, a little louder, he said soothingly, 'Good afternoon, Sir Hugh. At least we've got the weather for it today. The last time I was here it rained cats and dogs as I remember.'

Sir Hugh started and turned around. Monica smiled at both men, but couldn't help but notice the look on the old gardener's face. For a man who regularly got fired and didn't take any notice, he certainly seemed upset. She felt the urge to go over to him and reassure him that everything would be all right, but she did no such thing, of course, sensing that it would only embarrass him.

And with a muttered word that could have meant anything, Malvin excused himself and shuffled away.

But once at the entrance, she noticed, he turned and cast the white gladioli a strange and distinctly malevolent look before stomping out.

For some reason, it made her shiver. Which was silly, of course, because it was only about flowers.

'Ah, there you are, Sir Hugh,' James Davies's teddy-bear-like figure joined them. 'Are we all gathered?'

To Monica's surprise, she saw a look close to consternation appear in Sir Hugh's eyes as the local vicar smiled at him. ''Fraid not, Jim,' Sir Hugh said, sounding friendly enough. Perhaps too friendly? Monica wondered. There was almost too much of the hail-fellow-well-met about him now. Was there some problem between the squire and the vicar that Graham hadn't thought to tell her?

'We're still missing your better half, I'm afraid, and Daphne, of course,' Sir Hugh added with a somewhat strained smile.

James nodded knowingly. 'Ah yes, Her Ladyship. She'd be late to her own funeral, I fear.'

Sir Hugh's eyes didn't quite meet James's but he laughed heartily, his glance moving on to a spot just over his shoulder. Yes, he's definitely uncomfortable around James, Monica thought now, with a glimmer of interest in her eyes. She glanced across at Graham to see if he'd noticed it, but her husband was looking as bland-faced as was possible.

'Well, I suppose I'd better give yet another call to arms,' Sir Hugh said. 'See if we can't roust out your good lady and our other straggler.'

They watched him walk off toward the entrance with his loudhailer, detouring on the way to the rose table to bend over the display of Peace, cupping the biggest bloom in his hand and inhaling heartily. He admired the flowers for some moments before stepping outside and bellowing orders to recalcitrant judges.

Monica, unable to stand it any longer, walked up to him, touched his arm gently, and said, 'I think they're both in the tea tent. Or they were when I just left them. I'll go and fetch them for you, shall I?' She smiled sweetly.

* * *

In the tea tent, both Wendy and Vera heard the impatience in Sir Hugh's voice as he called yet again for the judges. 'Oh dear, I'd better go. Vera, are you sure you can cope on your own?' Wendy said, sounding harried.

'Of course I can, love,' Vera said comfortably. 'I told our Ernie, as soon as he hears Sir Hugh calling you to the tent, he's got to come and give me a hand. And he will,' she added meaningfully, a gimlet look in her eye. He knew what would happen if he didn't. Then she smiled in evident satisfaction. 'Look, here he comes now.' And indeed, through the tent's open doorway they could see Ernie's rather ape-like figure cutting a swathe through the crowd. He gave a strange sort of hand-to-forehead nod as he approached the tent, and Vera realized that the countess must still be standing just outside. Poor old Ernie never did quite know how to act around her.

It amused Daphne no end.

Wendy removed her pinafore and looked around for her handbag, a small, neat affair in white leather. 'Does my hair look all right?' she asked, without any real interest. As she spoke, Monica stepped into the tent.

Vera glanced at her friend's damp strands and smiled. 'You look lovely,' she lied pleasantly. A customer, who'd just purchased some lukewarm squash, finished it thirstily and put the plastic cup back on the table. 'Oh, hello, Mrs Noble,' she said, catching sight of Monica. 'Come to round up Wendy?'

Monica smiled and spread her hands helplessly. 'You know Sir Hugh,' she said, stepping aside to let the customer pass her. Just as she was leaving, however, the woman, who looked to be in her fifties, stumbled over one of the guy ropes and, her arms flailing and unable to find anything to hang on to, took a rather spectacular and nasty tumble onto the hard-packed grass. She gave a little grunt and a pained 'Whoof!' as she hit the ground, and instantly Wendy, Monica, Vera, and Ernie were all rushing to help her.

'Hey, missus, you ought to take a little more water with it next time,' Ernie grinned teasingly as he reached down to help haul her, rather unceremoniously, to her feet.

The poor woman was beetroot red with embarrassment by now, and was cupping her elbow protectively.

'Good grief, I'm a clumsy so and so,' she said, her voice a little uneven with fought back tears of surprise and pain.

'Here, let me get you a nice cup of tea and a chair,' Vera said, instantly making herself truly useful. 'Lots of sugar too. That's the thing for a shock. And falling over at our age *is* a bit of a shock,' she added over her shoulder, as if somebody was arguing with her.

Wendy quickly got a deck chair and placed it on the ground and, still muttering about her big feet and not watching where she was going, the older woman sank into it gratefully.

Monica, in an effort to ease her embarrassment, related a story of her own, telling how she'd fallen over in the street once whilst shopping, and how foolish it had made her feel when she'd burst into tears. Vera came back with the tea, and then nodded at the guy rope. 'Ernie, that thing's a menace. I've seen one or two other people trip over it today,' she added, casting a comforting glance at the older woman, as if to say she was not the only one with two left feet. 'Can't you have it up and hammer it in somewhere else?'

Ernie, knowing that it was useless to argue about proper tent construction with his wife, obediently nipped inside, where he'd stashed his tools out of sight, and set to with a jemmy and a mallet. 'Soon have this fixed, love,' he said with a wink to the woman in the deck chair, as if that would make her feel any better.

She blushed even harder, then rubbed her elbow ruefully and smiled.

Daphne Cadge-Hampton pulled out a tiny silver flask from the beaded bag on her arm (a 1920s flapper special) and handed it over. 'Try some brandy,' she said succinctly. The lady demurred modestly, then took a hefty swig.

Daphne nodded in approbation. That'll make her forget about her elbow, she thought smugly. It was nearly 100 proof.

Ernie, swinging the mallet with precision onto the newly placed tent peg, finished his labours and casually tossed the jemmy and mallet behind one of the boxes of crisps lining the inside of the tent, careful to make sure they were out of sight. You never knew when his Vera would get it into her head that other pegs needed moving about, and he didn't want to spend the rest of the day hammering away.

'Wendy, love, you'd really better get to the flower tent before poor Sir Hugh throws a fit,' Vera reminded her.

Wendy gave a sudden little cry of guilty assent. 'Oh my word, yes! I'll just pop inside and get my bag.' She ducked back into the now deserted tent and reappeared a few moments later.

'Ah, we'd better all make a move, I reckon,' Daphne spoke up. 'He doesn't like to be kept waiting, old Hugh,' she added, and smiled in such an impish way that all four ladies (and Ernie) glanced at her in astonishment.

Daphne, chuckling as if at some amusing secret, led the way.

* * *

In the flower tent, Sir Hugh saw with relief the little gaggle of judges making their way in, and ran a quick check over the tent. Good, no civilians were left inside.

'Right then, ladies and gentlemen,' he said loudly. 'If we can all gather over here.' He indicated the prize table, and looked set to embark on his speech. Graham heaved a great big sigh. Monica, coming to a halt beside him, slipped her hand beneath his arm and shot him a hard-luck grin. Just then, Daphne Cadge-Hampton turned her head. Monica had a brief glimpse of too-red lipstick and the impression of a liberal application of face powder, but it was the expression in the old lady's eyes that had Monica feeling suddenly cold.

Once again she had that strange sensation of undercurrents. Of menace. Of something being off.

Daphne was looking at someone specific, Monica noticed, but, in the gaggle of judges now grouped around the table, she couldn't quite be sure who it was. In vain, she tried to follow the line of the countess's gaze. It could have been Ross Ferris she was watching so assiduously. Or perhaps James. Or any of those immediately surrounding him.

As Monica's wide, apprehensive blue eyes returned to the aristocrat, she knew that there was no mistaking the look on the old woman's face now. She simply *couldn't* tell herself that she was imagining things this time. She'd caught the old woman, Monica realized, in a rare moment of vulnerability. And she looked almost frightened. No, Monica corrected herself barely a moment later, so engrossed in her thoughts that she actually shook her head. Not frightened exactly, but grim. And worried.

Yes. Monica nodded, knowing that she'd got it right this time. Her Ladyship, Daphne Cadge-Hampton, was definitely worried about something. The question was what? What could an indulged, still-powerful, lofty old aristocrat possibly have to fear at her own local flower show?

CHAPTER 8

In the tent, all eyes were now turned respectfully to Sir Hugh.

'Ladies and gentlemen,' he began, clipboard firmly in hand. 'For all you old hands, I hardly need to tell you the rules and regulations governing your own areas of expertise,' he smiled affably around the tent. 'However, for the new judges amongst you,' and here he shot a withering glance at Ross Ferris, 'I'd like to take the time to point out just a few things . . .'

* * *

Outside, the tombola stand was doing a cracking trade, and the five-a-side football was edging towards its final match. Nobody paid particular attention to the flower show, but such was the size of the crowd, it was almost inevitable that a few people would notice Malvin Cook approach the big tent and, avoiding the main entrance, slip craftily around the side instead.

Of those who did notice this, however, only two saw what he actually did next. One of them was Dr Gordon Trenning.

* * *

'As you know, we have three separate cups, donated over the years to the gladiolus class, the leek class and the chrysanthemums,' Sir Hugh nodded at those specific judges, 'so special care has to be given to these. All the rest of the classes have rosettes for first, second and third prize.'

Beside Monica, Graham stifled a massive yawn and tried to look as if he was engrossed in being lectured on his judging duties.

* * *

Malvin Cook had never given his short stature much thought. True, as a boy he'd often been the target for bigger bullies at school, and growing up, he'd also discovered that a lot of ladies preferred taller men; but since he'd only ever had eyes for his Phyllis, that had never been a problem for him. That afternoon, however, as he bent down to sidle under the loose side flap into the back of the main marquee, he had reason to actively thank his lucky stars that he was so squat, small and fit. For in only a matter of seconds he'd managed to wriggle and slip inside the tent with almost no noise and very little fuss. And, far more importantly, without being detected by those within.

As he'd expected, Sir Hugh was giving his speech at the top end of the tent, so Malvin, in a crouching walk that years of bending and manual labour had made easy for him, began duck-walking his way towards the flower tables. There was something he just *had* to do . . .

* * *

Back outside, Gordon Trenning paced and sweated as he watched the small man duck inside the flower tent. He noted the point of entry and quickly looked around to see who else had noticed, feeling as if all eyes must be on him, or on the tell-tale loose side flap of the tent. But with children running around with ice creams, and the fancy-dress competition getting underway, it was hard to see if anyone had noticed Malvin's illegal entry, and it was doubtful that they'd care if they had. The villagers, although avid gossips, also had a blithe live–and-let-live philosophy.

Gordon, his nerves unable to stand being so close to the flower show tent, slowly circumnavigated the football pitch instead. He was beginning to have real regrets about what he'd done.

He should never have parted with the capsule. Never. It had been a moment of weakness on his part. Yet another one, he thought, in self-disgust.

He set off along the length of the football pitch again, avoiding the spectators. 'What the hell was I thinking?' he muttered, making a beautiful blonde girl, just passing, shoot him a quick, half-amused smile in response. Not that the scientist took particular notice of her.

Carol-Ann tossed back her hair and sighed. Some poor soul muttering to himself was the least of her concerns. Still, at least it went to show that she was not the only one at this wretched shindig having problems, and the thought that at least the misery was being spread around gave her some small, if rather mean-minded comfort.

Gordon continued around the field until he'd come full circle. Restlessly, and with a kind of desperate hopelessness, his eyes returned to the flower show tent, and he began to chew his lower lip anxiously. He caught sight of the beautiful Melissa, and quickly turned away, taking refuge beside the small wooden pavilion. The last thing he wanted to do now was cross swords with that hellion. Besides, it was cooler there, in the shade, and he needed time to think.

Hell, he was in a mess.

Fantasizing about killing Ross Ferris had been wonderful. If only he'd let it *end* there. If only he'd destroyed the damn capsule when he'd finished making it. But no, he'd *had* to put it in his pocket and come here with it. And now look where it had got him. He had no idea now what was going on in that tent.

But surely *he* wouldn't be betrayed? But what if . . . He'd been stupid. Gordon knew, deep down, he'd been incredibly, mind-blowingly stupid. He could go to prison.

'Shit, what an idiot,' he groaned, making one of Ernie Gant's friends, still sipping beer in the shade of the same building, glance across at him and nod.

'You're right, mate. Anybody could see the goalie would get a hand to that effort.'

Startled, Gordon turned and looked down at the bleary-eyed man sitting propped against the wall of the pavilion, his eyes fixed to the football field.

For some reason, Gordon started to laugh. And then found it almost impossible to stop.

His companion affably offered him a bottle of beer.

* * *

In the flower tent, Sir Hugh's speech finally came to an end, but not before a few more pointed barbs had been directed at Ross Ferris.

'Water off a duck's back,' Daphne Cadge-Hampton muttered, quite audibly, and several of her fellow judges had to quickly hide a smile behind their hands and pretend that they hadn't heard. The group broke up and began to saunter back to their particular tables.

By then, of course, Malvin Cook was long gone and safely away. What he'd had to do hadn't taken him long at all.

* * *

'Well, they're lovely, of course,' Wendy Davies said to Monica as they approached a table which had asters on one half and roses on the other. 'But why on earth James roped me into this I can't imagine.' Her voice lowered. 'I really can't tell one flower from another.'

Monica nodded in understanding, and whispered back, 'I've got much the same problem.'

For the next few minutes, there was more or less silence in the tent as the serious business of competition began. Monica noticed that several of her fellow judges were making notations on their clipboards, and glanced down at her own pristine sheet of paper with a feeling close to panic. What on earth was she supposed to be writing down, exactly? Serious-sounding notes on sepals and stalk length? Or more poetical, whimsical thoughts on hues and scent?

Deciding to just enjoy herself, she began to inspect the flowers in detail. They were lovely. She really was fond of sweet peas. And they smelt even better than they looked. She noticed that one pale purple bloom had a slight yellowing at the edges and ticked those off her list. Another pink bloom had two tiny black beetles in them. Scratch another. She grinned. She supposed that arriving at a winner by way of elimination wasn't the way it was supposed to be done, but it would do for her. Should she now just choose the ones she liked the best? The trouble was, she liked the wine-coloured ones, which were so beautiful, but also the blush pinky-white ones as well. But weren't pastels, traditionally, the best option? Or was that old hat now, with all the new, modern and more vibrantly coloured varieties coming into play? So, which got the first prize?

She sighed and started all over again.

* * *

Sir Hugh was judging the chrysanthemums that year, but his eyes followed Ross Ferris's progress to the dahlia table. He was so engrossed in heaping mental coals upon his enemy's head that he failed totally to realize that Ferris was supposed to be judging the roses, not the dahlias.

* * *

Wendy Davies stared blankly at her half of the table and the jars of asters. She was feeling so tired it was almost pleasant. She reached for the rosettes and placed them totally at random beside the displays. There. Once again, she'd done what was expected of her.

And she smiled savagely.

* * *

Ross Ferris was surprised and pleased at the size of his new table, and realized at once that he'd picked the winning ticket. The dahlia entries were all impressive, and there were far more of them than in any other class. He rather thought that he liked the big ragged, pink-tipped lemon ones best. He glanced up and caught Sir Hugh glowering at him.

He smiled beatifically back. He would show the pompous old bastard yet. Oh yes, he would show him . . .

* * *

James Davies was very self-disciplined, and made himself examine all the other rose entries first, before approaching the magnificent display of Peace. He handled a bud, and smiled down at its perfection. Of all God's creations, he liked flowers and birds the best. He put the bud back, and bent down towards a huge open blossom. It was crammed with layers upon layers of petals of pink, cream, and lemon, and even before he began to bend his head, he could smell the lovely scent wafting up to him. He put one hand on the table to steady himself, then buried his nose into the bloom.

He drew a long, deep breath and slowly breathed out. Wond—

A strange noise emanated from his throat — a sort of gurgling, choking sound — and a sharp, strange almond scent hit him.

And then, so did death.

* * *

The strange, spine-tingling choking noise made everyone turn their heads. Wendy, who shared the table with her husband, saw him fall first. He seemed to hit the grass like a kind of black-and-white deflating balloon. 'James,' she said simply, her voice curiously flat. She watched her husband lying ominously still for a long, blank moment. She didn't move.

Sir Hugh, Graham, Monica, and many others glanced at Wendy, then across to look for her husband. Who now suddenly wasn't standing beside her.

'Hey, the vicar's fallen over.' The worried voice came from one of the vegetable judges at the other side of the tent, who had a clearer view of the event.

'It's the damned heat, I 'spect,' someone else said, but a sharp anxiety belied the prosaic words, and there was a general shifting of movement towards the rose table as people went to help. 'I expect poor Vicar's fainted.'

Sir Hugh, Graham, and Monica got there first.

'Shouldn't we get him some water?' Monica asked, looking around and noting that someone had already had the same idea and was heading for the top table, where there was a jug of mineral water and some plastic glasses.

Graham reached his friend first, and quickly knelt down beside him. He put a hand on James's pudgy shoulder.

'Hey, Jim, are you all right? Can you hear me?' he asked worriedly, and with a little grunt, succeeded in pulling his rather heavy friend over onto his back. The moment he did so, the sight of his friend's face had him rearing back and bumping into Sir Hugh, who was standing right behind him. Both men stared down into a face that was slightly blue, distressingly contorted, and totally devoid of life.

James Davies's death had been so sudden, so instantaneous, that he hadn't even had time to close his eyes. Graham, looking at the contorted expression on his usually friendly face, wanted to reach down and do it for him, but felt unable to touch him. The reluctance shamed him.

'Bloody hell!' Sir Hugh said, his breath exploding out of him in stunned shock. 'Bloody hell!'

Monica, who'd seen what they'd seen, clapped a hand to her mouth and stepped back.

Abruptly, somebody began to cry. Shock, hard, sharp, and painful, sliced through the air, affecting the whole crowd.

Wendy Davies stood at the other end of the table by her asters. She still hadn't moved.

'Vicar!' someone yelped, as if a shout would somehow rouse him. It seemed to affect everyone, for in a frozen moment in time, nobody seemed able to move. Then Graham, forcing himself to overcome his cowardly reluctance, leaned forward and closed his friend's eyes, put his hands together, and, on his knees, began to say a short, silent prayer. Some of those who realized what he was doing also bowed their own heads. Several more women began to sob quietly into their handkerchiefs, and were led away towards the back by their friends.

After a moment, Graham lifted his head. 'Is there a doctor at the fete, does anybody know?' he asked, his voice calm and somehow restoring a sense of reality to the group.

James had been well liked, a popular figure. Nobody seemed quite able to grasp, until that moment, that he was actually gone.

'Yes, Dr Clarke. He's here,' someone said, in little more than a whisper. 'I've seen him around.'

'Then someone ought to go and fetch him,' Graham said practically. 'And someone else must ring for the police and an ambulance. Right away.'

'I'll fetch the doctor,' Pete Drummond, the shallot judge piped up, and without another word turned and rushed from the tent. He looked green and sick and glad to leave.

Sir Hugh, aware that his authority was in danger of being usurped, opened his mouth, then found himself unable to say anything. Instead, he held his hands out in a sweeping gesture and began to gently usher the crowd further back into the tent. They went willingly enough. Nobody, after all, liked to be in the presence of death.

Graham slowly got to his feet, his face pale and shocked but perfectly in control. He looked around, seeking out his wife, who was still standing, leaning back against a table, a hand clasped to her mouth. Slowly he made his way over to her. 'Are you all right?' Graham whispered as he took her hand in his. It felt ice-cold.

Monica gulped and nodded, although she felt anything but all right. 'He *is* dead, isn't he?' she whispered.

'Yes.'

'Poor James.'

'Yes,' Graham said, but he sounded far away.

Monica squeezed his hand tightly. But Graham wasn't thinking so much about his own loss of a good friend at this point; something else was puzzling him. The speed of it all. The sheer, shocking, silent speed. One second he'd been fine, the next a choking cry, and then . . . Did heart attacks really happen like that? Wasn't there supposed to be some evidence of chest pain, or pain in the victim's left arm? Or was it a stroke? An embolism?

He stirred, looking around, as if seeking some kind of an answer. He wasn't the only one who was feeling lost, as many of those in the tent were obviously also feeling strange and off-balance. Things like this didn't happen. Not to them — not to their neighbour, their friend.

Surprisingly, no one had yet given a thought to Wendy Davies. It was only when Monica saw the familiar blonde head that she realized with a start that James's wife hadn't moved an inch. Shock, of course. She was about to walk towards her when someone else beat her to it. The gaudy, eccentric figure of the Dowager Countess of Fulcome suddenly appeared at the stricken woman's side, and a comforting and beefy arm was looped around her shoulders. Wendy didn't seem to notice.

Seeing that James's wife was being taken care of, Monica leaned back once more against the table, relieved (and feeling guilty for it) that someone else was handling it. Her knees felt quite weak.

At that moment, Pete Drummond returned with the doctor.

CHAPTER 9

Dr John Clarke was in his fifties, and an altogether round sort of man. His body was round, his big, bald head was round, and his big brown eyes were very round indeed. Those who elected to be his patients tended to be straightforward and down-to-earth people who liked and trusted him implicitly. Dr Clarke had a reputation for not suffering fools gladly, and evidently saw little use or need for a phoney bedside manner. He was, however, unmistakably a very competent and able doctor, and one that was almost universally and instantly trusted. Everyone seemed to feel infinitely better that he was now present.

After he'd entered the tent and satisfied himself that signs of life were indeed extinct, and that CPR would be pointless, he stood for a moment and simply looked down at his patient, for James had been one of the many who'd appreciated the GP's way of practising medicine.

It seemed to Monica that Dr Clarke was imprinting the scene on his memory, and then with the sort of grunt that could have meant anything or nothing, he squatted down beside his patient, his portly figure somehow managing to look both grave and ridiculous. He reached again for James's wrist and felt once more for a non-existent pulse. Then John Clarke glanced at his watch. Fixing the time that he could certify death, Monica thought automatically, then shuddered.

'Had a heart attack, I suppose?' Sir Hugh's gruff voice broke the silence, voicing, no doubt, what many of the others were also thinking.

But Monica herself wasn't so sure. Neither was Graham. And neither of them missed the fact that John Clarke made no effort to confirm this diagnosis. Instead he reached down and peered very closely at James's face. It seemed almost macabre, and certainly disrespectful, for the very much alive and vibrant GP to be nose-to-nose with the very dead vicar.

Restlessly, Monica turned away, unable to watch the spectacle further.

As she did so, she saw Daphne Cadge-Hampton very firmly pull on Wendy Davies's arm. 'Come along, m'dear. I think we'll go to the tea tent and have a strong cup of tea,' she murmured, loud enough for those nearest to her to hear. Some of the other ladies helped usher Wendy out of the tent. The very new widow moved with a curious kind of stiff-legged walk, and her face was still totally blank and white.

It suddenly hit Monica that Wendy had also recently lost a son. And now this. She shook her head, unable to imagine such suffering. Would it really be so surprising if Wendy *was* heading for a complete nervous breakdown?

Unable to stay still, she wandered around to the other side of the table, where she found herself next to the impressive display of Peace, the rose bred to celebrate the end of war and the end to all the killing. As she thought about that, she felt a pang of poignancy ripple through her. Just to think, these lovely blooms were the last things that James had smelt.

Slowly, she bent down to cup a bloom in her hand and breathe in the scent of the flower. It was the big, open bloom, and suddenly, as if having received a douche of cold water, she found herself unable to breathe. For just an instant, it seemed that she tottered on the edge of something monstrous and black that threatened to engulf her. Something invaded her, tightening a grip on her throat, on her heart, on her very being, attempting to rob her of the ability to exist.

In a gesture of sheer instinctive panic she reared up, took a step away, and suddenly she was all right again. Her throat no longer felt constricted. She dragged a deep, ragged breath into her lungs and clutched the end of the table for support. Nothing like that had ever happened to her before.

Was it a panic attack? she wondered wildly. She knew of people who suffered from those frightening, debilitating attacks; they'd often described it as being unable to breathe, of feeling as if your heart was going to stop, which certainly went some way to describing just how she'd felt.

Puzzled and scared, Monica sought Graham's reassuring presence. Just the sight of his handsome, calm face made her feel better. Feeling more like her old self again, Monica turned once more to the display of Peace. Curious, and this time very careful not to get too close (and feeling silly because of it), she inspected the bloom. It looked like the innocent rose it was, of course. But then, just because she *was* looking so closely, she saw a slight distortion in the centre of the flower. A tiny part of it seemed to ripple, like the shimmer of heat haze on a hot day. But *this* phenomena had to have been caused by something unnatural . . .

For a second she was totally baffled, and then her eyes suddenly took in the real cause of it. Like one of those pictures that are all just random squiggles and dots at first, but then, after you've stared at them for long enough, they suddenly turn into images of shipwrecks or unicorns or what have you, Monica suddenly saw what it was. A tiny glass capsule, no more than a centimetre long, lay nestled securely in the petals. Narrow. With a barely perceptible dark square dot at the end. She squinted in an effort to focus on the tiny item. For a second she stared at it as if unable to believe what she was seeing. For another second, she thought she must be having a nightmare.

She tried to wake up, but couldn't. This was real. And in that instant she knew, just as surely as she knew her own shoe size, that what she was looking at was a murder weapon. No matter how tiny and insignificant it seemed, it was, in reality, as real and as ugly as any gun or knife. She didn't know what it was, and didn't understand what it had done, but that made no difference. It, whatever *it* was, had killed James Davies. She just knew it. She took a quick step away, and then began to hurry around the back of the table towards Graham. She had to tell him.

'I hope someone's called the police?' It was John Clarke who spoke, for the first time since entering the tent.

'Yes, they've been called,' Sir Hugh answered. John nodded, and got ponderously to his feet.

'Just routine, I suppose,' Sir Hugh added, and became unusually flustered when John's big round eyes looked at him levelly. 'I mean, in a case of sudden death and all that,' Sir Hugh mumbled.

'Nothing routine about this,' John Clarke said quietly, looking down at his patient with a very odd expression on his face. 'Nothing natural about it, either, I'm thinking,' he added, even more quietly. The crowd, even though they'd been ushered by Sir Hugh to the top end of the tent and thus were well out of the way, nevertheless heard this last comment. Not surprisingly, it caused a bit of a stir.

Monica heard him too, and abruptly decided to keep quiet about the glass capsule in the flower until the police arrived. It would serve little purpose in telling Graham now, especially if others might overhear and start speculating, perhaps alerting the killer to the fact that someone was already on to the truth of the matter. No, she had to secure the evidence and stop any possible contamination of the crime scene.

Pure fortitude made her take up her position again beside the vase of Peace. If somebody thought they were going to retrieve the little glass killer lodged in its petals, and thus remove all evidence of foul play, Monica thought grimly, they'd better think again.

* * *

A little less than half an hour later, Chief Inspector Jason Dury unsnapped his seat belt and climbed from the passenger seat of his unmarked police car.

It was nearly four o'clock now, and the afternoon was sweltering. It reminded him of another hot day last year, when he'd come to a village not far from here to investigate another suspicious death at a newly converted vicarage. For a second, the vision of a dark-haired, blue-eyed woman swam into his mind, but he quickly thrust it back out again.

He shut the car door behind him and looked around. He was wearing a dark blue suit, white shirt, and maroon tie. His corn-coloured hair had been recently cut, and the two wings from a centre parting tapered neatly to the nape of his neck. His pale blue eyes narrowed as they took in the two police cars and the constable on duty at the gate. In the unlikely event that this should turn out to be a murder case and not death from natural causes, he only hoped that someone had had the brains to put some uniforms at the other, less obvious exits as well. Although anyone who had wanted to leave had probably already left, long before the police showed up at the scene.

It was going to be one hell of a job trying to find out who might have been present earlier but wasn't now. He only hoped the fete-goers all had good memories for faces and names.

He nodded at the man on the gate, who nodded back very respectfully. By his side, Sergeant Flora Glenn smiled at the young copper and waited for her superior to step into the playing field.

Once inside, Jason looked over the scene carefully. It was an odd mixture of carry-on-as-usual and stop-and-gawp. Somebody was bowling for a pig on the stall just to his right, but others were staring at him openly. An old lady bought the last of the fairy cakes from the WI stall, but the woman who absently handed them over gave out the wrong change, her gaze avidly fixed on the smart-looking couple who'd just entered the playing field. A uniformed copper, a tall, ginger-haired man with freckles and a hangdog look, approached Jason and Flora and nodded smartly.

'Sir. The victim is in the big tent over there.' He didn't point, and unknowingly earned himself brownie points with the chief inspector for his discretion. 'It's the vicar, sir. Just dropped dead, apparently.'

Flora stirred restlessly at his side, sensing a mere routine investigation stretching ahead of them. Flora Glenn was thirty-two, divorced, with a cap of black hair and deep green eyes. Many of her fellow policemen had made advances and been rejected since her divorce, and speculation was running rife as to whether or not Jason, who had a bit of a reputation as a ladies' man, was more than just her superior officer. Nobody, as yet, was daring to offer odds.

'Hot in the tent, is it?' Jason asked quietly.

'Yes, sir. Boiling.'

'The vicar — an oldish man, is he?'

'In his fifties, I believe, sir.'

'And you've called us in . . . why?'

The constable, who was called Brian Gilwiddy and had been in uniform for over five years, flushed nervously. 'The local doctor . . .' he lowered his voice carefully, 'is unhappy. Very unhappy, and quite insistent about it.'

Jason looked at him with a clear gaze. 'A GP?'

'Yes, sir.' Brian took a deep breath and looked his superior in the eye. 'But one that I believe should be listened to.'

It was Brian, as the oldest and most experienced of the men at the scene, who had taken the decision to call in a senior man. And if it turned out that James Davies had indeed died of nothing more sinister than a heart attack, he knew that it wouldn't be forgotten that it had been he who'd wasted the chief inspector's valuable time.

But Jason merely nodded. He was a good judge of people, and he found himself respecting young Gilwiddy's own instincts. Besides, if a doctor raised a question about a death, it simply had to be investigated, so there was no point giving anyone a rough time over it. 'Right then, let's see what we've got,' he said mildly, and Flora noticed Gilwiddy's shoulders relax as the tension suddenly left him.

'Yes, sir,' he said, and quickly led the way.

Flora was aware of the many eyes boring into her back as they made their way to the tent.

Inside, because the constable had taken the decision to allow no one to leave, the interior was getting uncomfortably hot despite the open tent flaps. The scent of human sweat and fear competed with the more sickly sweetness being given off by the flowers, fruit, veg, and baked goods. Flora, dressed in a knee-length black skirt, a smart white blouse and black blazer, felt the heat prickle her skin the moment she stepped inside.

Jason, looking as cool and elegant as a male model, didn't seem to notice. He looked around at the scene with a jaundiced eye, his gaze instantly falling upon the body on the flat, trampled grass, then moved on. The bright splashes of cheerful flowers contrasted jarringly with the funereal atmosphere of the people, who all turned to look at him with hopeful, curious eyes.

'Well the crime scene's well and truly contaminated,' Jason said quietly to Flora.

'Yes, sir. I think Gilwiddy did the right thing in keeping them all in here, though,' Flora said.

Jason nodded. Since the damage was already done, he agreed with Flora's assessment. Even so, the SOCO and forensics boys weren't going to be happy.

'Harrumph.' A throat being cleared drew Jason's attention, just as it was meant to. A tall, silver-haired gentleman, complete with moustache and a military way of walking, detached himself from the edge of the crowd and approached. From the way Gilwiddy made no demur, Jason assumed that the man had made himself spokesman. And, for the moment, Jason didn't mind that. There were so many people in the tent that, until he'd got a team assembled to interview them all, it would be much easier to get the full story from only one of them.

'Sir Hugh Featherstone, sir,' Gilwiddy said quietly as the man approached. 'Local squire and lord of the manor.' There was just a touch of warning in his voice, and Jason was careful to take note of it. Sir Hugh had influence, and Jason was no idealistic tyro who thought that he could buck the system. Like it or not, it was always a good policy to treat the local bigwigs with respect, since most of them knew your boss, or were friends of the chief constable.

But it was also necessary to make sure that you never let them get the upper hand.

Sir Hugh held out a hand. 'Good . . . er, afternoon, Inspector . . . ?'

'Chief Inspector Dury, Sir Hugh,' Jason introduced himself smoothly, and from somewhere in the crowd he heard a small, sharply indrawn breath.

It came from Monica, who, still standing by the rose table and a little behind the doctor, hadn't yet seen Jason, but recognized his voice immediately. Alarmingly, her heart rate picked up a beat.

Jason, who'd instinctively glanced in the direction of the small giveaway sound, found his eyes running around the tables and then crashing to a halt. Over the shoulder of the rounded man standing in front of her, Jason saw the familiar dark head and big blue eyes of Monica Noble.

'Er, yes. Quite,' Sir Hugh said.

But Jason wasn't looking at him now. Instead, a nasty feeling was creeping up his spine, and his eyes swivelled once more to the body on the floor. From where he was standing he couldn't see the corpse's face, only the clerical garb.

'Did you say it was the vicar who was dead?' Jason suddenly asked Gilwiddy, his voice sharp with anxiety and something else the constable wasn't quite able to pinpoint.

Flora Glenn looked at Jason sharply, also hearing something unfathomable in her superior's voice.

'Yes, sir,' Gilwiddy said smartly.

Instantly, Jason's eyes went back to Monica, but she looked back at him steadily, her eyes bright but dry. She didn't look overly grief-stricken or in shock. Then he looked back at the corpse on the ground and felt his shoulders slowly slump. Graham Noble was tall and lean, but the man on the ground looked fairly short and bulky. But for one awful moment there . . .

He found himself letting out a long, low breath, even as Sir Hugh cleared his throat again and said, 'James Davies. Our vicar here.' And he gave a quick glance at the prone body before hastily looking away again. 'Glad you came so promptly, er, Chief Inspector,' he carried on, beginning to visibly swell as he sought to take charge. 'We thought—'

'Yes, thank you, Sir Hugh,' Jason cut in smoothly but firmly. 'Your local doctor is here, I believe?' It totally took the wind out of the old soldier's sails, and a look approaching respect appeared in his eye. If nothing else, Sir Hugh recognized command when he saw it.

Accepting his cue, John Clarke stepped forward. 'Yes, I'm Dr Clarke.' At first introduction he was not overly impressive, but then Jason met the level, wide-eyed gaze and suddenly understood why Brian Gilwiddy had listened to him.

'Chief Inspector,' John Clarke said. 'If you'll come with me?' Jason followed him the short distance to the body, eyeing the trampled ground around it with despair; but at least it meant that he could do no more harm in getting as close as he wanted. John Clarke knelt beside the body and leaned forward. 'Note the blue tinge to the face?' he asked, keeping his voice deliberately low-pitched.

Jason nodded.

'The man's eyes were open at the time of death,' he added.

'Who closed them?' Jason asked sharply, but still quietly.

'The dead man's friend and fellow cleric, I believe, a Reverend Noble,' John said calmly, his voice non-judgemental.

So Graham's here too, Jason thought. He hadn't spotted him, but then the tent *was* crowded. 'I see,' he said, his voice also totally lacking in censure. It had been a respectful and understandable gesture on the part of Graham Noble, but both professional men silently wished that he hadn't done it.

'So, why did you ask Gilwiddy to send for someone senior?' Jason asked.

To the others watching this gruesome, low-voiced conference, it seemed as if secrets were being traded and that made all of them feel uncomfortable.

Monica, who'd had previous experience of this feeling of guilt-cum-anger, understood what was happening, and was therefore able to feel more patient about it than the others, who suddenly all wanted to be allowed out of the tent. They probably felt the first stirrings of fear and unease now that the forces of law and order had arrived. But someone, somewhere, wasn't innocent, Monica thought grimly. Someone, *one of us*, she added to herself silently, was very much guilty.

Over the body of James Davies, John Clarke said quietly, 'You might not be able to smell it now, but put your nose close to the victim's mouth.'

Jason blinked, but did as he was told.

He had to sniff several times before he picked it up. When he did so, he felt himself stiffen incredulously. He straightened, staring at the doctor with disbelieving eyes. 'Surely not?' he said, his voice more of a croak now than a whisper.

Flora Glenn, who knew her boss well, even though she'd only been working with him for a few months, felt her pulse quicken. Something was up. Jason Dury was one of the coolest, most professional coppers she'd ever met, and if something could surprise him, she wanted in on it.

'Yes, I know how you feel,' John Clarke said. 'Incredible isn't it. But true, I think.'

Jason continued to stare at him. In all his years as a serving officer, he'd investigated many kinds of murders — from brutal beatings by a husband resulting in a wife's unexpected death, to the mess caused by a shotgun blast. From street killings with a knife — usually gang- or drug-related — to arson.

But this . . . this belonged on a television programme. Or in an Agatha Christie book.

'But people just don't kill other people in this way any more,' Jason said, sounding, even to his own ears, almost comically petulant.

John Clarke nodded knowingly. 'I understand all too well. In all my years as a doctor, I've never come across anything like it either. But that smell is unmistakable, and it was still quite strong when I first got here.'

'Bitter almonds,' Jason said.

'Yes,' John Clarke agreed flatly. 'The cyanide was probably in gas form, since I've had a quiet word and nobody saw the victim eat or drink anything just prior to his collapse. And as you know, cyanide — or any of its close derivatives — works very quickly indeed.'

For a long moment the two men merely stared at one another, then Jason nodded curtly.

He rose, walked to his sergeant, and said quietly, 'Call in SOCO and the pathologist. Get some more uniforms in here to cordon off the body and make sure nobody leaves.'

Flora nodded gravely, but was quivering with excitement. Her first murder case with Jason Dury! And something spectacular too, by the looks of it. 'Yes, sir,' she said crisply, and turned to walk quickly back to the car and its ever-present radio.

Murder, and fantastic murder at that, had definitely come to Caulcott Green flower show.

CHAPTER 10

'Right, I need an overall picture of events,' Jason said, still looking at John Clarke as he spoke. He knew it wouldn't take SOCO long to arrive, so he thought he might as well make good use of the brief lull.

'Don't look at me,' the GP said evenly. 'When I got here, the poor sod was already dead.'

Jason, if surprised by the doctor's rather abrupt and seemingly irreverent manner, certainly didn't show it, but glanced around instead, openly considering Sir Hugh. If he knew the type (and he did), he was bound to be chairman of the show and would have seen the whole thing, and be more than willing to tell his story. The only trouble was, Jason was sure that it would be just that — *his* story. Most witnesses, of necessity, tended to give very biased viewpoints.

What he needed was . . . Graham Noble, he thought suddenly. It had been to the vicar of Heyford Bassett that he had turned during the murder at the vicarage last year. The massive old building had been recently renovated into very elegant and sought-after flats, and when one of the new residents had been killed, both of the Nobles had been very useful to him in helping him to close the case. Both had kept their heads in the situation, and their eyes and ears open. He'd be a fool, he told himself flatly, not to take advantage of their presence at a crime scene once again.

He nodded at John, turned to Gilwiddy, ordering him to make sure that nobody moved or touched anything near the body, then moved away. He glanced towards the back of the tent at the group of silent and shocked judges, most of whom found it hard to meet his eyes, but Jason was too experienced to read anything into that; even the most innocent and innocuous member of the public could feel nervous and guilty when confronted by a full-scale police investigation. Also, it was obvious that James had been a popular man, and that his death had come as quite a blow to the small community.

And then he saw Graham. The vicar was a tall man, and had the kind of face that tended to stand out in a crowd. He looked like a Victorian poet, or an artistic academic, with that kind of fine-drawn elegant handsomeness that you didn't see much of nowadays.

As Jason approached him, he saw the man begin to smile a warm welcome and felt the usual ambivalence begin to creep over him. He liked Graham Noble a lot, but he sometimes wished that he didn't. More than that, he wished above all else that the man wasn't married to Monica Noble.

Quickly, he caught the direction of his thoughts and rapidly applied his internal brakes. Even so, he was aware of feeling slightly uneasy as he halted in front of Graham and held out his hand in greeting. He'd thought when he left Heyford Bassett after arresting the culprit in what had turned out to be a particularly nasty double murder case that he'd never see the Nobles again. Either one of them. And that that would probably be for the best. Now, just a year later, here they all were, back at the scene of another murder.

Talk about a bad case of déjà vu.

'Chief Inspector,' Graham said pleasantly, unknowingly interrupting the policeman's grim line of thought.

'Reverend,' Jason acknowledged, a shade more curtly than he'd meant to. Because of that, a slightly puzzled expression creased Graham's brows above his chocolate-coloured eyes. Instantly feeling guilty, and just a little foolish, Jason nodded vaguely towards the corpse. 'We seem doomed to meet in tragic circumstances,' he said quickly, by way of apology and explanation.

Graham's face clouded. 'Yes. James was a good friend of mine,' he said simply.

Jason sighed with genuine sympathy. He'd thought that might be the case, of course, and he could only hope that Monica wasn't too upset by what had happened to their friend. 'I was wondering if you could give me an idea of what happened, Reverend, but if you would rather do it later, I quite understand.'

'Oh no, I don't mind,' Graham said. 'I want to do all I can to help. And please, Inspector, call me Graham.'

Jason wasn't so sure about that, but nodded briefly. 'If you can just give me the gist of what you know, and some of the background,' he asked, taking out a small recording device.

As he made sure it was working, he half-turned to scan the crowd in the tent once more, and found Sir Hugh trying not to stare at them. Graham noticed as well, and had to hide a small smile, knowing that the ex-soldier was feeling extremely put out. No doubt Sir Hugh considered that the constabulary was wantonly ignoring him.

'Well, I don't know much,' Graham began, trying to be succinct but not miss out anything important. 'Every year there's a flower show here, and James Davies, he's the local vicar here, and the . . . er . . . deceased is on the committee that organizes it. This year he volunteered Monica and me to be judges.'

Jason nodded, his eyes still randomly sweeping the people he could see around them. Sometimes body language could give away many a secret.

'The judging was supposed to begin at three, but I suppose it was more like a quarter past before everyone arrived and Sir Hugh gave his pep talk,' Graham continued.

'Can you remember when Mr . . . er . . . Reverend Davies entered the tent? Early? Late?'

Graham thought about it and shrugged. 'Well he wasn't the first in, but not the last either. He always tried to be punctual, when possible.'

Jason nodded. 'I see. Please carry on.'

'Well, as I said, Sir Hugh gave us his pep talk, we collected the rosettes and such like, then returned to the tables to start the judging. James was judging the dahlias this year, and his wife . . . er . . . the asters, I think. But I'm not sure about that.'

Jason ignored the politics of flower show judging. 'And he seemed fine? He was acting as normal? He didn't seem scared, or worried or distracted?' he pressed.

'No,' Graham said firmly. 'I'd seen him on and off all afternoon, and he seemed very much the same as always. Nothing unusual.'

Jason sensed the pain in the other man's voice, but the factual, no-nonsense statement was a great help. He glanced up and met Graham's level gaze. 'Are you sure you want to carry on?' he murmured.

Graham straightened his shoulders. 'I'm fine. Anyway, James went to his table and we went to ours. I didn't see what happened because I was doing my own judging — the lilies. But after a while, about ten minutes or so, I heard a kind of gasping, gurgling sound. I looked around, but it took me a few seconds to realize what it was, and that James had fallen onto the floor.'

His gaze moved across to his prone friend, then hastily away again. He wished the medical examiner would get here quickly so that the body could be taken away. Odd, that. Already James was 'the body.' Of course, his soul had already gone . . .

'I see. And then what?' Jason's crisp, matter-of-fact voice rescued Graham from his painful thoughts and he dragged his mind firmly back to the task in hand.

'I went over to him, along with several others. Someone, I think it was my wife, suggested that we get him some water. At that point, I think we all thought he'd just fainted, you know? Because of the heat. It's been so very hot in here all afternoon — everyone's commented on it.'

Jason nodded. 'And then?'

'I bent down and turned him over. Yes, I know, sorry about that,' Graham added hastily as Jason looked up sharply from his contemplation of a nervous-looking little man who had entered a fine array of shallots in the vegetable section. 'But at the time I had no reason to suppose that he was dead. Or that it was in any way suspicious,' he added quietly but firmly.

Jason's pale blue eyes narrowed slightly. 'What made you first think it might be suspicious?' he asked quickly.

Graham looked vaguely troubled. 'I'm not so sure. It was just the quickness of it, I suppose. The moment I saw his face, I could see that he was dead. And he was such a strange colour. Anyway, I closed his eyes and said a short prayer for him, as I know he would have wanted, and asked someone to go and get the local doctor and call the police. Everyone was very shocked and upset. James was well liked, Inspector,' he said, once again in a firm voice. 'Sir Hugh then ushered everyone else to the back of the tent.'

Jason had not missed the firmness with which Graham had stressed how popular James was, and had received the message loud and clear. Muck-raking over the victim's character or the circumstances of his life would not be appreciated. And Jason could only hope that there would be no muck to rake, but, in his experience, people didn't get themselves murdered for nothing. Still, if he should come across any unsavoury facts about the dead man, he would certainly be very discreet about it.

'I see,' he murmured non-committally. He had been remembering the case in Heyford Bassett with more and more clarity as Graham had talked, and with it, his recollection of this man's cool but compassionate intelligence grew. His account of the past hour or so had been clear and to the point, and it was obvious that he'd carefully thought about everything he'd said before speaking, so that he didn't let his own opinions and thoughts cloud his memory of the events. Like it or not, Jason thought, sighing heavily, it looked as if Graham's presence was going to come in handy yet again. As a witness, he was a policeman's dream.

'And then?' he prompted gently.

'Then the doctor came — Dr Clarke. He's resident in the village and had been attending the fete. Someone had gone to fetch him — I'm not sure who, exactly; I think his name might be Drummond. Sir Hugh asked him if it was a heart attack. He didn't commit himself to that, but I could tell that he wasn't satisfied about the circumstances surrounding James's collapse. Wendy, that's James's wife, left with some of the other ladies at that point, I think. And then Dr Clarke openly declared himself unhappy with things and asked if the police had been sent for. It was then decided that we should all stay more or less where we were until you arrived,' Graham finished.

'Who decided that?' he asked sharply.

Graham blinked, thought about it for a few moments, then frowned and shrugged. 'Well, it was more or less a joint decision, I think. Myself, Sir Hugh and the doctor all thought it best, under the, er, circumstances,' Graham stumbled a little at the last. Even now he didn't really want to think the impossible.

The word 'murder' hung between them, unspoken but shouting louder than thunder.

Jason nodded and switched off the recorder. 'Thank you . . . Graham,' he said stiffly. Then he very quickly jotted down a few notes. Well, the preliminary facts were certainly clear enough.

Just then, Flora Glenn returned with a four-man team dressed in white overalls. Some of them looked around the crowded tent in obvious surprise and disapproval.

Jason beckoned to Brian Gilwiddy.

'Sir?' He approached smartly.

'More help should have arrived by now, so chivvy them up,' Jason said. 'Get this crowd organized. I want them led outside, but cordoned off from the rest of the people in the field. Needless to say, I want them all interviewed and statements taken where appropriate.'

'Sir.'

As the constable began to shepherd them out, finding no unwillingness to co-operate since everyone was happy to get out in the fresh air, Sir Hugh and Monica both made moves towards Jason. Monica got there first. She saw Jason's shoulders tense, just for a moment, as he watched her approach, but his pale blue eyes were giving nothing away.

She smiled tentatively. 'Chief Inspector,' she greeted him softly. Like Jason, she'd never expected to set eyes on him again, and found herself feeling, for some absurd reason, almost shy. Shoving aside such foolishness, she got straight to the point. 'I've found something that I think you ought to see,' she added determinedly. She wanted to get this over with.

Jason's eyes narrowed ominously. It had been Monica Noble who had all but handed the solution of the Heyford Bassett murder case to him on a plate. Which was just one more thing about her that he was never going to forget. And the fact that she was now mixed up in another crime scene didn't exactly fill him with joy.

He smiled briefly. 'In that case, Mrs Noble, perhaps you'd better show me,' he said simply. He couldn't help but notice her husband give her a quick glance, and felt — ridiculously — a quick shaft of pleasure that, whatever it was she'd found, she hadn't thought to confide it to him.

'It's over here,' Monica said, leading him to the table of roses and pointing out the display of Peace.

Jason stared at the blooms blankly. 'Sorry?'

'You have to look closely,' Monica said. 'I only just saw it myself. It was this rose that James was inspecting just before he died.'

By his side, it was Flora now who was making notes in her notebook. At this statement, however, both of them looked up at her.

'You saw him?' Jason asked, surprised.

Monica hesitated, looked a little abashed, and then finally shook her head. 'No, but I'm sure it must have been this flower. Look inside and see for yourself.'

If it had been anyone else, Jason might have suspected that he was having his leg pulled, but one quick glance at Monica's earnest blue eyes had him peering down into the flower. Even so, it took him a few moments to spot it. When he did, he stiffened. 'Flora, get a SOCO over here quickly,' he said quietly.

A short, dark-haired man in overalls came over, obviously intrigued by the leading officer's interest in the rose. 'Benson, get some tweezers and a bag,' Jason said, and the lab man produced them from a case he was carrying. Jason then stood a little to one side to allow the SOCO man to stand beside him. He pointed into the centre of the flower. 'See it?'

The man peered in, eyes squinting a little. 'No. Oh yeah.' He called over to a SOCO with a camera and had some pictures taken of it before carefully, and with perfectly steady hands, retrieving the tiny glass capsule from the rose. Both Graham and Flora peered at it with fascination, as did Sir Hugh, who'd managed to sidle up unnoticed.

'What do you think it is?' It was Flora who spoke first.

'I don't know,' Jason admitted grimly. But whatever it was, he doubted it had anything to do with improving the growing of roses.

Benson looked across to one of the men scraping the grass around James Davies's body and called calmly, 'Hey, Frank, come and take a look at this.' To Jason he added matter-of-factly, 'Frank's a bit of a boffin when it comes to stuff like this.'

Jason watched the other man approach. He was tall, slightly stooped and grey-haired, with wire-rimmed spectacles and a rather ragged white moustache; he really did look like the archetypal absent-minded professor. As the technician reached them, he pushed his gold-rimmed glasses a bit closer up the bridge of his nose. He peered at the proffered capsule for several seconds, his slightly myopic grey eyes widening as he did so.

Then he let out a long, low, admiring whistle. 'That's some piece of equipment,' he said at last.

'It's tiny,' Flora said, apropos of nothing.

'I know. That's what makes it so interesting,' Frank said. 'State-of-the-art with a capital S.'

'But what is it?' Jason said impatiently.

'It's a capsule, and would have contained some kind of gas, I'd say. Perhaps liquid, but much more likely a gas. See the almost microscopic chip at the end there? At a guess, I'd say that was some kind of trigger, or release mechanism.'

He reached into his own bag for a lens, and peered closer. 'Yes, there's a tiny little gizmo attached. It's ruptured the seal on the end, and yes, the gas must have been compressed. When the seal broke, it would have ejected a tiny amount of gas from the capsule. Probably a gas that had been modified in some way — made more intense and therefore more toxic would be my guess. Whoever made this little darlin' certainly knew what he was doing, all right.'

Jason stared at him, aware that his jaw was quite literally dropping, and quickly snapped his mouth shut. Even so, he felt as if he'd just wandered onto the set of some spy film.

Tiny exploding gas capsules? Give him a break!

But then again, what had Dr Clarke told him about the poison probably being in gas form? No one had seen the victim eat or drink anything close to his death, he'd said. Perhaps these inventions weren't just reserved for fiction, after all . . .

'What activated it?' he asked. 'It surely wasn't on a timer. Not a thing that size.'

'Oh no,' Frank said. 'See the back of this chip? It's got a tiny sponge on it. No bigger than a large pin head. My guess is that it was soaked in some kind of chemical.'

Jason was lost and he knew it, but he had no choice but to show his ignorance if he wanted to get to the bottom of this. 'And exactly what purpose would *that* serve?' he asked, a touch acidly.

The boffin shrugged. 'Could be any number of things. But my guess is that it was put there so that it would react to another, very specific chemical signal, and thus trigger off the release mechanism.'

Flora Glenn, sensing her chief's discomfort, took over. 'Can you put that into English for me?' she asked sweetly.

Monica saw Jason glance at her gratefully, and felt a tiny tug of jealousy, deep down in the pit of her stomach. It shocked her, and made her look quickly away.

'Well, anything could have triggered it, of course, but my guess is that it's rigged to respond to one of the chemicals present in human breath,' Frank said matter-of-factly, as if discussing the weather or the winner of the two forty-five at Aintree.

For a second, though, there was a stunned silence.

Then Jason spoke. 'Are you telling me that that thing was set off just because James Davies *breathed* on it?'

'Could be. I can't know for certain, of course, until I get it back to the lab and can run some tests on it. But this little beauty is easily capable of that kind of sophistication. Of course, to kill anyone the gas itself would have to be a very potent one to begin with, even with some modification. The amount in a capsule this size would be tiny.'

'How about cyanide?' Jason suggested quietly, having even more confidence in the doc's theory now.

Frank, showing no apparent sign of surprise, nodded and almost smiled in approval. 'Yes, that would certainly do it. There are other possibilities, of course, but not many.'

'But isn't it rare?' Flora asked. 'Cyanide, I mean.'

But already the boffin was shaking his head. 'Not as rare as you might think. You'd be surprised just how much of it is still used commercially, even nowadays, especially in industry. And what with the internet and everything, almost anybody could, with a little due diligence, track down a source of it.'

Jason leaned closer, and Frank discreetly but firmly put a hand against his chest. 'Don't get too close to it, sir. Even a whiff of cyanide can kill. My old professor at Durham wouldn't let us med students near the stuff when . . . I say, miss, are you all right?' He broke off to look at Monica, who'd gone dead white and was swaying alarmingly.

'Yes. No,' Monica mumbled confusedly. 'I . . . When I first found it, it felt as if I couldn't breathe for a moment,' she explained faintly, suddenly realizing that what she'd felt had had nothing to do with an anxiety attack after all. Some of the gas must still have been in the air near the rose. She might have *died*! For a second, the tent spun around her and she took a hasty step forward to try to regain her balance. Jason and Graham both moved abruptly towards her, Jason, at the last moment, pulling back to give her husband priority.

Graham's arms came around her, and she smiled up at him tremulously. 'Sorry,' she said, feeling ridiculous. 'I'm just being a bit feeble.'

Jason didn't know it, but beside him, Flora Glenn was staring at him with wide, surprised eyes. Her boss looked unusually pale and grim-faced and she shot the vicar's wife a rapid, thoughtful, and assessing gaze. What she saw was a slim-waisted woman, with dark curly hair, a thirty-something face, and wide blue eyes. Attractive, if you liked mature women. But hardly a supermodel.

'Do you need a doctor?' Jason asked quickly, still looking at Monica with worried eyes.

And, because he hadn't been asked to leave with the others, John Clarke heard the sharp question and hurried forward. 'Everything all right?' he asked calmly.

111

'No,' Jason snapped. 'Mrs Noble might have had a whiff of that damned cyanide gas.'

The doctor moved at once to her side. With Graham supporting her on one side, and him on the other, she began to feel even more of a fool.

'No, honestly, I'm all right now,' she protested. 'It was just the shock of thinking . . . that thing . . .' She stared at the innocuous piece of glass, now safely contained within an evidence bag, and shuddered. 'That I was so close to it so soon after it was activated. That I might have breathed in some of the poison too.'

'I think you'll be all right, Mrs Noble,' John Clarke said bracingly. 'If you were going to die, you'd have done it long before now,' he added, with his usual tactless cheerfulness.

Both Graham and Monica found themselves grinning at him in appreciation.

Jason turned abruptly away. 'OK, Benson, get that thing back to the labs,' he said roughly. 'And treat the damned thing with kid gloves — it might still be dangerous. I want a thorough analysis of it as soon as you can. At least it shouldn't be hard to track it back to its origins. There can't be many places, or people, with the know-how or ability to build such a thing. Right, Frank?' he added, shooting the boffin a don't-you-dare-say-no look.

But Frank was already shaking his head. 'I should say not. There can't be many men in this country who would be able to construct it, that's for sure. He'd have to be a bit of a chemist, an engineer and a computer-chip technician all rolled into one. Mind you, having said that, it could have been made anywhere. Even abroad.'

'But—' It was Sir Hugh who spoke up, and then, finding all eyes were on him, wished heartily that he'd kept his big mouth shut.

'Yes, Sir Hugh?' Jason asked levelly, wondering why he hadn't been shepherded out along with all the others.

'Nothing,' Sir Hugh mumbled, then saw that he wasn't going to get away with that, and added reluctantly, 'only there's Ferris Labs, you see. Right on our doorstep. They've got some good brains in there, or so I've heard, and I daresay they'd have access to cyanide. I just thought—'

'Right, Ferris Labs,' Frank chipped in. 'I knew the name of Caulcott Green sounded familiar for some reason.' He turned to Jason. 'They'd have the know-how and equipment in that place to produce a gizmo like this, right enough.' His myopic eyes suddenly widened. 'And doesn't Gordon Trenning work there?' he added, rather as a movie buff might talk about a film star.

Sir Hugh looked more uncomfortable than ever. 'Who?' Jason asked sharply.

Frank obliged. 'Dr Trenning, sir. I've read one or two of his papers. He's something of a genius. I . . . er . . . follow things in his area of research,' he mumbled, as if admitting to subscribing to porn.

Jason's eyes began to gleam. Perhaps this was going to be one of those cases where it was handed to him on a silver platter after all? If the murder weapon was such that only very few people could have made it, and one of them was right on the victim's doorstep, so to speak . . .

'Is Dr Trenning at the fete today?' he asked generally.

'Yes he is.' It was John Clarke who replied.

Sir Hugh opened his mouth to speak, and then abruptly closed it again with a snap.

Jason turned to Flora. 'Sergeant Glenn, get some help and find this Dr Trenning. I want a word with him as soon as possible,' he added ominously.

* * *

Outside, speculation was buzzing. The fete-goers hadn't missed the fact that no one was allowed to leave the playing field without producing ID for the policemen at the exits, and being granted permission to go. So far, though, few people had opted to leave. Human nature being what it was, everyone wanted to stay and watch the drama unfold.

By now it was widely known that the vicar was dead. It had given Carol-Ann a very nasty stomach-churning moment, until someone else had confirmed that it was James Davies, and not her stepfather, who had died. She wanted to find her mother and stepfather and make sure that they were both all right, but she suspected that if she did so, their protective instincts might take over, and they might insist she return home. Which was the last thing she wanted. She was still actively engaged on a plan of action to get herself photographed by the famous Marc Linacre. And whilst, in the face of such a tragic event, she couldn't help but feel a flash of shame for being so selfish, she sturdily reminded herself that all the top people, when being interviewed, always stressed how you had to be tough to get to the top.

So, tough she would be. Like nails. But perhaps, later, she'd just find her mother and see if there was something that she could do to help out.

Marc Linacre and his wife were standing with a group of others, pretending to watch the football, but really watching the flower show tent. Taking advantage of their distraction, Carol-Ann sidled up to Marc. As she did so, however, she noticed a man in a suit slipping around the back of the tea tent. For a moment, she had that weird, slightly giddy feeling that you get when you feel as if you've been here and done it all before. And then she realized that it was the same man that she'd seen earlier in the afternoon, and that he'd been doing exactly the same thing then — sneaking around behind the tea tent.

Not again, Carol-Ann thought, wrinkling her nose. He must have a weak bladder or something. Gross. But at least this time nobody followed him.

Then she took a deep breath and let her hand very 'accidentally' and lightly brush against Marc Linacre's. As he half-glanced down and across at her, his face comically dropping at the sight of her, she beamed at him beatifically.

'Hello again,' she said cheerfully.

On the other side of him, Angela Linacre's head whipped around.

'Who'd have thought that all this was going to happen . . .' Carol-Ann said, trailing off as, with a visible yank, Marc was pulled away. Angela, with a firm grip on her husband's arm, pulled him further into the crowd. Carol-Ann watched them go, her eyes narrowing in despair. Just what did that wife of his have against her? she thought mournfully. Then, with a concerted effort, she stiffened her backbone. If Mrs Linacre thought that she was going to keep Carol-Ann Clancy off the cover of *Vogue*, the old harpy had better think again! She gave a brisk nod of her head, causing a young boy passing by to stare at her in surprise.

She'd just have to think of something that would really grab his attention.

As she turned away, she noticed the eye-catching figure of Daphne Cadge-Hampton emerging from the tea tent; even Carol-Ann had to admire the old girl's style. She certainly was a scene-stealer. A thought crept into her head. She'd bet that old sour-faced Mrs Linacre was a bit of a snob. If she could just get on the countess's good side, and score points by introducing Her Ladyship to Marc Linacre and his wife, maybe even get them to think that the Nobles hobnobbed regularly with local aristocracy, well . . .

Carol-Ann watched the old woman thoughtfully. She already knew her slightly from when she'd volunteered to help run a jumble sale for one of the countess's favourite charities, and they'd got on like a house on fire. The old lady had liked her 'spunk,' whatever that meant. And from what she'd overheard, the dowager countess had been a bit of a goer too, in her day, so she might well approve of Carol-Ann's plans to become a model. It was certainly worth a try to get her on side.

As she watched, though, Lady Daphne lowered herself onto a deckchair just outside the tent, and even from that distance Carol-Ann could see that she was deeply unhappy about something. She was breathing deeply, and her jaw was clamped as tight as a vice. Perhaps she should offer to go and get her something to drink — or fetch a doctor? Although she looked more angry or worried than in distress.

Either way, now was definitely not the time to approach her for a favour. And with rare insight for one so young and single-minded, Carol-Ann reluctantly turned away.

CHAPTER 11

Jason stepped outside the tent and looked around. Of all the murder scenes he'd had to cope with, this was by far the most unusual, and the most nightmarish. There had to be hundreds of people in the playing field. How to start eliminating them?

He heard a shout from the football field, and a ragged cheer went up. Well, those playing football could be knocked off the list for a start, he mused, and felt himself smile ruefully.

The question, of course, was *when* was the capsule planted? If it had been deposited fairly early in the day, it could have been anybody who'd done the deed, although Dr Gordon Trenning surely had to be top of the list.

He got out his notebook and began making memos to himself.

Question the rose-grower.

Question those in the tent to see if anybody went near the rose, or smelt it, at any time. That might give him a time frame for the planting of the murder weapon.

Find out who hated the vicar . . . At this he paused and shook his head. A *vicar*, for pity's sake! Although he knew that attacks on the clergy were, in this modern day and age, sadly on the rise, even so, this killing was so bizarre. He couldn't help but feel that it just didn't fit somehow. It felt off. A high-tech crime committed against a harmless clergyman just didn't gel.

And yet, James Davies was dead.

He'd already sent out constables to find Dr Trenning. If he had indeed been responsible for the outlandish murder weapon, what on earth had possessed the man to make it?

'The preliminary interviews are almost over, sir.' Brian Gilwiddy's voice interrupted his dire musings.

Jason sighed heavily. 'Right. We need a temporary incident room,' he said, looking around the area vaguely. His eyes alighted on the fortune-teller's tent. It was small but private. It would do at a pinch.

'Right, clear the fortune-teller's tent, will you? We'll use that for an interview room. If she's any good, it won't come as much of a surprise to her,' Jason added, with a wolfish smile.

Gilwiddy, surprised at his chief's sudden flash of humour, grinned appreciatively and trotted off.

Jason was still writing memos to himself when Flora Glenn walked quickly up to his side. 'Sir,' she said sharply.

Something in her tone had Jason's head rearing up quickly. His eyes quickly scanned around her, but she was alone. 'No Dr Trenning?' he asked archly.

Flora took a deep breath. 'Yes, sir. That is, I've found him. But he's dead.'

* * *

Flora led her superior officer around the big tea tent to the rear. Here Jason looked over the scene with a jaundiced eye.

The tent had been set up only about a foot from the perimeter fence. Lying in the narrow alleyway it created, face down, was the figure of a man. He looked pathetic. He was wearing a suit that was now hopelessly crushed and sweat-stained. The back of his head, showing already thinning hair, had been caved in by what looked like a single, massive blow. There was surprisingly little blood. For a few moments, Jason simply stood and stared down at him.

'I've checked for a pulse, sir,' Flora said, unable to stand the silence. All her previous excitement had suddenly evaporated with her discovery of yet another body. Perhaps it was because she had found him personally. Perhaps because she too thought there was something rather pathetic about the dead man. So unbearably sad. In some ways, she felt, it was worse than seeing the vicar dead, although, if asked, she wouldn't have been able to say why exactly.

But Jason knew why. Whereas the vicar's death had caused much shock and dismay amongst his friends and community, he already sensed that nobody much would mourn for this man. The vicar had at least died amongst his friends. This man had died alone.

Jason sighed. 'Go and get John Clarke. Then the SOCO team,' he said flatly to Flora. They were certainly going to be busy today. He'd just known this was going to be a bugger of a case. He'd just known it.

A green-faced constable, whom Flora had commandeered to stand guard while she fetched Jason, hastily looked away from the sight of the body as Flora brushed past him.

Jason bent down gingerly and peered into the profile of the dead man. His had been a nondescript sort of face — neither old nor young. Not handsome, but not ugly. The sort you wouldn't look at twice, in fact. And yet it was looking more and more likely that this anonymous man had indeed been responsible for that fantastic capsule of death, and had thus started off this whole chain of tragic events.

But if this murdered scientist *was* the catalyst for all this death and mayhem, what on earth had gone wrong? Why had he wanted James Davies dead? *Had* he wanted James Davies dead? Obviously, something, somewhere, was seriously amiss here, or else why would a possible killer now also be lying dead? So there were two killers? Had they, in fact, formed a partnership? It was unusual, he knew, for two people to collaborate to kill, but it was not unheard of.

Jason backtracked his thoughts a little and rose stiffly to his feet.

Taking it for granted that Trenning was the maker of the capsule — and that, he felt sure, was now a fairly safe bet — was it possible that he'd constructed it for someone else, and that another party had stolen it for their own purposes and then killed him? Or had Trenning and someone else indeed been in collusion to commit the murder of Caulcott Green's vicar, and then, for some reason, Trenning's partner had killed him afterwards? Perhaps in order to make sure that he would never be able to talk to the police about it afterwards?

A scientist and a vicar, both dead at a country fete. Why?

'Hello — another one?' The hearty voice, naturally, belonged to Dr John Clarke.

Jason nodded, and as the doctor brushed past him — difficult in that narrow space — Jason said curtly, 'Try not to disturb anything, Doctor. Just ascertain death, and if possible, identify him for me.' No doubt the police's own surgeon would have something to say about local amateurs being given first shot at his corpses, but it seemed a shame not to take advantage of the local GP's knowledge.

John grunted, knelt down, peered at the wound, checked the pulse and stared down at the face. Then he nodded once, and got cumbersomely back to his feet.

'Yes, that's Trenning all right. Killed by what looks like a single heavy blow to the back of the head. And not long ago, either. Not more than half an hour, I'd say, but probably much more recently than that, even. Say five to fifteen minutes ago. Of course, your chaps will be able to give you every little bit of info once they've had him on the table for a few hours.'

Jason sighed and nodded. So he'd been killed whilst the police were already present at the playing field. Wonderful. He could imagine what his superiors would have to say about that!

Not to mention the media, if they found out. 'Any thoughts on the weapon?' he asked gloomily.

'Something big and blunt, or there'd be more blood. Whatever it was, it caved his head in with a large circular indentation, but it didn't cut him up much. So it had no sharp edges. A mallet, maybe? A rounded cudgel of some sort?'

Jason sighed. 'Right. Flora, we need a search team set up. And we need this field emptied of all non-relevant witnesses.' He was getting tired of having such vast numbers to think about.

Flora, glad to be given something positive to do, nodded and quickly got to work.

Jason looked beyond the body, then ran his eye along the tent and spotted the open tent flap, which seemed to have been loosened about halfway down the canvas wall. Careful where he put his feet, he stepped over the prone Gordon Trenning, and noticed the doctor disappearing back the way he'd come. With his girth, it wouldn't have been very easy for him to follow Jason anyway.

The chief inspector found his nose wrinkling as he crouched down and then wriggled under the flap and through the back of the tent. He quickly realized why: he was in a narrow, dog-legged space with portable loos on either side of him. Taking a few steps forward, left, then right, he suddenly came into the main body of the tea tent itself. There, several female eyes turned his way in obvious surprise, no doubt wondering how he'd managed to appear from seemingly nowhere, and for an instant, Jason felt as if he were back at school, being given the evil eye by his disapproving teachers.

Sitting on a chair, a blonde rag doll of a woman was listlessly sipping tea. There was a curiously blank look to her eyes, which told him at once that he was looking at the widow.

Beside her was a big, buxom woman with brown hair turning to grey, big grey eyes and a normally cheerful mouth, now turned down and looking anxious. For her part, Vera Gant stared back at the blond, handsome man who could only be a policeman, and her lips thinned ominously.

But it was the third woman, a little sparrow of a thing with bright button-black eyes and an energy that probably never seemed to diminish, who got to her feet and attacked first.

'You must be a policeman,' she said. 'I'm Mrs Dinwiddy. And poor Mrs Davies should be home in bed. She's already had to rush to the loos to be sick once, and with this heat, I'm sure it can't be doing her any good to just be sitting here, waiting around for you lot.'

She paused for breath, and as she did so, Vera Gant took over. 'My Ernie says there are men at the gates, and they ain't letting people out unless they go through some rigmarole about showing 'em their driving licences or something. A damn disgrace, that is,' she pronounced, vigorously nodding her head. 'As if we all carry things around with us that have our names and addresses on 'em.'

Then her hand fell to Wendy's shoulder and gave a gentle squeeze, but the woman didn't seem to feel it.

'She should have a doctor,' Mrs Dinwiddy added, when Vera had said her piece.

Jason nodded. 'Dr Clarke is around somewhere. Perhaps you'd like to bring him in?' He took the wind right out of her sails by neatly agreeing with her.

Mrs Dinwiddy stiffened, then inclined her head graciously, and marched out of the tent.

As she passed, the dowager countess, Daphne Cadge-Hampton, who'd been sitting in a deck chair in the sun, got ponderously to her feet. She'd heard voices inside, and was anxious to hear what was being said.

'Mrs . . . er . . . ?' Jason turned to Vera, who stiffened her backbone and straightened her shoulders as if getting ready to face Armageddon.

'Gant's my name. Vera Gant,' she said challengingly, as if expecting the police to doubt her word.

Jason smiled his most winsome smile. 'Mrs Gant. Tell me, have you heard anything strange in here in the last . . . oh, I don't know, half an hour or so?'

Vera's big grey eyes widened. Whatever she'd expected to be asked, it obviously hadn't been that.

'Hear anything? Whaddya mean? What sort of thing?' she demanded.

Jason shrugged. 'A cry. A thump. Anything odd.'

Vera's eyes narrowed. She was obviously puzzled, and half suspected a trick of some sort. Slowly she shook her head. 'No,' she said cautiously. 'I never heard nothing like that. Did you?' She turned to look down at Wendy, her eyes softening in pity as she saw the vicar's wife raise a tea cup to her lips with badly shaking hands.

She turned back to Jason. 'No, there was nothing,' she said firmly, and Jason believed her. For all her self-protective belligerence, he got no sense that she was being dishonest.

He looked around the tent thoughtfully, then back the way he'd come. The tent was big, and the loos being outside meant the women were a good distance from the back of the tent. It would probably have been possible for the killer to sneak around the back and kill Trenning without being heard inside. Especially if Trenning didn't have a chance to cry out. And if he'd been hit from behind, he wouldn't have known it was coming. It was a very quiet way to kill someone. Even so, whoever had done it must have known the tent was occupied. To take such a risk!

Unless, of course, Trenning was killed earlier on and then dumped here. No, that would never do. You couldn't go lugging a body about and not be spotted in a field this crowded. Besides, the murder had only just happened.

'Has there always been someone in this tent?' he asked, and seeing Vera's puzzled look, added patiently, 'since it's been set up and open for business, I mean. Has there always been someone here, inside?'

'Of course,' Vera said, as if he were a moron of the first order. 'It's the tea tent. What's going on?' she added abruptly. She could almost hear the wheels turning in the copper's brain. She always felt nervous around men who looked as good in a suit as this one did. With his perfect haircut and quiet, give-nothing-away face, he was like a foreign species to Vera. And she didn't half feel funny when he looked at her. As if he could see right through her.

'So, let's see what we can do, eh?' Once again John Clarke's loud and cheerful voice interrupted Jason's thoughts as he came into the tent, followed by the inimitable Mrs Dinwiddy.

Then Jason's eyes widened at the sight of the figure coming in behind them both. For a second, he wondered if he was hallucinating.

The first thing he noticed was the amazing gown. It looked like something Queen Victoria could have worn, mainly because it *was* something that Queen Victoria could have worn. It was certainly the right age and style. Then his gaze went to the huge diamond necklace, hung around a very scrawny, baggy neck. His gaze rose to the face of the woman herself, and met eyes that would have put lasers to shame. This time it was Jason who felt himself stiffening his backbone and squaring his shoulders.

She beheld Jason for a long, silent moment.

He was peripherally aware of John Clarke competently and cheerfully attending to Wendy Davies, but he was unable to take his eyes off the old woman. Slowly, she moved forward. 'How de do?' she said, her voice so upper crust it would cut glass. 'I'm Daphne Cadge-Hampton.'

Jason nodded. 'Chief Inspector Dury, madam.'

'Your Ladyship.'

'Pardon?'

Daphne smiled beatifically at him. 'I'm the Dowager Countess of Fulcome. You call me "Your Ladyship,"' she explained helpfully, only a twinkle in her eyes letting him in on the fact that she thought such protocol to be a jolly old joke.

Jason felt that little tug, that nebulous sensation that always alerted him when he was on to something. He smiled. 'Do you have anything to tell me, Your Ladyship?' he asked quietly.

Daphne grunted, then abruptly turned away and walked towards Wendy, leaning on a slender silver and ebony cane.

'She should be allowed home,' Daphne said gruffly, and both Vera and Mrs Dinwiddy cast triumphant glances at Jason. No doubt they were used to seeing the countess's word as law, and expected him to respond immediately to it; it instantly niggled him.

'I'd rather Mrs Davies stayed available for questioning,' he said stiffly, then realized he wasn't being fair. 'But only if the doctor, and Mrs Davies herself, feel that she's up to it,' he added quickly.

Wendy Davies, suddenly thrust into coming to some sort of a decision, made weak, demurring noises. 'Oh, I don't mind, really,' she murmured. 'I feel quite all right.'

She didn't look all right, Jason thought sympathetically, and glanced at John Clarke.

'Any of you ladies have a little snifter of anything?' he asked prosaically, but he was looking mainly at the countess. Daphne smiled at him approvingly and reached into her beaded bag for her silver brandy flask.

John unscrewed it, filled the little silver top with brandy, and handed it to his patient.

Wendy obediently drank it with a little shudder. 'Do you want to go home, duck?' he asked bracingly.

Wendy shook her head. 'No, no, I'm fine, really I am,' she said again, more firmly this time.

Vera sighed. 'Brave little thing,' she muttered, turning away.

Daphne shook her head. 'She should be home,' she said sharply. Couldn't they see that she'd had enough? And she didn't like the sharp-eyed, no-nonsense look in the young policeman's eye. He was obviously a man who knew what was what and, in her experience, that sort of thing invariably meant trouble.

John got up and walked over to Jason. 'I think she'll be fine, but can you leave off the questioning for a little while?'

Jason nodded. It wasn't, in truth, much to ask, despite the fact that the spouse of the murder victim was usually high up on the list of suspects. Besides, he had plenty of other witnesses that he wanted to question first.

'Fine.' He pulled the doctor to one side. 'Tell me, what do you know about the Davies couple?'

The doctor shot him a quick, shrewd look, and sighed. 'Nothing that's going to help you, I'm afraid. James wasn't one of those stick-your-nose in, holier-than-thou types that get people's backs up. Neither was he a sneaky quick-grope-of-the-choir-boys type. And their marriage seemed to be steady and happy. Certainly there was no hanky-panky on either one's part, or you can be sure the whole village, down to Miss Simpkins's cat, would know about it.'

Jason bit back a smile. Whatever else he was getting, he was sure that John Clarke was giving him an honest opinion.

'He was a decent enough sort of chap. Put his money where his mouth was,' the doctor added fairly. 'I often found him visiting my patients when they were down. And he knew how to make himself useful, giving lifts and things to those without cars. He was a big voice in local affairs, of course, as you'd expect, but he wasn't the steamroller type. Unlike Ross bloody Ferris.' John's face darkened.

'You don't like this Mr Ferris, I take it?' Jason asked, grinning.

'You won't find many that do,' John said bluntly, and gave him a quick rundown on the Ferris situation and the local opinion on Ferris Labs.

'But James,' John finished, 'was well liked. Well respected too. He and his poor wife suffered a tragedy earlier this year. Lost their little boy to meningitis. A terrible thing.' John shook his head. 'Mrs Davies called me out late one night. Snow was bloody awful. James was giving last rites, or whatever, to some old duck with bad legs in a village a few miles away. They thought young Tommy just had a cold. It often seems that way, with meningitis. But Wendy got worried. A mother's instinct, I suppose. Course, I called the ambulance in right away, but . . .' The doctor shrugged fatalistically. 'Of course, a lot of the villagers muttered about it being down to having the lab nearby, poisoning the water, the air, what have you. And whilst I don't like having it here either, there was nothing suspicious about poor little Tommy's death. It was meningitis, plain and simple. Still, that didn't stop a lot of folks blaming the lad's death on the lab.'

Jason, who'd gone a little pale, looked across sympathetically at Wendy. First her son, now her husband. 'Perhaps she *should* be at home,' he said dubiously.

John glanced over and shook his head. 'I'm not so sure. If she went home now, to a home that'll never have her son or husband in it again . . . I think she'll feel better here, surrounded by friends and other people for now.'

Jason bowed to his superior judgement.

'So there's nobody you can think of who bore a grudge against James, then?' he prompted. 'Dr Trenning, perhaps?' he added cunningly.

John shook his head. 'I doubt that they'd have had much to do with each other. I mean, what would they have in common? And as for anything else, I know what you're thinking. Vicars are only human too. But I honestly don't think you'll find anything of that sort going on with either James or Wendy.'

Jason sighed. He had a feeling that he wouldn't either. So why *was* James Davies dead? And who had killed Gordon Trenning? He thanked the doctor and walked outside into the afternoon sunshine.

It was now getting on for five. The slow, painstaking process of elimination was taking place, and already about twenty or so people, who'd seen nothing, knew nothing, and heard nothing had been questioned and allowed to leave. Jason sighed and started adding to his memo list.

Who was killed first, James or Gordon Trenning? From what Dr Clarke had said, it seemed likely the vicar had died first, but he couldn't take that for granted. He'd have to have a word with the MO and the SOCO boys when they were finished, but it seemed logical that James had died first. If someone had seen Gordon Trenning after the vicar's death then that would clear it up immediately, but Jason was yet to find that out.

So, who'd noticed Gordon Trenning's movements, and had he been seen with anybody? Maybe quarrelling?

Money. Who benefitted?

As he wrote and thought, and went through the usual police procedures in his mind, he still had that niggling, worrying feeling that all of this was going to be a waste of time.

If Gordon Trenning had planted the capsule himself, why was he then killed and by whom? The only one who would want to avenge James's death by killing Trenning would be Wendy Davies. But that pre-supposed that she knew that it was Trenning who had made and planted the capsule in the first place. So far, there was no evidence that anybody at the fete knew what Trenning had been doing.

Besides, Wendy Davies, after being escorted from the flower show tent, would have been fussed over and constantly watched by her two companions. What chance would she then have had to go wild and bash the scientist over the head with a blunt instrument? No, this still wasn't making any kind of sense.

So, what if Trenning had made the capsule for someone else, as he'd previously been speculating. That meant that he had probably handed it over to his accomplice at some point during the fete. The big question there was, who had he given it to, and why had he been so willing to implicate himself in murder? He must have known that the very complicated nature of the capsule's construction would point the finger straight at him. Unless, of course, he'd intended to retrieve the capsule after the murder before the police arrived on the scene, but had been killed himself before he could do so.

Or might he have been blackmailed into making it?

Jason sighed. He knew that he didn't have anything like enough information yet to even start exploring all the various possibilities. As usual, he was jumping the gun.

He snapped the notebook shut and headed for the temporary incident room. Time to start questioning in earnest.

Jason usually liked this part of a job. It was when he found out what everybody else knew and he didn't. What would they tell him, what would they lie about, and what would they try to conceal?

And one of those witnesses would be Monica Noble. He shook his head and entered the tent. It would definitely be a good idea to keep his mind firmly on the job at hand.

CHAPTER 12

Carol-Ann spotted Jason Dury right away, and her interest quickened. Ever since he'd solved the murder of one of the flat-owning residents at her vicarage, she'd been inclined to think about him often.

Of course, he was quite old. Nearly forty. But he was still a hunk. She was half tempted to reintroduce herself, but at that moment she spotted Marc Linacre, seemingly arguing with a policeman guarding the stile at the bottom of the field, and she grinned. If he was trying to sneak off home early, he could forget it. She remembered police tactics from the last time. They never let anybody off the hook until they'd asked about a zillion questions at least.

Nonchalantly, she made her way to the bottom of the field. Here a big makeshift car park had been established, and as she watched, the photographer pointed to a low-slung sports car. Carol-Ann's eyes widened. Was that a Ferrari, maybe? Or an Aston Martin? Truth to tell, Carol-Ann wasn't sure, but it was one cool car. Obviously the man appreciated the fine things in life.

He walked towards her, shoulders slumped in defeat, and she coughed gently as he passed. Like a cornered rabbit, his head shot around and his eyes widened.

'Look, miss . . .' he began hotly.

Carol-Ann studied her green-painted nails casually. 'The police won't let us go for ages yet,' she told him coolly. 'Believe me, I know about these things. So you might as well find something to help pass the time. You can take pictures of me if you like,' she offered brightly.

'You are joking, right?' As he looked at the annoying blonde pest, a slow, angry red flush suffused his face. 'Look, why don't you just go away? Can't you comprehend the fact that I don't take cute little pictures of cute little girls any more?' The photographer began to huff and puff, like an out-of-control steamroller.

Carol-Ann's big blue eyes widened in alarm.

'That episode with Olivia Gee cost me my marriage, a fortune in alimony, and it embarrassed the shit out of everyone around me. I'm through with all that.' He was getting spectacularly red in the face by now, and his voice was rising dangerously, attracting the attention of those nearest to them. 'I take *real* photographs now, can't you understand that?' Linacre was almost jumping up and down with impotent rage, he was so beside himself. Carol-Ann had never seen a performance like it, and was fascinated and appalled in equal measure. A grown man, throwing a tantrum that a five-year-old would have found impressive. What was she supposed to do now? Go and get Graham maybe? He was probably the best one to calm him down.

'Are you capable of getting it through your dizzy little blonde head?' Linacre yelped patronizingly. 'I'm an *artist*.' He finally blew his top, aware that he was shouting now, but unable to stop. 'I take artistic shots only!' he screeched. Then he spotted his wife Angela, charging towards them through the crowd, no doubt alerted by her mate's bellowing, and Marc felt his heart sink, all sense of power deserting him like air escaping from a deflating balloon.

Quickly, he hissed at the now open-mouthed Carol-Ann, 'Scram. Hide. Shoo. Get away from me, you—' And with that, he quickly headed towards his wife (something he rarely did) in the hope of intercepting her and thus avoiding an almighty scene.

Carol-Ann watched him go, her mouth hanging open, her heart thumping a little uncomfortably. Then she told herself that she was being lily-livered. It was just artistic temperament, right? All the great artistes were supposed to throw wobblies, weren't they? If she was going to make it in this business, she had to grow thicker skin!

'All right,' she forced herself to say nonchalantly, watching his figure disappear into the interested crowd. 'Way to go, Markie-boy.'

Then her mind finally registered something else he'd said. Something pertinent. Namely, that he only did 'artistic' shots now. That meant nudes, even she knew that. And there was no way she could do that. Her mother would have a fit! And, she had to admit to herself, the very thought of it made her squirm.

On the other hand, if they were done really well, with nothing really showing . . . some talent scout might see an 'artful' shot of her in some posh magazine and realize that she'd look even better modelling the latest fashion designs of the great and the good. Then it would be 'Hello!' to Milan, Paris, New York, and Rome. The fabled cities seemed to beckon tauntingly. But was she really prepared to do what it took, and risk all . . . ?

On the other hand, if she wanted to be one of the greats, she couldn't be faint-hearted, right? Carol-Ann gulped. Hard. And so, frowning thoughtfully, she wandered back into the midst of the field.

The football was over now. She wondered where Jason Dury was, and if she oughtn't to say hello after all. The good-looking detective wouldn't have forgotten her, she was sure. She had to remember to build self-confidence. She straightened her back. Nobody forgot Carol-Ann — especially men nearing forty. Again she nodded emphatically, just to underline the point. There. That felt better.

She smiled, lifted her chin, and practised her sashaying walk. And wondered what her mother would think if they started dating.

* * *

Jason, blissfully unaware of Carol-Ann's designs on him, glanced around the small fortune-teller's tent. There was a desk, cleared now of its crystal ball, and three chairs. He wondered if he should have left the crystal ball where it was; if things got *that* desperate, he might just need it.

All in all, it was barely adequate, but it would have to do. He took a seat, and indicated one to Flora. 'How are the eliminations going?' he asked mildly.

'Not too bad, Chief. Most people weren't interested in the flower show tent at all, but several did have a wander around it before the judging. We're keeping those back.' Jason nodded. 'Those who've been running their own stalls are being told to pack up and go. The fact that they've had to stay put in one place all afternoon fairly rules out any chances that they might have seen or heard anything interesting.'

'Right,' he agreed. 'Tell Gilwiddy I want his officers on the alert for anyone who saw Dr Gordon Trenning go into the flower show tent prior to the judging. If we can place him in there, we'll at least have a starting point. And I want those reports on the life and times of Dr Gordon Trenning as soon as they come in. They're interviewing his friends and colleagues as we speak, right?'

'Yes, sir,' Flora confirmed crisply. That task was being made easier by the fact that a fair few of the lab people were also at the show. Ross Ferris seemed to have made it clear that he wanted a good showing of his employees at the village's biggest annual event. But if he'd hoped to win the natives around, Flora mused to herself, he was probably wasting his time. None of the villagers who didn't actually work there seemed to have a good word for the place.

'Good. The sooner I know what made him tick, the better I'll like it,' Jason said, interrupting her thoughts.

Flora nodded. 'But so far, nobody has said that they saw Dr Trenning anywhere near the flower tent. And we've already spoken to over a hundred people.' She sounded as discouraged as he felt.

Jason's lips thinned gloomily. 'I might have bloody well known,' he muttered. 'Right. We might as well start. Let's have Sir Hugh in first — he'll blow a gasket if we don't show him preference.'

Flora Glenn smiled conspiratorially, and left to fetch the squire.

* * *

Jason looked up as Sir Hugh entered the tent. It was now nearly half past five, and the accumulated heat wasn't helping anyone's temper. Because of the privacy Jason required, the tent had no open flaps save the front one, and as he stepped inside Sir Hugh was reminded of his army days training in the Sudan. He ran his handkerchief over the back of his neck and nodded at the blond policeman.

A good chap, this one, Sir Hugh's instincts told him. Sharp and clever. Good officer material.

'Sir Hugh,' Jason said pleasantly. 'Please, sit down.' The chairs, of necessity, were of the slatted, wooden folding variety, but sturdy enough. He watched the old man sit down, and didn't fail to notice the way his eyes strayed briefly to Flora Glenn's legs as she too took a seat and crossed them.

Jason didn't blame him — Flora had very nice legs — but it gave him a little insight into Sir Hugh's personality.

'Now, Sir Hugh, if I could just have a few personal details,' he began, and quickly learned his age, address, marital status, telephone number and profession. 'Right,' he continued, 'perhaps you can help me get the flower show setup straight in my mind. You're the chairman, I believe?'

'That's right.'

'Can you, first of all, run me through the timetable of the fete? What was supposed to happen when and did it all go as scheduled?'

He listened for a good five minutes as Sir Hugh explained the various workings of the Caulcott Green flower show. Flora, he noticed, made few scribbles in her notebook, but then she knew that Jason had asked the question mostly to relax the witness and get him in a voluble mood.

'Thank you, that's very clear,' Jason said smoothly, when he'd finished. 'Now, could you tell me a little about the judges themselves?'

Once again, Sir Hugh launched into conversation. It was obvious that many of the men and women in the flower show tent that day had been doing the same job for years. It wasn't until he began to talk about the flower judges, however, that Jason really started to pay attention, and something in particular had him sitting up straight in his chair.

'I'm sorry to interrupt you, Sir Hugh,' he said loudly, stopping the ex-soldier in mid-flow. 'But you've just made a mistake. You said that James Davies was judging the dahlias this year.'

Sir Hugh's face darkened. 'And so he was, Chief Inspector. So he was. I don't make mistakes like that.'

Jason slowly leaned forward in his chair. 'But, Sir Hugh, all the people I've talked to so far agree that James Davies was judging the roses. In fact, the . . . er . . . murder weapon was planted in a rose.'

He watched as the old soldier's face crumpled in disbelief. His watery eyes widened. 'Bloody hell,' Sir Hugh said succinctly. 'So he was. I never noticed . . .' He shook his head, as if unable to believe that he'd failed to spot such a breach of the rules. Then his face reddened alarmingly. 'Well he had no damned right to be judging the roses!' He began to splutter, such was his anger. 'That was that . . . that . . .' Sir Hugh was almost incandescent with rage now, 'that . . . *bastard*, Ross

Ferris's job. The dahlias were the real challenge this year; that's why it was agreed at committee level that James should judge it. He was always fair, and the entrants were more likely to accept his judgement without getting into a tizz over it,' Sir Hugh explained, talking so fast now that his words were almost tripping over themselves. 'Are you telling me that . . . that . . . *Ferris*,' he spat the word out as if it were a choice swear word, 'was actually judging the *dahlias*?' The last word came out as an outraged squeak.

It would almost have been funny if it weren't so significant. Jason cast Flora a quick look, and saw that the sergeant was also sitting on the edge of her seat, and trying not to stare too obviously at the witness.

Jason took a slow, deep breath. 'Sir Hugh, tell me. Was it widely known that Ross Ferris was going to be judging the roses this year?' he asked casually.

'I'd say it was!' Sir Hugh exploded, and proceeded to tell them, with much bitterness, the saga of the roses, and how poor Millie Fletcher, the proper rose expert, had been steamrollered aside by Ferris. 'The man was absolutely blatant about it.' Sir Hugh finally came to the end of his bluster, leaving only white-faced bitter rage in its place. 'And now you tell me that we could have had Millie after all, because he swapped with James? How the devil did James let him get away with that? I wouldn't have done,' he added unnecessarily. 'Damned if I would. And James knew it was against the rules to swap—' He broke off, appearing to suddenly remember that James was dead. 'Yes, well, he was a vicar, I suppose,' he muttered more forgivingly. 'He did it to keep the peace, no doubt.'

'Sir Hugh, could someone in Ferris Labs, for instance, have known in advance who was supposed to be judging which class?'

'Nothing simpler,' Sir Hugh stated flatly. 'The list of judges is always printed in the edition of the village newsletter just prior to the show. And nowadays, it's even online. Anybody could look it up.'

Jason sighed and rubbed his forehead wearily. 'So anyone would have known that Ross Ferris was judging the roses this year?' he clarified miserably.

'Yes,' Sir Hugh said flatly. Then he scowled. 'Except that he didn't, did he?'

Jason wondered if the ex-soldier could be as oblivious to what this really meant as he seemed to be.

'Just one more thing, Sir Hugh. Did you yourself go anywhere near the display of roses? Or the display of Peace in particular?'

A strange expression suddenly crossed Sir Hugh's face. A sort of sickly fascinated expression that made Jason sit up and take notice.

'Well, as a matter of fact, I did,' Sir Hugh said reluctantly, looking embarrassed. 'Everyone knows it's my favourite of all. I took a good hearty sniff . . .' he paled, then carried on bravely, 'just before the judging started.'

Jason stared at him, his mind racing. Had his witness just gone pale because he realized that he'd just admitted to having the perfect opportunity to plant the capsule? Or was it because he suddenly understood that if somebody had planted it sooner, then it would be him lying dead now, and not James Davies? And then another ugly little thought slid slyly into Jason's mind. If, as Sir Hugh claimed, everyone knew he had a fondness for Peace, could *Sir Hugh* have been the intended victim all along?

He looked across at Flora, who managed to get Sir Hugh to his feet and out of the door with very little fuss. When she returned she looked at Jason with a gleam in her eye.

Jason smiled grimly. 'All along I've had trouble with a harmless vicar as a murder victim, Sergeant,' he said with quiet satisfaction. 'But Ross Ferris . . . now he's just the sort that *would* go and get himself murdered.'

Flora nodded. 'I've been getting that impression all afternoon. Nobody at the fete has had a good word to say about the man. So you think Ferris was definitely the intended target all along, sir?'

'Don't you?'

Flora nodded. 'It makes much more sense,' she agreed.

'And Dr Gordon Trenning worked for Ross Ferris,' Jason said. 'Which is a definite connection. That's more than we have for Trenning and James Davies. So far we haven't found one thing that links the scientist and the vicar together. Flora, go and find out what's taking so long for those reports to come in on Trenning. I want to know if there was any bad blood, or even the tiniest hint of trouble between him and his boss. From what we've heard of Ross Ferris so far, it's doubtful that he's a candidate for an Employer of the Year award.'

Flora nodded. 'Yes, sir,' she said, and got to her feet.

Of course, what he needed was more basic background, Jason thought. Someone who could give him a truthful, unbiased opinion of the personalities involved. And he knew just the man to do it.

'Oh, and Flora, ask Graham Noble to come in next.'

Flora shot him a surprised look. She'd have bet a month's salary that he'd have asked to see Ferris.

'Yes, sir,' she added, a bit less crisply.

* * *

Sir Hugh, contrary to what Flora or Jason might have believed, had *not* missed the implications of the dahlia/rose swap at all. Furthermore, he had a shrewd idea what connotations the chief inspector had put on it.

The moment he left the interview tent, his outraged expression vanished, and he looked around at the slowly thinning crowd with sharp, seeking eyes. He needed to see someone, and urgently. At last, his eyes found the one he sought, and he marched across the field towards the tea tent, and the quietly sitting figure of Daphne Cadge-Hampton.

* * *

'Graham. Sorry to drag you away from Monica. Is she really feeling all right?' Jason stood up as the vicar of Heyford Bassett came in. Flora, her face a picture of bland blankness, left to hurry along the reports.

'It's fine, I know how it is,' Graham said, taking a seat without being asked. 'And yes, Monica's perfectly well, thanks for asking.' He looked at Jason patiently, his hands folded across his lap.

'Tell me, Graham, what class was James judging this year?' Jason asked casually.

'The dahlias.' The reply came promptly and without any doubt.

Jason's eyes flickered, just a bit, and Graham sat forward on his chair as he suddenly caught on. 'But in the tent, it was the roses . . .' he added quietly. 'Funny, I never gave it a thought at the time.'

Jason nodded. As he'd remembered, there were no flies on Graham Noble. 'What can you tell me about Ross Ferris?' he asked crisply.

Graham looked at him a shade uncomfortably. Jason sighed. 'Yes, I know. It feels like you're "sneaking" on friends and neighbours. But two people are dead—'

'*Two?*' Graham echoed sharply.

Jason nodded. So, the grapevine hadn't yet picked up on the other murder; SOCO must be being very discreet.

'Yes, I'm afraid so,' Jason said, but didn't elaborate. 'I really need to know what's what.'

Graham sighed. 'Well, Mr Ferris isn't very popular with anyone much, but that's hardly a secret.'

Jason pursed his lips. 'I find that a little puzzling. Don't his labs employ a fair few locals? Surely the job market isn't so great around here that people can turn up their noses at an industry right on their doorstep?'

'Oh, some people are glad of the jobs, of course,' Graham said hastily. 'But the majority don't work there and never wanted the old mill to be turned into a lab complex in the first

139

place. You know how scared people can get of something they don't know much about. Even in Heyford I've heard rumours that they're making chemical weapons for the government out here, and that one day everyone will be poisoned in their beds while they sleep. Others are sure that the labs are an ecological disaster just waiting to happen.'

Jason smiled. 'Like that, is it?'

'With some reason, Chief Inspector,' Graham rebuked him mildly. 'Haven't you heard what happened to Sir Hugh's angling business?'

Jason's eyes sharpened. 'No. Tell me.'

So Graham did. When he'd finished, Jason slowly nodded. No wonder Sir Hugh hated the man's guts. And he'd bet that there was even more to it than the loss of his fish stock and the strain of the upcoming court case. If he knew Ferris, and he was beginning to, he'd bet his last pound that the interloper was also trying to oust Sir Hugh from his role as squire. And that would cut deep.

So here was one man at least who'd wanted Ferris dead. But not James Davies. And by his own admission, Sir Hugh hadn't noticed, or hadn't known, that the two men had swapped judging roles. And he'd inspected the display of roses himself . . .

'I see. Anything else?'

'Well, there was that tragedy with Malvin Cook's son,' Graham said uneasily.

'Who?' Jason was sure he hadn't heard this name before. 'Sir Hugh's gardener. His son was one of the first to get a job at the lab. Apparently they're a big producer of fertilizers and stuff. A sort of lucrative sideline, you might say. That's the area where the majority of their unskilled workers come in; loading and transporting lorries and the like. Anyway, Stephen, Malvin's son, was killed in an accident barely a few months after starting work there. A big crate of fertilizer toppled off a forklift truck and killed him.'

Jason stared at Graham intently. 'What happened?'

'Oh, it was found that the forklift truck hadn't been maintained properly. Ross Ferris, from what I can remember from reading about it in the local papers, tried to argue that he'd bought the equipment from another firm, and that they were therefore responsible for seeing to it that the forklifts were OK. But the safety inspection people and the court judges didn't agree. They found in favour of the Cook family and awarded Malvin and his wife a huge amount in damages. Well, Stephen was their only son and main breadwinner,' Graham added meaningfully.

Jason nodded in total understanding. But what was all the money in the world compared with losing your only child? 'And you say this Malvin Cook works for Sir Hugh?'

'As his gardener, yes. One of those men who has worked for the same family since he was fourteen. Not many of their kind left, nowadays,' Graham mused sadly.

And there's another man with a good reason for wanting Ross Ferris dead, Jason thought. He wondered ruefully just how many more he was going to find before the day was out.

It was looking more and more likely that James Davies had died by mistake, in the place of Ross Ferris, and as a direct result of the vicar's own charitable action in agreeing to swap judging classes. He wondered what James Davies would have thought about that, had he been given the chance to comment.

'I see. And what can you tell me about your friend James? Know anybody who might have wanted to hurt him?'

As expected, Graham couldn't help him there. He heard once again about the loss of the Davies's son, Tommy, and that it was generally thought that Wendy Davies wasn't yet over it. He also confirmed John Clarke's view of the vicar's character. When he was finished, Jason was more convinced than ever that the potential victim must have been Ross Ferris.

Just then, Flora came back, clutching a folder of papers and looking, even to Graham's eyes, flushed with excitement. She took a seat next to her superior and carefully kept quiet.

Graham cast a quick questioning look at Jason, who nodded back in response, and guessing himself to be dismissed, the vicar rose to his feet, bade them a brief farewell, and left.

Flora watched the good-looking clergyman go with eyes that were openly curious. 'A very handsome man that, sir,' she said, watching Jason Dury closely.

'Yes, so I've been told,' Jason said mildly. 'What have you got for me, Sergeant?' he asked, meeting her gaze levelly.

Flora had enough sense to drop it. 'News from Ferris Labs, sir. It seems that there *was* some big trouble between Gordon Trenning and his boss.'

'Why am I not surprised,' Jason said dryly. 'So what was it all about, then?'

'Some sort of computer chip or gizmo patent that Trenning came up with. Apparently it's all set to revolutionize the computer world, sir. It would have made Trenning very rich indeed. Maybe even billionaire rich, if his fellow workers are to be believed.'

Jason whistled under his breath. 'I notice you said it "would have" made him rich?'

'Yes, sir,' Flora grinned. 'Except that Ross Ferris successfully registered the patent under the name of Ferris Labs first. Got his lawyers to argue that Trenning made the gizmo on firm time, using the company's facilities, and whilst under contract to the lab.'

'Ergo, it belongs to them.'

'Yes. Dr Trenning was not happy, they tell me,' she added in massive understatement, unable to stop herself from being facetious.

'No, I don't suppose he was,' Jason said dryly. 'So he decides to get revenge by making a killer capsule that has his name written all over it. Not very clever, for a very clever man,' he added thoughtfully.

'Losing all that money would unhinge anyone, sir,' Flora pointed out. 'Perhaps he didn't care if he got caught, just so long as his enemy was dead.'

'And killing him in such a clever and outrageous way probably *would* appeal to a boffin like him,' Jason agreed slowly.

'So he planted the capsule . . .' Flora put in.

'Except that we can't find anyone who can put him anywhere near the tent and the rose display,' Jason added flatly.

'And then he promptly killed himself by hitting himself on the back of the head with something and then tossing the weapon away before he died,' Flora finished ironically. 'You're right, it still doesn't fit, does it?'

Jason sighed. 'Still no sign of the blunt instrument, I take it?'

'Not yet, sir. I noticed the uniforms are in the field opposite the tent now. With all those deep ruts and covering stubble, half a dozen murder weapons could have been tossed over the fence and be lying out of sight.'

Jason sighed, rubbed his eyes, and brought Flora up to date on what he'd learned so far.

'So that's three people that we know of who might have wanted this man Ferris dead,' Flora mused.

'Perhaps the question should be who wanted *Trenning* dead?' Jason said. 'He must have had an accomplice. He must have made the capsule, then passed it on to someone else to plant it and thus kill Ferris. He must have had one hell of a shock when he heard that it was the vicar who was dead by mistake. Who knows, perhaps that's why he was killed himself? He wasn't going to stand for an innocent man dying, and threatened to confess all. So his accomplice had to kill him to keep him quiet. Which means that his accomplice almost certainly had to be one of the judges. They were the only ones who would have had the opportunity to plant the capsule at the right time.'

'Sir Hugh?' Flora hazarded.

'Perhaps. But then again, there were people in and out of that tent before the judging even started. It might have been a villager we don't even know about yet. No, wait a minute, that won't wash now. Sir Hugh admits to smelling the rose just before the judging started, and he's still in the land of the living. So unless he was lying, it must have been planted more or less at the last minute.'

'At least we've got somewhere to start now, sir,' Flora said encouragingly.

Jason nodded. 'We've got to find out how and when James and Ross Ferris came to an agreement about changing their judging roles,' he mused. 'I've got a feeling it might be important.'

Flora didn't quite see why, but she wasn't about to argue with a superior who had a clearance rate as high as Jason Dury's.

'We'll have Ferris in now, I think,' Jason said, his pale blue eyes glittering. 'It should be interesting to see what he has to say for himself.'

CHAPTER 13

After all they'd heard about him, their first actual sight of Ross Ferris came, perhaps naturally enough, as something of an anticlimax, although there *was* just a whispered hint of something out of the ordinary about him. A miasma of power, perhaps. He had well-cut blond hair and a good-looking enough face in a heavy, portentous sort of way. His clothes and accessories must have run into four figures.

He looked very much like what he was, Flora thought archly – a rich, self-important, self-made man.

'Please, take a seat, Mr Ferris,' Jason ordered him crisply.

Ross had been doing assessments of his own, and the man in front of him looked every bit competent enough to be in charge of a murder investigation. And the fact that there was no respect whatsoever in the ice-cold blue eyes looking him over was something that Ross found particularly unforgivable. He was used to being treated with far more cautious awareness than this policeman was affording him.

Restlessly, his gaze turned to the female officer, and his grey eyes widened appreciatively. Now she was quite a looker.

'Thank you,' he said, taking a seat as if he were doing them all a great favour. 'I must say, I don't appreciate being told that I can't leave this damned playing field. Isn't that illegal imprisonment, Sergeant?' he demanded, holding the younger man's pale blue gaze in a blatantly obvious power struggle.

Jason merely smiled. 'It's Chief Inspector, Mr Ferris,' he corrected him mildly. 'And no it isn't.'

Acknowledging that locking horns with this man would accomplish nothing, Ross merely linked his hands over his knees and stared at Jason with a bored expression, a bare smile lifting the corners of his fleshy lips.

Jason felt antagonism stir within him, and quickly crushed it. No doubt that was just what Ross Ferris wanted. If you could rile a man, you could distract him and dictate the terms of a conversation. Jason had no intention of letting Ross Ferris play his little games here.

'Now, sir, if you can tell me how you came to be judging the dahlias this year, and not the roses as everyone supposed, I'd be much obliged,' Jason said, with such sardonic politeness that it was Ross's turn to grit his teeth in anger.

Ross sighed. 'Really, as if that could in any way be relevant, Inspector—'

'Chief Inspector,' Jason interrupted him blandly.

Ross smiled wolfishly. 'Chief Inspector,' he repeated drolly. 'If that's a sample of the kind of questions you're going to ask, I must say I'm rather disappointed. What on earth can it possibly matter what class of flower I was judging? And why are we going through all this rigmarole for a vicar who died of a heart attack anyway?'

Jason stopped himself from smiling in anticipation. Nevertheless, he was certainly going to enjoy this. 'Firstly, sir, who said that James Davies died of a heart attack?' As Ross's mouth dropped open, he added silkily, 'And what class of flower you were judging, and why, is vitally important, or I wouldn't have wasted my time asking you. Now, Mr Ferris, answer the question please,' he added, a definite warning bite to his voice now.

Ross's wide grey eyes narrowed cunningly. 'You're treating his death as suspicious then, Inspector?'

Jason began to feel like killing Ross Ferris himself.

'It's *Chief* Inspector. And yes. We're treating the death of James Davies as suspicious in the extreme,' Jason gritted.

Ross leaned back in the chair, making it creak. 'In that case, perhaps I should call my lawyer.'

He was only doing it to be obstructive, Jason realized that at once, but two could play at that game.

'Oh?' he leaned forward, suddenly looking keen. 'Are you admitting then that you have reason to be worried, Mr Ferris? Did you have a grudge against the vicar of this parish by any chance?'

Ross jerked upright, his hands falling apart, totally losing his carefully created image of amused observer. 'What? No, of course not. I hardly knew the man,' he blustered.

'I see. Do you know of any reason why anyone should want to kill Reverend Davies?'

'Of course not. The man was totally harmless,' Ross said scornfully.

'And yet he was murdered, Mr Ferris. By a tiny exploding gas capsule containing cyanide.' Even now he had trouble describing the method of murder without feeling like he'd stepped into a James Bond film. It obviously had the same effect on Ross Ferris, for he suddenly burst out laughing.

'What?' he barked scornfully.

Jason smiled. 'I know — sounds ridiculous, doesn't it? But we found the remains of just such a device secreted in a rose head.'

Ferris slowly felt himself growing cold. 'In a rose, you say?' he asked, his voice suddenly croaking hoarsely. He nervously flicked out a thick pink tongue to run over his dry lips. His eyes darted to Flora, then away again, his gaze flickering around the tent as if searching for answers in the bland canvas awnings.

'Yes, Mr Ferris,' Jason said succinctly, and with distinct pleasure. 'In a rose. The class of flower that *you*, and not the vicar, were set to judge. In fact, every person I've spoken to so far was sure that you were judging the roses this year. Sir Hugh tells me that a list of judges was even sent out in a newsletter to every house in the parish just a few weeks ago. So perhaps you can tell me how it came about that when the judging started, you were at the dahlia table instead?' he asked sweetly.

By now, Ross Ferris was quite white. 'You think that someone meant to kill me, don't you?' he demanded, his pupils dilating in shock, his voice a hoarse croak.

'Either that, or you planted the capsule in the roses in order to kill James Davies, and then convinced him to swap places with you so that you could judge his class of flower in complete safety,' Jason said calmly, watching him carefully.

With a wave of his hand, Ross Ferris dismissed the idea, apparently without even thinking about it. And then he blinked. Twice. 'Wait a minute. This . . . capsule. It must have been tiny, like you said. Microscopic, almost.'

'It was.'

'And it was filled with cyanide gas, you say? How was it activated?' He was leaning forward now, the colour flooding back. He was breathing fast, obviously a man under extreme stress and excitement.

'Our experts believe some chemical in human breath probably triggered it,' Jason said reluctantly. 'But until they can run proper tests, that can't be proven.'

'Trenning,' Ross Ferris said flatly, leaning back once more in his chair, a hard, ugly look crossing his face. 'It could only have been made by Gordon Trenning, one of my top people. Only he has the right mix of expertise in both gas and micro-technology. You have to arrest him right away.'

Jason watched the conflicting emotions cross the other man's face — fear, anger, and, finally, a sort of reluctant admiration. 'Who'd have thought he'd have had the guts,' Ferris murmured, shaking his head in disbelief.

'And who exactly is Gordon Trenning?' Jason asked, as innocent as a lamb.

Ferris snorted. 'The man who made that capsule, that's who,' he snarled. 'The man who tried to kill me. And I want him arrested, *now*!' he finished, his voice decibel level rising dramatically.

'That might prove rather difficult, Mr Ferris,' Jason said mildly.

'Oh?' Ferris shot out the word challengingly, and leaned forward aggressively in his chair. 'And why's that? Did you let him get away?' he sneered. 'Don't tell me. He's done a runner, and you let him,' he snorted disgustedly.

'No, Mr Ferris. Dr Gordon Trenning isn't going anywhere.' And much as it annoyed him, he was sure that the puzzled and frustrated look that crossed the businessman's face was perfectly genuine.

'I don't understand,' Ross said, a shade more cautiously now. He was beginning to think that this fresh-faced copper was playing him for a fool, and he didn't like it. He didn't like it one bit. He was sure to know someone who both owed him a favour and who knew the chief constable. When he got back home, he'd soon arrange for a rocket to be lit under the bum of *Chief Inspector* Jason bloody Dury.

'I'm telling you, only Gordon Trenning could have done this,' he snarled, frustration making him go puce in the face. 'He is brilliant in his field, and—'

'Oh yes, I'm sure you're right,' Jason interrupted, anxious not to get lost in techno-babble.

'Then it's obvious that he must have made the damned thing,' Ross yelped. 'So why can't you arrest him and get this over with?' He was all but huffing indignation now, and Jason was pleased to see that it made all his good looks vanish.

'Because he's dead, Mr Ferris,' he said flatly.

For a few long seconds there was total silence in the tent. Then, 'What? What did you say?' Ross Ferris croaked.

'He's dead.'

'When?'

'A matter of an hour or so ago.'

'Here?'

'Yes. Here.'

The grey eyes flickered. 'He was . . . killed?'

'Yes.'

'Like . . . like the vicar?'

'No.'

'Oh.'

It was quite a sight to see, Ross Ferris demoralized and bewildered, Jason mused. 'Now, if you'd just answer some more questions. Sir Hugh tells us that he passed the display of roses, and bent to smell and handle the display of Peace. Did you see him do this?' Jason would feel better once he'd got this little snippet of information confirmed by a (more or less) unbiased witness.

'Yes. As a matter of fact I did notice him by the roses,' Ross said, a little too hastily. 'You think he and Gordon were in it together? That Sir Hugh planted the capsule then?'

Jason smiled. 'Now why would he do that, Mr Ferris?'

Ross flushed angrily. Now he was sure this copper was playing games with him. 'Oh come on. You must know by now. Both Trenning and that old duffer had reason to hate my guts.' He said it as if it was something to be proud of, rather than the reverse.

No doubt for all his life Ross had been trampling over people and expecting nothing less than rancour and repugnance in response. He must have grown a hide inches thick, Jason mused. 'So I've heard,' he agreed calmly, the mocking tone of his voice going straight over Ross's head.

'Well, there you go then. Why don't you arrest him?'

'Who?'

By now Ross was on the point of blowing his top altogether, and Flora felt like getting up and applauding her boss. He was by far one of the best wind-up merchants she'd ever come across. And after years in the police force, that was really saying something.

'Sir Hugh, of course!' Ross yelped. 'It's obvious that he must have planted the capsule. He and Trenning were in it together.

Trenning made the capsule, Sir Hugh planted it, thinking I'd be killed, and then he killed Trenning to shut him up.'

Jason shook his head patiently. The fact that he'd just repeated their current top theory was beside the point. 'Well, that's one way of looking at it, Mr Ferris,' he said mildly, as if humouring a child. 'But you still haven't told me how it was that the Reverend Davies came to be judging the roses in the first place,' Jason reminded him.

'Oh what the hell does *that* matter?' Ross all but yelled. He took a deep breath and made an obvious effort to bring his temper under control. Until he did, it was clear he was not going to be able to regain the upper hand.

He began, in a much more reasonable tone, to explain himself. 'I happened to be in the tea tent when Mrs Davies told me that her husband was going to have a hard time judging his class this year. It was by far the largest entry, and according to local gossip it was going to be particularly contentious, with several contestants expecting to get the top prize. I thought a vicar might find it hard to tread on so many people's toes, so I thought I'd find him and offer to swap; the roses are much easier to judge. I thought I was doing him a favour, that's all.'

Jason had to hand it to him. He'd said that with almost total conviction and innocence.

'I see,' he said flatly. 'And you told Mrs Davies about this sudden attack of altruism of yours?'

Ross, this time, began to look slightly uncomfortable. 'Well, no. I mean, I didn't think of it at the time. I just got my tea and left. But later, when I saw the vicar, I remembered what she'd said and approached him.'

'I see. And was he . . . er . . . pleased about your offer to take the terrible dahlias off him?' Jason asked sardonically.

Ross flushed. 'Yes, as a matter of fact he was,' he lied boldly. Jason nodded. 'And who heard you making these arrangements to swap with the vicar?'

'No one. We were alone at the time.'

'In a crowded field? Surely someone could have overheard you?' Jason pressed.

'No. We had a spot to ourselves.'

Jason's eyes glinted knowingly. 'I see.'

Ross saw too. Say what you like about him, Jason thought grimly, the man had brains, and had seen at once the significance of what that private chat with the late James Davies had meant. No one could have known that he and James had swapped, so everyone thought it would still be him who'd be judging the roses. Jason checked the businessman for signs of overt panic, and couldn't see any. Which was a little unexpected, perhaps, but was it significant?

Could he have put two and two together much sooner, and then killed Gordon Trenning to ensure that his employee never got another chance to try to murder him? A nice little case of retroactive self-defence that would have been!

Jason considered Ross Ferris a little harder. He certainly had a temper. And he was obviously a man who could keep his head and think fast under fire. And Jason wouldn't put it past him to act as judge, jury, and executioner — especially where his own safety was concerned. So far, he'd been thinking along the lines that the person who'd killed James Davies had also killed Gordon Trenning. But was there really any evidence for that? The killings, when you came to study them, were so vastly different. James Davies's death smacked of premeditation. Careful planning. Cunning. Gordon Trenning's murder, on the other hand, had all the hallmarks of a hasty, opportunistic killing — a quick bash over the head with something blunt and hard when nobody was looking.

Jason sighed. He had to admit that the thought of being able to arrest Ross Ferris was tempting.

Realizing that Flora and Ross were staring at him, both almost able to hear the wheels turning in his head, Jason forced himself to concentrate.

'Can you think of anyone else who might want you dead, Mr Ferris?' he asked, making it sound as if he expected the man to come up with a list at least twenty strong.

Ross, picking up on it, angrily opened his mouth to deny it, and then a sudden, thoughtful look took over. 'Well, yes, as a matter of fact, I do know of someone else,' he was forced to admit quietly. 'And she's here today,' he added. 'But she wouldn't have the guts,' he scoffed, and shook his head. Then his eyes narrowed in more ominous thought. 'Or would she? I thought the little witch had showed up just to embarrass me, and try a spot of blackmail, but perhaps . . . Yes, *and* I saw her talking to Trenning earlier on,' he continued excitedly, leaning forward in his chair once more.

'Mr Ferris,' Jason interrupted, his voice as sweet as honey. 'Perhaps, under the circumstances, you might care to share your thoughts with us. Who exactly are you talking about?'

Ross smiled grimly. 'Certainly, Inspector. It's my wife. Or soon-to-be ex-wife, I should say. Melissa. What's more, as I said, she's actually here at the fete. Although she shouldn't be. She's no longer resident in the village, and I doubt very much that anyone would have gone out of their way to invite her. She must have just remembered the fete was today and decided to come.'

'Is that so surprising?' It was Flora who slipped in the question, unable to prevent herself.

Ross snorted. 'If you knew Melissa, you'd think so. We're separated and she's currently living in London. She hates and loathes the countryside and Caulcott Green in particular. When she left, she swore never to grace us with her presence again. I'd have said wild horses wouldn't have been able to drag her to an event so bucolic and unimportant as this.'

'But you're sure that she's here?' Jason asked sharply.

'Oh yes. Positive. I haven't spoken to her, but I've seen her around once or twice. Believe me, she's rather hard to miss.'

'And you're going through the process of a divorce? From the way you've been talking, I take it that it's not a particularly amicable process?' Jason added drolly.

Ross grinned wolfishly. 'Hardly. She signed a pre-nup and I'm not letting her out of it. She's wild with fury.'

And she's right here at the fete, Jason thought, with ample motive and opportunity; yet one more contender for the role of Gordon Trenning's accomplice.

Wonderful.

CHAPTER 14

Monica spotted Pete Drummond standing by the coconut shy, sipping warm beer and watching the white-suited members of the SOCO team toing and froing around the tea tent. It made her pause, and fight a brief inner battle with herself. On the one hand, she was dying to have a nose around to see what she could find out about what was happening. On the other, she was inclined to think that having been involved with *one* murder should be enough for anybody. And she really had no justification for going around asking questions.

'Hello, Pete.' She greeted her fellow judge with a weak smile.

'Mrs Noble.' Pete straightened up a bit as she approached, and looked around for a place to hide his beer bottle. Monica pretended not to notice.

'Well, none of us thought the day was going to end like this, I'm sure,' she said sadly, and Pete sighed heavily. He was a well-padded man of middle age, and worked in insurance somewhere over Cirencester way.

'That's a fact to be sure,' he said grimly.

'You did well to get Dr Clarke so quickly,' Monica said, sensing the other man's very real depression, and trying hard to think of anything positive to say.

'A bit of a football fan, is Doc Clarke, so I went to the field first off, and there he was.' He seemed almost childlike in his desire to be praised, and Monica smiled encouragingly.

'It's not everyone who can think clearly in a crisis,' she said approvingly.

The coconut shy man, an older villager that Monica didn't know, nodded wisely. He made no effort to hide the fact that he was blatantly listening in, and seemed to take it for granted that he was invited to join in the conversation. Monica could have kissed him. Well, hypothetically speaking, of course.

'It comes to something when you're not even safe in your own village,' he said, tossing a hard white ball casually in the air.

'It all feels very strange, doesn't it?' she murmured, as she looked around. The sun was on its downward slide into evening, and the shadows were slowly elongating. The football pitch was deserted now, and the stalls were slowly winding down. People were milling about, laden with their purchases and prize winnings. Even so, the evening had an odd, unreal feel to it — as if they were all having a communal dream.

'I feel as if I've been wrong-footed somehow. The world just doesn't feel right or as it should, and the worst thing is I just don't know what to do about it,' Monica sighed.

Both men nodded, relieved that someone else had put into words their own sense of unease. And Monica was wise enough to know that being a vicar's wife gave her a certain amount of authority. She was also well used to encouraging, and being the recipient of confidences, and Pete Drummond was no exception.

'It's not just that, though, is it?' he said, rather ambiguously. 'I mean, I'm beginning to think things. Really stupid things.' And he looked at her out of the corner of his eye, trying to assess her reaction to this overture.

Monica was careful not to look at him too quickly, or too curiously.

'You all know about that nasty affair of our own last year, of course, over in our village?' she began craftily, referring to

155

the murder they'd had there, and noticed how the two men cast quick looks at each other.

'Ah. Most upsetting,' the older man said profoundly, still casually tossing his ball up and down. Everyone and his mother knew that the Nobles had had a murder up at their place, which put Monica and Graham in the unique situation of being 'experts' now.

'It was really strange at the time,' Monica went on, anxious to capitalize on it now that she had their full attention. 'After the body was found I began to go over and over things in my mind that had seemed perfectly ordinary before, but then, afterwards, had become somehow sinister. And it only got worse; suddenly, everything anyone did or said seemed suspicious. But it was mostly in my mind, of course,' she added with a light little laugh. She glanced at Pete to see if she was on the right track, and found him staring at her intently.

'Right. That's exactly what I mean,' he said. 'Take that business with old Malvin Cook for instance,' he blurted. Then abruptly stopped, looking a bit like a wild-eyed horse suddenly confronted with a fence it wasn't sure it could jump.

Monica felt her heartbeat quicken, but merely nodded. 'Let me guess,' she said, seeing that Pete was beginning to look as if he was having second thoughts about carrying on. 'It meant nothing to you at the time, whatever it was,' she mused, 'and it seemed innocuous enough then, but now, with everyone talking about murder and things . . .' she trailed off tantalizingly and looked at him openly.

'Just so,' Pete agreed, with barely concealed relief. 'I never thought nothing about it before. Old Malvin's always treated the flower show tent like it was his own private property. Him and Sir Hugh both. So I never gave it another thought, like. I just smiled, and thought to myself, "Old Malvin's got something up his sleeve," and never thought no more about it.'

Monica took a careful but surreptitious breath. 'Yes, I imagine both Sir Hugh and Malvin feel like they have special privileges. After all, the show wouldn't be the same without them, would it?'

'That's a fact,' the coconut man said dryly.

'Thing is, I could have sworn I saw Malvin in the tent after it had been cleared of the general public, like, but that probably doesn't mean a thing, right?'

As Pete suddenly blurted out what had been bothering him, a little nubbin of worry in the back of his eyes as he looked at Monica made her wonder exactly who was using who here. She might well be treading carefully, scared that she might do or say the wrong thing that would put him off talking. But she was beginning to think that Pete was just as anxious to offload what he knew onto her shoulders, as a way of avoiding his responsibility to approach the police directly. In which case she was more than happy to be a buffer zone for him.

'I'm sure it probably means nothing,' she agreed obligingly. 'I daresay he does it every year. Just to have a last check or something, when nobody's watching.'

'Probably. He and Sir Hugh were really keen to win the Gladiola Cup this year,' the coconut shy holder chipped in.

'Yes, I'd heard that,' Monica said mildly. What she was doing wasn't a totally selfish act on her part. She knew he'd feel a lot better once he'd got it all off his chest. 'So, what time approximately do you think you saw him?' she probed gently.

Pete hesitated for just a moment, then shrugged. 'I'm not sure. I think it was when Sir Hugh got us all up to the top end to deliver his annual speech.'

'I daresay Malvin just forgot something and didn't want to bother anyone,' she said airily.

Pete sighed. 'Most likely he only wanted to give one of his displays a last-minute check over, like you do,' he agreed quietly.

Monica smiled and brushed a strand of hair off her cheek. 'Well, I'd better go and find that daughter of mine before she gets into any mischief,' she mused, and caught Pete Drummond's eye as she turned.

He looked both guilty and relieved.

No doubt about it, Monica thought wryly. She'd been had. Pete didn't want to drop Malvin Cook in it himself, but he felt obliged to tell *someone* what he'd seen, knowing, no doubt, that it was bound to get back to official ears at some point. But by then at least the cops would be asking him direct questions and, as an honest man, he couldn't be expected to lie, could he? Thus his conscience could remain clear.

As she set off to find Carol-Ann, Monica tried to remind herself about just what it was that curiosity did to the cat. But she knew that she wouldn't be able to resist talking to some others, and seeing what else she could find out from them. And then, of course, she'd have to pass all the information on to Jason.

James had been a dear friend, after all, and just like everyone else, he deserved justice.

* * *

In the fortune-teller's tent, Jason watched the man who'd been judging the carrots that year get up and go. The vegetable judge had also confirmed that Sir Hugh had taken a sniff of the Peace rose, just as the squire had admitted, but, like all the others, he *hadn't* seen a man in a suit anywhere near the flower show tent.

It took them no further forward, but at least it confirmed the other interviewees' stories, and it was looking more and more as if Gordon Trenning hadn't done the actual planting of the capsule himself.

The reports on the scientist had been coming in to Jason all afternoon, allowing him to build up a solid mental picture of Gordon Trenning. The impression he was getting of the man was that of a clever, isolated, bitter, and rather lonely figure — his romance with a local village girl notwithstanding.

'Right, who's next?' he asked Flora. Just then a uniformed man came in, trying to look professionally detached, but with an unmistakable air of suppressed excitement about him.

'Sir,' he said smartly, 'we're getting several accounts coming in of a near-physical fight between one of the victims and a man here at the fete.'

'Not the vicar, surely? I can't see him resorting to violence,' Jason replied drolly.

'No, sir, the other victim — the scientist. Apparently he and one of the locals, a Mr Sean Gregson, had a very loud argument. According to some, they very nearly came to blows.'

Jason sighed. 'Right. Well, let's have this Gregson in, then, and get it sorted.'

'Sir,' he said smartly, and left.

'Another twist, sir?' Flora asked. Even in the hot tent, her boss looked good enough to eat. She'd really have to make a few overtures, very tentatively of course, and see what happened.

* * *

Monica found Carol-Ann standing in front of the sports pavilion, looking at herself in the window glass. As she approached, Carol-Ann turned to one side, and checked her profile in the glass, one hand resting on her extremely flat stomach.

'Mum, do you think I've got the figure for art shots?' she asked, seeing Monica's reflection appear next to her own.

Monica, as might be expected, promptly lost her head. 'No,' she said flatly.

Carol-Ann turned slowly around. 'Oh? Do I look fat?' Visions of anorexic girls flashed quickly across Monica's inner eye, and she paled even further. 'No, you look lovely and slim,' she said firmly. 'That's just the point. Women who get asked to do "art" shots are more like those women you see in paintings by Rubens,' she lied shamelessly. 'You know, plump.'

Carol-Ann's big blue eyes narrowed in thought. 'Oh. You mean my boobs aren't big enough?'

Monica, caught on the horns of a dilemma, wanted to kick herself. 'You don't need a boob job, Carol-Ann,' she said, struggling to keep her voice even. 'I think you've got the perfect figure for fashion modelling just as you are now,' she temporized craftily. 'If you start tinkering around with it — either trying to put on weight, or take it off — you're probably not going to wind up with the right look to do anything.'

She held her breath as her daughter mulled this over.

'Besides, if your exam results are good enough, you'll be going to college. Right?' She tried not to sound too desperate, she really did, but even Monica could hear the tinge of hysteria in her voice now.

Carol-Ann turned back to the glass, and put a hand on her flat tummy again.

Hastily, Monica changed the subject. 'Reverend Davies is dead,' she said.

'I know,' Carol-Ann said flatly. 'I'm so sorry, Mum. I know he was your friend. Are you all right?'

'Thanks, sweetheart, I'm fine,' Monica said, even if she wasn't quite so sure that she was. 'They're saying now someone else is dead too.'

'Really?' Carol-Ann looked at her mother with troubled eyes. 'Who?'

Monica wasn't sure, but the consensus of opinion had more or less agreed on the identity of the second victim. 'I don't know his name, but he's one of the scientists from the nearby lab.'

Carol-Ann's eyes flickered. 'Not the man in the suit? The one who kept going behind the tea tent to have a crafty pee?' As she finished speaking, both mother and daughter turned to look at the tent in question. No doubt about it, there was a lot of action from the men in white overalls around the back of the tent now.

Monica felt her blood begin to freeze. This was an afternoon for shocks all right. First her daughter was threatening to pose in the nude, now she seemed to have knowledge about the murders.

'What makes you think it was him?' Monica asked.

Carol-Ann shrugged. 'He just looked like a scientist type. Thin, wearing a suit. You know the kind.'

Monica wasn't so sure that she did. 'What made you think he went behind the tent to pee?' she asked, curious in spite of herself.

'Well, what else would he be going behind there for?' Carol-Ann snorted, and wrinkled her nose.

Monica went even colder. If someone had been killed there, as it was now beginning to look, then . . . 'Carol-Ann, did you see anybody follow him? Behind the tent, I mean?'

'Yeah. The big cheese.'

'The big . . . you mean the countess?' Monica squeaked.

Carol-Ann heaved a massive sigh. 'No, not her. The other one — the bloke. The one who walks around as if he owns the place.'

Monica felt her heart sink. 'You mean Sir Hugh?'

'That's him.'

Carol-Ann began to turn towards the glass again, but Monica quickly headed her off.

'Look, I think we should go and talk to Jason about this,' she said, missing the way her daughter's eyes suddenly lit up. 'It might be important. I'm not saying that Sir Hugh killed him, of course, but—'

'Oh, Mum, of course he didn't,' Carol-Ann sighed. 'When he went around there the second time I'm pretty sure that he wasn't followed. At least, I didn't see anyone.'

Monica blinked, thoroughly confused now. 'What do you mean, the second time?'

Carol-Ann shrugged. 'The second time,' she repeated carefully, 'I saw the man in the suit go around the back of the tea tent twice. That's why I thought it must be some sort of a make-do, open-air gentleman's lav! The first time Sir Hugh followed him, but the second time all you lot had already gone into the tent to start judging the flowers.'

'OK, this is important. We have to get this right, Carol-Ann. So concentrate! You say that the second time the man went behind the tent he wasn't followed?'

Carol-Ann began to look unsure. 'Well, I don't think so. Not right away he wasn't, anyway. But I was . . . talking . . . to someone at the time, so I wasn't really paying that much attention. So someone could have gone around after a while, and I might not have noticed.' She sounded rather doubtful now. And she was worried that she was going to have to spill the beans about hassling Marc Linacre to take photos of her. Her parents would be sure to stop her pocket money for a week, then. Or maybe even two.

Monica, unaware of her daughter's angst, shook her head as she mulled over this latest evidence. It didn't make much sense to her. But one thing was for sure.

They needed to talk to Jason. And fast.

* * *

Flora Glenn looked up as a second policeman poked his head around the tent flap.

'That was quick,' Jason said. 'You've got this Gregson chap?'

The constable looked puzzled. 'No, sir. But there's a lady out here who says she needs to speak to you. Urgent, like.'

Jason sighed. There was always someone who wanted to get in on the act. The last thing he needed now was some busybody matron bending his ear with a thin story and a useless piece of gossip, trying to pump him for information.

'Not now.'

'Yes, sir.'

Flora looked back down at her notes. 'Sir Hugh had the motive and opportunity. All we need is for someone to link him to Dr Trenning . . .' she trailed off wistfully.

'Sir?'

Jason's head snapped up to spear the constable again, who already looked miserable. Jason's furious gaze did nothing to improve his plight.

'She says to tell you that she's Mrs Noble, sir, and that she thinks her daughter may have some vital information.' He relayed the message in a rush. 'She's most insist—'

'Show her in,' Jason said quickly. 'And if the others return, keep them outside until we've finished.'

'Sir!' The relief in the constable's face was almost comic. A moment later, Flora watched the dark-haired vicar's wife come in, a striking, leggy blonde princess beside her.

162

Jason rose. 'Mrs Noble,' he said, his mouth just a shade dry.

Monica smiled, a little uncertainly, Flora thought. 'Chief Inspector. You remember Carol-Ann?' Beside her, her daughter tossed back her mane of long blonde hair and looked at him boldly.

Jason took a deep breath. 'As if I could forget,' he said, half amused, half wary.

'Carol-Ann, tell the chief inspector what you just told me,' Monica prompted.

Carol-Ann, who didn't appreciate being told what to do as if she were a five-year-old, deliberately moved forward and took the seat in front of Jason, crossing her long, long legs conspicuously. Monica, glaring at her offspring, took the second chair and cast an apologetic glance at Jason.

'Well, it's about the man in the suit,' Carol-Ann said, instantly gaining the two police officers' attention. Nonchalantly, Carol-Ann described Gordon Trenning's two trips behind the tea tent. When she was finished, Flora's notebook was crammed with shorthand.

'And you're sure the man who followed him the first time was Sir Hugh?' Jason prompted.

'Sure. You can't mistake that head of white hair of his. Or the way he walks — like he was changing the guard at Buckingham Palace personally.'

Flora's lips twitched.

'Right. And — this is important, Carol-Ann,' Jason said, leaning forward. 'You're sure that the second time that you saw Dr Trenning go behind the tent, the flower show judging had already started?'

Carol-Ann rolled her eyes. 'Yes! Didn't I hear his nibs' voice over the loudspeaker ordering his troops into battle?'

Jason's eyes sharpened. 'You never mentioned that before!'

'Well, excuse me!' Carol-Ann huffed. 'I only just remembered it. The only reason I remembered it at all was because his nibs was sounding so cheesed off. I think he'd called for the judges at least twice before.'

Monica nodded. 'He did. I remember. Both Wendy and Her Ladyship were rather late getting in. I went to fetch them.'

Jason nodded, glanced at Flora, then back across at Carol-Ann. 'Well, thank you for coming forward, Carol-Ann. You've been most helpful,' he said, aware of sounding almost pompous.

Carol-Ann smiled widely. 'Anything for you, Jason,' she responded huskily.

Monica blushed. Jason paled.

Flora almost laughed. But it wasn't the little vamp blatantly coming on to her boss that had her worried. It was the way her boss was being so careful *not* to look at the little vamp's mother.

'Carol-Ann, if you'd just wait outside for a moment,' Monica began, her tone distinctly holding the threat of deferred retribution to come. 'There's just another little matter that I want to discuss with the chief inspector, then I'll join you.'

Carol-Ann got up, tossed her head, and stalked off.

'She hasn't changed much,' Jason commented drolly the moment she was out of earshot.

Monica sighed. 'I'm afraid not. Her latest wheeze is to get into nude modelling. Over my dead body,' she added grimly.

Jason laughed. 'Your husband's already been very helpful,' he said, his voice strangely loud. He coughed, and tried again. 'And whilst I appreciate your help, I want to make it quite clear that I will tolerate no interference with my investigation this time.'

Monica stared at him, feeling ridiculously hurt. 'Of course not,' she said, her pain rather more evident than she'd have liked. 'I just thought that you ought to know what someone told me a short while ago,' she added crisply.

Quickly she told him about Pete Drummond, and how he'd been sure that he'd spotted Malvin Cook in the tent during Sir Hugh's pep talk. A place that, as a non-judge, he had no business being in.

Jason listened in grim silence. 'I see. Flora, have we talked to this Mr Drummond yet?'

'No, sir,' Flora said, without even glancing at her notes.

Jason nodded, then turned to Monica again. 'Well, thank you for this information, Mrs Noble. And of course, if you hear anything more, be sure to tell us. But please, don't go around soliciting information. Leave that to us.'

Monica was definitely feeling miffed now. She'd fondly imagined, after that business at her own vicarage last year when she'd proved so helpful, that Jason Dury might at least think of her as a friend, if not an ally or even an asset. But right now he was treating her like a total stranger. Moreover, like a stranger who was poking her nose in where it wasn't wanted.

Well, never let it be said that she couldn't take a hint! Her colour angrily high, she nodded stiffly and got to her feet. As she did so, she spotted the woman sergeant smiling cattily. Flushing even more furiously, she walked to the door, Jason not far behind her.

Outside, Graham Noble turned and smiled at her. 'Finished?' he asked mildly, noting her high colour and the angry flash in her lovely blue eyes.

Monica nodded, stalking forward quickly to stand close beside him. Urgently, she sought his hand and felt his warm fingers close comfortingly around hers.

Instantly, she felt better. 'Yes,' she murmured, then glanced over her shoulder at Jason and said pointedly, 'all finished now.' She turned her back and began to move off, unaware of the pain and regret that flickered across the policeman's face.

Graham Noble, however, didn't miss it at all. And his hand tightened instinctively around the fingers of his wife as they walked away together.

CHAPTER 15

A few minutes later, Monica found herself watching her husband talk to a rather distrait old lady, and smiled tenderly. The poor old thing had been, she suspected, one of James's stalwarts, and was feeling in need of succour and comfort. For someone so set in their ways, the loss of their vicar was bound to take some getting over.

So naturally, when the old lady had spotted Graham, his dog collar had worked like a homing beacon, and now he was leading her to a deckchair and was leaning over her, holding onto her hand, and talking to her earnestly. Any minute now, Monica thought with a soft little tug of indulgence, he'd set off and get her a cup of tea.

Knowing he'd be some time, Monica looked around and spotted Sir Hugh. He was standing alone beside the pavilion, looking bleak. And suddenly Monica found herself remembering that strange little scene in the tent just before all the mayhem had started. Sir Hugh had been talking to them and then James had come over, and for some reason, the squire had gone all uneasy.

Totally forgetting Jason's strictures to cut out the modern-day Miss Marple act, Monica set off. She noticed that the old soldier, on spotting her, straightened up courteously as she approached.

'Mrs Noble,' he greeted her pleasantly.

'Sir Hugh.' Monica eyed him surreptitiously, wondering what might be the best and most successful way to tackle him. In the end, she relied on the most tried and tested of all tactics: she simply cut the ground out from under his feet, with no messing about. 'I hope you don't have any old skeletons in the family cupboard, Sir Hugh,' she said lightly. 'The last time I had to deal with the police — the murder over at our place, you know — you'd have been amazed at the facts that they dug up. Old family secrets; things that you might have thought buried and forgotten about; irrelevant but embarrassing misdemeanours. You name it, they found out about it.'

Sir Hugh, as expected, looked at first startled, and then downright alarmed. 'Eh?'

'Oh yes,' Monica went on blithely. 'Every one of us had our friends questioned and our backgrounds checked. You'd be absolutely stunned at the things they were capable of finding out about — things that had nothing whatsoever to do with the crime, of course. But to be fair to them, I don't suppose they could possibly know that, until they'd eliminated all the possibilities. Still, it was very embarrassing, I can tell you.'

She was telling the truth, of course, but she was also shamelessly fishing. And from the puce colour that Sir Hugh was slowly going, she knew that she'd managed to hook a very big fish indeed.

'Take the situation between you and James, for instance,' she carried on conversationally. 'I noticed that when you were talking to him earlier on, you seemed a bit awkward around him. And it started me thinking.'

'Now look here, Mrs Noble—' Sir Hugh blustered.

Monica quickly cut him off by waving a hand airily around. 'Oh, I know it's probably *nothing*,' she smiled understandingly. 'But you see, the point is if I noticed it, you can bet your life that someone else did too. And human nature being what it is, and Jason Dury being such a good officer and all, well, he's bound to hear about it in the end. And being a policeman with a case to solve, he'll start digging around. He'll start asking what kind of a quarrel or difference you must have had with the vicar, and sooner or later the rumours will start circulating that you and James were deadly enemies!' She laughed, but with a touch of bite. 'Believe me, I'm not exaggerating. I know from bitter experience how these things can escalate. There'll be so much paranoia about, that's the trouble. Everyone starts looking at everyone else with suspicion or fear. After that affair last year, some of our oldest friends started putting distance between us. It was the same with others in the village, too. And all the time, the police kept coming up with something new about us all. Some secret that seemed ominous. Some family crisis that would have been better kept buried.'

She paused for breath, and risked a full look at him. He was watching her with a mixture of wry respect and near anger.

'Are you trying to make a point, Mrs Noble?'

Monica smiled wryly. 'I suppose I am,' she admitted.

'I think, Sir Hugh, that you and James had some kind of a history together. And now he's dead, I think Jason Dury and his team will eventually find out what it was. And if they have to find out the hard way, there's every chance that everyone else will get to know about it too. So not only would it look better for you to come clean, it gives you the opportunity to do it discreetly. Simply take him aside and tell him yourself, privately. I can assure you that he's a reasonable man, and that he'll consider it calmly and logically. He won't just jump to conclusions. You can trust him,' she added firmly.

Sir Hugh sniffed, obviously not totally convinced by her testimonial, but it was obvious that he was also seriously mulling over her advice. He looked at the fortune-teller's tent and then, strangely, over towards the tea tent. Monica followed his gaze and felt a small jolt of anxiety shoot through her, for the first person she saw was Graham, emerging with the old lady's cup of tea. Then she realized that it wasn't her husband that Sir Hugh was watching, but the eccentric figure of the Dowager Countess of Fulcome, who was still sitting in a deck chair outside.

'Hmm,' Sir Hugh said. He glanced back at Monica, a little sparkle in his eye. 'It's as you say, Mrs Noble,' he said gruffly. 'A family matter, best left buried.'

'Did it give you a motive to kill James?' Monica said crisply. 'That's what matters, you know. To the police, I mean.'

The question was direct enough, and honest enough, to make Sir Hugh stare at her. She could almost see the wheels going around in his head. Finally, reluctantly, he nodded, as if coming to some internal decision.

'You're a wise woman, Mrs Noble,' he said with some respect. 'So I'm going to tell you something in confidence. And if you feel it needs to be said to your chief inspector chap,' Monica felt her breath catch, 'then you can tell him.'

My chief inspector chap, she thought. Why did people keep assuming that the infuriating Jason Dury was anything to do with her?

'It goes back years,' Sir Hugh rushed on, anxious now to get it over with. 'And I do mean years,' he added, his voice barely above a whisper. 'When I was a younger man, I fell head over heels for an older woman. Of course, nothing would ever come of it. She had a wild reputation, and was considered a great beauty of her day. Trouble was, she was married, and very respectably married at that, and . . . well . . . as you can imagine, it burned brightly between us for a while and then fizzled out. I've always liked her enormously, and we're still the best of friends, even to this day.'

'That all sounds very human,' Monica said gently, knowing what her husband thought about adultery, and wisely keeping it to herself. 'Not something that should have happened, of course,' she felt compelled to add, 'but perfectly understandable.'

'Exactly,' Sir Hugh said gruffly. 'Nothing should have come of it. And nothing would have, except . . . well, my wife found out about it. Oh yes, I'd been married for about three years at the time.'

Monica blinked. *Definitely* a good job Graham wasn't hearing any of this. 'I see.'

'She wasn't happy to learn of the affair, of course, but I assured her that it was over. As it was. And because the lady's family *was* very prominent around these parts, my dear wife agreed to, well, forgive and forget, as they say. Not to make a fuss.' He seemed to swell with sudden pride. 'A good sort, my Dora,' he added, with very real affection in his voice now.

Monica's mind buzzed. So his mistress's family had been prominent, had it? Slowly, and with her eyes widening with incredulity, she turned her gaze once more towards the dowager countess.

Of course, she was in her eighties now, but take away forty odd years or so . . . Yes, Monica could well see that Daphne Cadge-Hampton would have been considered a great beauty of her day.

Sir Hugh watched Monica's realization and gave a subtle nod of acknowledgement as she turned back to him. There was no point him denying it when he was giving her the rest of the story.

'But I don't see how James comes into this,' she said, puzzled.

Sir Hugh coughed grimly. 'Yes, well. The thing is, you see, Daphne had her son round about then. The present earl.'

Monica gasped.

'No, no, not that,' Sir Hugh said hastily. 'The boy isn't mine. Daphne swore he wasn't and she's not the sort to lie about a thing like that,' he assured her earnestly.

But Monica wasn't so sure. A young countess with a wild reputation wouldn't have been about to rock the boat by admitting to bearing a son not of her husband's lineage. Still, on the whole Monica tended to agree with Sir Hugh that it *was* one of those things best left buried. After all, what good would come of digging up old scandals now?

Sir Hugh launched into whispered speech again. 'The thing is, when Dora became so ill and came home from hospital that last time, we all knew that she was coming home to . . . well, to die.' He cleared his throat gruffly, then plunged on. 'Well, her last lucid night, she asked for James Davies to come. And I think she told him all about it. She needed to be comforted and told that she'd done the right thing keeping quiet, I suppose,' Sir Hugh was pale now. 'And I never begrudged Dora her confession. It put her mind at rest and allowed her to go in peace. But, well, you can see how it left me.' He shot Monica a pleading look. 'Even though James never mentioned it, or even made any sign that he knew . . .'

Monica nodded. 'Yes,' she said thoughtfully, and not without sympathy. 'I can see why you've felt so uneasy around him ever since.'

Sir Hugh sighed. 'The thing is, Mrs Noble, I've always liked James. I did before my Dora died, and I do now. I never once felt that he'd betray Dora's confidence. I never even seriously considered that he might take advantage of the situation, and of course he never did. But, well, damn it, when a man knows your deepest, darkest secret . . .'

'You just can't act as if he didn't,' she finished for him. 'Yes, I understand.'

Sir Hugh sighed. 'But will the police? As far as they're concerned, it gives me a motive, doesn't it?' He was, she realized with some admiration, very pragmatic about his tenuous position. 'And I did smell that damned rose,' he further admitted. 'I was right there. I could have planted that thingamajig.'

Monica nodded. Her eyes narrowed in thought. 'Does the countess know? About James knowing about your aff— how things had been between you, I mean?'

'She does now. The moment I left the tent after being interviewed, I realized what a sticky patch I was in, and went and told her. But I got the impression that she might have already guessed as much, probably from the way James might have acted around her,' Sir Hugh admitted, thinking he might as well be hung for a sheep as a lamb. 'She agreed with me that we should just keep our mouths firmly shut.' He looked at Monica frankly. 'And I'm still not convinced that we shouldn't do just that.'

'No, neither am I — now,' Monica admitted, surprising him a little. Now that she knew Sir Hugh's secret, she wasn't sure that it would do anybody any good to share it. After all, it had all happened so long ago. And if Sir Hugh had wanted James dead, why wait until now? Besides, this Dr Trenning man was also dead, and according to Carol-Ann it would have been impossible for Sir Hugh to have had anything to do with *his* murder. No, she was sure that Sir Hugh was innocent. She just felt it. Not that her instincts should come into it, of course — she could so easily be wrong. On the other hand, did she really have the right to interfere with other people's lives and future happiness?

Even so . . . Her eyes turned thoughtfully to the figure of the countess. Sir Hugh, seeing her interest, misinterpreted it. 'It wouldn't be fair to dump the old girl in it now, either, would it?' he said softly. 'Not after all these years. Think what would happen if the tabloids got a hold of it. Her son's life would be made a misery.'

But Monica was thinking of something else entirely. Daphne had been a flower judge. Theoretically, all the judges had to be at the top of Jason's list of suspects. Perhaps she *had* already guessed that James Davies had dangerous knowledge about her, as Sir Hugh had said. Would a woman like Daphne kill to keep her son's suspect parentage a secret? The earl would lose an awful lot if it ever came out that he wasn't a true Cadge-Hampton. His title, for a start. The estate. And any money the family might still have. Always supposing that the current earl *wasn't* her husband's legitimate offspring, would a mother kill to protect her son from all that scandal?

Monica rather thought that she might. No doubt about it, the countess was obviously one of those strong-minded women and, moreover, she'd been raised to think that she was a cut above the rest of the mere mortals. She might well have decided to act and damn the consequences. But that meant that she must have been in cahoots with the scientist. Could she have killed Gordon Trenning too? Was she strong enough to wield a blunt instrument? She was so old. Besides, if Carol-Ann was right, the countess was in the flower show tent along with the rest of them when Gordon was killed. Unless . . .

Sir Hugh moved restlessly beside her. Monica, making a snap decision, said quietly, 'If I were you, Sir Hugh, I'd keep this knowledge to yourself for a while longer. With a bit of luck, it need never come out at all.'

Sir Hugh, not surprisingly, let out a huge sigh of relief. Monica, however, felt no such sense of release. Instead, she wandered away, her mind whirling.

* * *

Sean Gregson thrust his chin out belligerently. 'Yeah, I nearly decked the prat. So what?' He'd been folding down his stall when two coppers had come and all but dragged him into the fortune-teller's tent. 'I don't deny it. He was messing my Linda about.'

Jason looked at the man in front of him, accurately pigeonholing him. Hard-working. Not over-bright. Probably good-hearted. 'I see. And in what way, exactly, was he messing her about?' he asked mildly.

'Two-timing her, wasn't he?' Sean said aggressively. 'With some bird over Banbury way. I told her, but she wouldn't listen. Said she was going to marry him. Hah!' Sean snorted.

'Tell me about this fight,' Jason said patiently.

Sean sneered. He was sitting in a chair in front of the two police officers, looking more miffed than guilty. 'T'weren't no fight. Not what anyone would call a *real* fight anyways,' he said disgustedly. 'I never hit him or nothin'. Just told him to lay off my Linda. He sort of blubbed and went all weird.'

Jason's eyes flashed. 'Weird? What do you mean?'

Sean, for the first time, looked a bit shamefaced. He stared down at his bare, hairy arms hanging limply between his denim-clad legs and shrugged. 'Well, it was when I sort of grabbed him, by the lapels, like,' he began, as the silence dragged on his nerves. 'The prat was wearing a suit. I ask you. And, well, he suddenly went weird. He went white as a sheet, the sissy, and sort of grabbed my hand.' He looked up, then quickly away again.

Jason slowly leaned forward. 'Mr Gregson, think carefully,' he said, with such gravity that the mechanic blinked nervously. 'Looking back, do you think he was worried about something he had in his jacket pocket? Up here, at the top,' Jason patted his own inside jacket pocket, saw Gregson follow his movements, and then watched as the other man's face suddenly lit up.

'You know, now that you mention it, yeah. I think he might've been. I've been wondering about that; I wondered if he thought I was gonna try and grab his wallet or summat.'

Jason nodded. He glanced at Flora to make sure that she'd also picked up the significance of it. She had. So Gordon Trenning still had the capsule on him when Sean Gregson had started threatening him. He noted the time the witnesses said the fight had started. The details weren't exact, but they were slowly and surely piecing together a picture of Gordon Trenning's movements that afternoon. Now they knew that the scientist had come to the fete with the deadly capsule in his top pocket. It was still there when Gregson had cornered him. No wonder he'd gone pale! If Gregson had broken the glass capsule, they'd probably both have breathed in the gas and died.

And the capsule must have been planted in the rose by 3 p.m., when the judging started. Some time in between, he must have handed it over to his accomplice.

But who? And when?

'Here, can I go now?' Sean complained belligerently.

Jason glanced at him. 'Is your daughter here today, Mr Gregson?'

'No she bleedin' ain't. She's working, see? You ain't laying nothin' on her. I didn't kill her boyfriend, no matter how it looks,' he added, a shade of real fear in his tone now.

No, Jason thought. I don't think you did either. But he could be wrong. Killers, he'd learned, were like those boxes of liquorice sweets you could buy. They came in all sorts.

'Yes, you can go for now, Mr Gregson,' he sighed wearily. 'But please don't leave the country without informing your local police station.'

Sean snorted. 'The last time I left the country was to go on one of them package holidays to Spain. I did nothing but sit on the loo because of something in the water, and get burned by the damned sun. It was Bournemouth for us after that.'

Flora bit her lip to stop herself laughing as Sean Gregson exited in high dudgeon.

Jason shook his head. 'Well, that's—'

'Sir!' Brian Gilwiddy rushed in, his red hair plastered to his hot, sticky face. 'We've found the murder weapon, sir. It's a bloody great mallet!'

* * *

A few minutes later, Jason and Flora were in the field at the back of the tea tent with a SOCO man knelt down in front of them, watching him work. As Gilwiddy had said, they were looking at a hefty, wooden-handled mallet, the iron head of which was tainted with an ominous, sticky red substance.

'No doubt about it?' Jason asked quietly, just to be sure.

'No, sir. The doc confirms the wound to the head corresponds perfectly.'

Jason nodded and started to walk back to the interrogation tent. 'Any idea where it came from, Gilwiddy?'

'Well, sir, I think we should talk to a man called Ernie Gant. He seems to be the handyman and general fixer-upper around here.'

'Right. Let's have him in then.'

* * *

By the time they'd walked back to the fortune-teller's tent, an ambulance had drawn up to the flower show tent, and the sheeted body of James Davies was being removed. It brought an aghast, general silence over the whole field.

Jason sighed.

* * *

Ernie Gant looked scared. As he walked into the tent he was as reluctant as a Christian walking into an arena full of lions. He looked nervously from the good-looking copper in a suit to the pretty, dark-haired Flora. He wasn't sure which one scared him the most.

'Please, sit down, Mr Gant,' Jason said gently, for some reason feeling in a compassionate mood.

Ernie did so. He turned scared, cow-like brown eyes to Jason.

'Everyone tells me you're the Mr Fix-it around here,' Jason smiled. 'That's a lot of hard work, I bet, what with all these tents and stalls and things.'

Ernie very nearly managed a smile. 'Ah, well. It's for the village. Got to have a bit of community spirit, ain't ya?'

Jason nodded. 'Not much of it about nowadays, unfortunately. Tell me, do you have to use a mallet? A big one?'

Ernie paled. 'Yeah,' he admitted reluctantly, sensing trouble. His throat was suddenly bone dry.

'When was the last time you used it?'

Ernie licked his lips nervously. 'Can't remember,' he mumbled.

Jason looked at him for a few moments, and then had a brainwave. 'Flora, why don't you ask Mrs Gant to come in? If I remember rightly, she's in the tea tent with Mrs Davies.'

Flora, surprised, but not about to second-guess his tactics, nodded and left. And Jason knew he'd done the right thing the moment Vera Gant stalked in. Ernie looked at her like a drowning man spotting an approaching lifeboat.

'Mrs Gant. Perhaps you can help us?' Jason said mildly.

'What are you doing to my Ernie?' Vera demanded, stomping up to her spouse and laying a hand possessively on his shoulder. Almost smugly now, Ernie turned to look at Jason. Get past her, if you can, he seemed to be saying.

'Nothing, I assure you, Mrs Gant,' Jason said mildly. 'But he seems to be having trouble remembering the last time he used the mallet. The one he needed to hammer in the tent pegs.'

Vera's fierce expression lightened as she looked down at her husband. 'You daft bugger,' she said affectionately. 'It were in the tea tent, just before Wendy and the others left. Don't you remember that poor old soul who tripped over the tent peg?'

'Oh, right! Course it was,' Ernie said, and between them they competed to tell Jason all about it.

Flora took notes with burgeoning admiration. No doubt about it, her superior was a dab hand at using psychology. When they were finished, Jason turned to Vera. 'Now, Mrs Gant, please think carefully. Was the tea tent left unattended for any period of time *after* your husband left the mallet there?'

'No, course not,' she said at once. And then instantly looked stricken. 'Well, I did . . . er . . . have to go to the back of the tent once or twice.'

Jason gazed at her blankly for a second, then twigged. 'Oh, you mean to visit the ladies'?'

'Yes. But I weren't gone long,' Vera insisted quickly. 'And there weren't no customers waiting when I got back, neither,' she said ferociously.

Jason smiled a little bleakly. 'No, I'm sure there weren't. Thank you.'

Ernie rose ponderously to his feet, and reached out touchingly to take his wife's hand in his own.

'Oh, er, Mr Gant,' Jason added, as they turned to walk out. 'I want you to go with Constable Gilwiddy here. He's going to show you a mallet. I want you to tell him whether or not it's yours.'

'T'ain't his mallet,' Vera said at once. 'All the tools belong to the social club. Ernie just looks after them.'

'I see,' Jason said, very nearly cheering her on; it wasn't often you saw such wifely devotion these days. 'But you will recognize it if you see it, won't you, Mr Gant?'

'Course he will,' Vera snapped. 'He ain't simple!'

When the couple had left, Flora burst out laughing. She couldn't help it.

Jason grinned back at her. 'Marvellous, aren't they?' he agreed mildly. 'Well at least we have a murder weapon now.'

'Yes, sir,' Flora agreed. 'But everyone seems to know that Ernie is the man with the tools, and anyone and their mother probably saw this woman take a tumble. Or heard about it afterwards.'

'And figured out that it was a good bet that Ernie had left the mallet in the tea tent area,' he followed her line of reasoning easily.

'Then all they'd have to do is keep an eye out for Mrs Gant to abandon her post for a few minutes,' Flora took it up.

'And hey presto, slip inside, find it, and you've got yourself a handy little murder weapon,' Jason said. 'No. Wait a minute. Our killer could hardly have gone about lugging a dirty great mallet with him. Someone would have been bound to notice. He must have taken it straight around to the back and hidden it there, which means definite pre-meditation.'

'And then lured Gordon Trenning around there on some pretext or other,' Flora concluded.

'So. What have we got?' Jason ran over the scenario so far. 'James Davies died first, almost certainly as a mistake, in place of Ross Ferris. Trenning is later lured around to the back of the tent and killed by someone, most likely his accomplice, in order to keep him from talking. And it's possible that he was killed whilst the flower show judging was actually in progress. Carol-Ann said she saw Trenning go around the back of the tent *after* Sir Hugh had called for the judges. The question is how much longer after was it? She didn't seem to know. Ten minutes? Half an hour?'

'But that lets off all the people in the flower tent as a candidate for his murder,' Flora said, exasperated. 'But they're *still* the most likely suspects to have planted the capsule. Since Sir Hugh was seen sniffing the rose after the tent had been cleared of the general public, it *has* to have been either Sir Hugh or one of the other judges who killed the vicar.'

Jason sighed. 'Perhaps Trenning went to the back of the tent not twice, but three times? The first two times he was spotted by Carol-Ann, but not the third time.' But he was already shaking his head as he spoke.

'Doesn't seem likely, does it, sir?' Flora pointed out miserably.

'No. It doesn't,' Jason concurred. 'Which keeps bringing us back to the idea of two different killers. And yet, that doesn't make sense either.' He rubbed a hand wearily through his hair. 'OK, who's next on the interview list?' he asked flatly.

Flora checked her list. 'Er, Her Ladyship, the Dowager Countess of Fulcome, sir,' she said uncertainly.

Jason groaned. That was just what he needed.

CHAPTER 16

Daphne Cadge-Hampton nodded curtly to Jason, cast Flora a thoughtful glance, then lowered herself gingerly onto the chair. It creaked loudly.

Jason fought back an urge to apologize to the grande dame for the makeshift nature of the tent, and instead smiled briefly. 'Your Ladyship. Just one or two questions.'

Daphne inclined her head. Her hair, which had been up in some sort of a chignon, was fast coming loose and sending little twirling tendrils of grey hair falling down around her face, giving her a rather rakish quality.

'Did you see anyone near the rose stand, specifically the Peace entry, before the judging started, Your Ladyship?' Jason began pleasantly.

'Only Sir Hugh, who could never resist 'em,' Daphne responded gruffly. 'He had a good whiff as the tent was being cleared of spectators.'

Jason nodded. 'Anyone else?'

Daphne smiled. 'No.'

She's lying, Jason thought instantly. He wasn't sure why he thought so, just that he did.

'I see,' he said, making his disapproval clear. Daphne's smile grew wider.

'Do you think many people noticed Sir Hugh's enthusiasm for the rose?' he asked next. If he could just get a *feel* about what it was that she was trying to hide then he might discover where best to start probing in earnest.

Daphne shrugged. 'Probably. He made some comment or other about them being his favourite.'

Jason felt a slight twinge as she said this. Was it a hint? If so, what exactly was she trying to tell him? Don't say Sir Hugh was the intended target after all!

'I see,' he repeated blandly.

Daphne shifted a little on her seat. She looked tired, despite her bravado, and he suddenly felt a shade ashamed of himself. She was an old lady after all. Nevertheless, she was definitely trying to keep something back from him, whilst at the same time, leading him in another direction, he thought, stiffening his shoulders.

'Do you know anyone who might have wanted to kill James?' he tried next.

'No.'

'How about Ross Ferris?'

'Why should he want to kill James?' she asked, eyes twinkling.

Jason grinned. She was a game old bird, he had to hand it to her; he'd walked right into that one.

'No,' he said patiently, 'I meant, can you think of anyone who might want to kill Mr Ferris? He was due to judge the roses this year, you know. Not Reverend Davies.'

Daphne's face seemed to close in on itself for a moment, then she shrugged. 'I daresay you can find scores of people who wanted to do in that atrocious little twerp,' she said finally.

'Yourself included?'

Daphne smiled. 'Not specifically. I'm probably the only one whose toes he hasn't managed to tread on,' she added, with a bark of truly amused laughter. 'Probably because I've not got anything that he wants. Still, I suppose I might have thought of knocking him off as a sort of public duty,' she mused in her extremely upper-crust accent, her head cocked mischievously to one side in mock contemplation. 'As a favour to my fellow man, as it were. *Noblesse oblige* and all that bilge.'

Jason grinned again. She certainly knew something that she wasn't telling, and he was experienced enough to know that he was never going to get it out of her. For form's sake, however, he asked mildly, 'Did you have any dealings with Dr Gordon Trenning?'

'Never heard of him,' Daphne said briskly, allowing herself to look majestically bored and then getting ponderously to her feet. 'That all?' It was, of course, more of a command than a question.

Jason nodded ruefully. But as he watched her go, his eyes narrowed ominously. He didn't appreciate being taken for a ride. Even such a classy ride as the one he'd just been given.

* * *

Carol-Ann noticed that the bottom gates were being opened to let out those people who had been cleared as free to go, and who had arrived in cars, and she quickly made her way down there, heading straight to the Linacres' low-slung sports car. It was a deep red in colour — a real classic. And thus, of course, went very well with blondes.

And as she stood looking down at the car, a sudden image came to her of car shows, where scantily clad women draped themselves over bonnets whilst photographers snapped away. It was all a bit naff now, of course, and couldn't even really be regarded as retro, but to a man like Marc Linacre, who was obviously of the older generation, he just might find a pretty girl draped over his car *très nostalgique*.

Doubtfully, Carol-Ann looked around, but for once luck was with her. Only a few cars remained, and she glanced anxiously behind her at the nearly empty field, reassuring herself that all the action was still over by the tents. Gawkers and gossipers were paying no attention at all to the bottom end of the field. So why not? Carol-Ann looked down at her blouse, tied in a knot above her midriff, and chewed her lip nervously. She was wearing a flesh-coloured bra underneath, so she wouldn't really be topless. But it would be dead easy to slip off her blouse and arrange herself across the bonnet as if she were.

Nevertheless, she felt a twinge of unease. Whenever she thought about being photographed, she'd always assumed it would be in a proper studio, with everyone being professional and hardly anyone even bothering to look at her. She'd read that all the top models went about at work half naked, and nobody paid the slightest bit of attention to them, because they were all in the business, and to them it was just like a secretary going to the office to type memos.

But this was a bit different. Suppose someone other than Marc saw her? But then, just rounding the pavilion, the distinguished figure of the photographer suddenly caught her eye, and the decision was made for her. Visions of being the new Olivia Gee flooded her head.

What he'd done once, for her, he could do again!

Telling herself not to be such a chicken, and before she could change her mind, Carol-Ann untied her blouse, slipped it off her shoulders, hoisted herself up onto the hood (which was hot! — *owww!*) and leaned back on one elbow. With frantic haste she made sure that her hair was falling forward over her shoulders and covering her bra. Rather distressingly, she felt her skin beginning to adhere damply to the paintwork.

Then Marc was walking towards her, reaching into his trouser pockets for his keys. She smiled. A rippling breeze, as if in cahoots, suddenly rustled the leaves in the hedge behind her, and gently moved her hair. She was just about to make a frantic move with her hands to make sure the breeze hadn't moved her hair *too* much, when, behind Marc, she saw the familiar dark head of Angela Linacre.

'Oh hell,' Carol-Ann muttered in despair. At that moment, Marc looked up.

His jaw dropped.

And Angela began to screech like a banshee.

* * *

Monica was listening to Vera Gant describe, in meticulous detail, her interview with Jason, and how she'd bested him. She barely recognized the description of Jason, who was by turns 'shifty-eyed,' 'snide,' 'a know-it-all smarty pants' and a 'bully boy of the first order.' After her fury at the way he'd treated her poor helpless Ernie, she garrulously went on to describe how the mallet had been found in the field. All horrible and covered with blood and gore, apparently, and how her poor Ernie had come to be so unfairly under suspicion just because everyone knew he was the handyman. And what man in his right mind would so much as dare to think that her Ernie would go around knocking people over the head with a mallet?

Monica soothed her ruffled feathers as best she could, but carefully filed away the information Vera had provided.

So, it now seemed almost certain that Gordon Trenning had been killed with the mallet behind the tea tent sometime after the flower show judging had started. It was all very interesting and perplexing, but before she began mulling it all over in earnest, there was something she really had to do first. She wasn't looking forward to it, because it was risky, but . . .

'I'd best be off,' Monica said, and then slowly, and very sneakily, made her way towards the flower show tent. Now that the body had been removed, and SOCO would be finishing up in there, it was, she hoped, going to be largely deserted. There was something she just had to look at inside. Something she had to find out about. It was important.

All afternoon she'd been worrying about Malvin Cook's secret visit to the tent. She was almost sure now that she knew what he'd gone in there to do, and why, but she needed to be certain. After all, for those mixed up in it, murder was a deadly serious business, and she had to be absolutely sure of her facts.

Luckily, with the field rapidly emptying now, she managed to get to the side of the tent with nobody noticing her. She didn't realize it, but she spotted the same gap as Sir Hugh's old gardener had done a few hours before, and just like him, she managed to duck and wriggle lithely underneath.

Even as she did it, she wished she hadn't. It was just asking for trouble to cross police lines and actively seek clues. If Jason found out, he'd be furious with her.

As she crouched on the grass under cover of the nearest table, her heart was beating sickeningly as she watched a pair of constable's boots walking about. She swallowed hard, finding her lips and mouth and throat as arid as the Sahara. In fact, she wanted to cough!

She quickly clapped a hand to her mouth and, with some difficulty, strangled the sensation. She could just slither back out again, of course, but even in her panic she'd counted only one set of feet. Just a token man to make sure nobody (like herself) interfered with the crime scene. And she was so close. The table she wanted to look at, in fact, was only a few feet to her left.

And now that she was here, she thought, she might as well make the best of it. Calling herself all sorts of a fool, she duck-walked to the neighbouring table and took a deep breath. Warily, she lifted her head. The constable was over by the vegetable stands, eyeing the beetroot. Perfect. Slowly, Monica shuffled along to the display she wanted, checked the constable again (he seemed to have a fetish for beetroots, seeing as he was now holding them up against the light) and, her heart in her throat, quickly half-rose and began to count.

She was right! She now knew exactly what Malvin Cook had been doing.

'Hey! You!' The surprised, squeaky voice had her heart almost skyrocketing into her throat.

Monica jerked upright and stared, aghast, at the constable. He was still holding a bunch of beetroot in one hand. For a second, the two of them simply stared at each other. It was hard to say which of them was the most surprised or dismayed.

For a wild instant, Monica had an almost irresistible urge to flee. Her whole fight-or-flight instinct nearly had her going up on her toes, ready to race for the exit.

Then the constable flushed. And in a few seconds he was beside her, and was holding her arm in a very firm grip.

Monica found herself wishing heartily that Graham was there.

* * *

Outside, the second ambulance had arrived to remove the remains of Dr Gordon Trenning. The dwindling crowd watched with continued morbid interest.

Jason and Flora were also watching the white-shrouded figure being removed, when Brian Gilwiddy sidled up to them. 'Sir, we found an intruder in the tent. You'd better come.'

Jason nodded curtly, following quickly on his heels.

Inside the tent, Monica was looking as miserable as she felt. Her upper arm was still being held in a worryingly firm grip, and her head swung to the front of the tent as the light was blocked out temporarily. Three figures marched in.

Her heart sank as she met Jason's furious icy blue eyes. 'Sir,' the constable said with some excitement, 'I found her tampering with one of the exhibits.'

'Oh now, really,' Monica felt compelled to defend herself, 'tampering surely isn't the right word! I never touched or moved a thing.'

Well, that at least was true.

By now Jason had reached her, and she could swear the fiery heat of his anger was scorching the air between them.

'I suppose we should be grateful for that, at least, Mrs Noble,' he said flatly.

Monica went pale and Flora Glenn began to smirk. She was rather enjoying seeing the pretty, normally oh-so-composed vicar's wife put out. In fact, it was making her day.

'What are you doing here?' the sergeant asked snappily, lest anyone forget that she was there.

'I just wanted to check my memory,' Monica began, only half lying. 'I needed to be sure of something before I came to you with it,' she added cunningly, and turned back to Jason, who, unfortunately, didn't appear to be in any mood to be mollified.

186

'If you have information for me, Mrs Noble,' he gritted, 'all you have to do is give it to me. I don't suppose it occurred to you that I would have gladly escorted you in here to "check your memory" if you'd simply thought to ask me?'

Monica swallowed. 'Well, no it didn't,' she admitted honestly. Besides, after the dressing down he'd given her, she hadn't really wanted to go cap in hand to him with such a simple-sounding request.

But before Jason could think of how to reply, another constable came rushing in. 'Sir, there's a disturbance in the car park,' the young man panted.

'Not now!' Jason barked.

'But, sir, there's a woman down there demanding that a teenager be arrested for indecent exposure.'

'What?' It was Flora who asked for a repetition, her voice rising incredulously.

The constable glanced down at his notebook. 'It's a Mrs Angela Linacre, Sarge. She's insisting that a Miss Carol-Ann Clancy be arrested for exposing herself.'

'WHAT?' This time the yell of anguish came from Monica. Jason swore graphically.

* * *

The scene at the car park was one of amusement (on the part of the police), outrage (on the part of Angela Linacre), cringe-making embarrassment (Marc Linacre) and feigned bored indifference (Carol-Ann).

When Jason, Monica, and Flora arrived at a brisk trot, Carol-Ann was once more decently dressed in her blouse, which she'd cunningly done up in the normal way, and thus was now looking the picture of innocence. Well, almost. Jason shot her a killing look; it was almost as withering as the basilisk-like glare of her mother. And in the face of this dual assault, Carol-Ann's lower lip began to tremble. In some deep dark part of her she knew she'd been stupid, and she had to fight a childish instinct to cry.

'Now then, what's going on?' Jason demanded coldly. The last thing he needed was a distraction like this!

'This . . . this . . . *creature*,' Angela began, pointing at Carol-Ann imperiously, 'is a menace.'

Monica stiffened. Her hackles rising, she turned on the other woman with a look so furious that even the redoubtable Mrs Linacre quailed. 'That's my daughter you're talking about,' Monica warned her quietly. 'So be very careful what you say.'

Angela sniffed, but sensed in the other woman a force to match her own. 'Yes, well, your *daughter* was draped half naked over my husband's car,' she hissed.

A constable tittered.

Monica looked grimly at Carol-Ann. 'Is this true?'

Carol-Ann shrugged nonchalantly. 'I wasn't to know that she was such a prude, was I?'

This, Monica took for a 'yes.' She heaved a huge, long-suffering sigh. 'Would you care to tell us why? I'm sure we'd all be most interested,' she added.

Carol-Ann tossed back her long blonde hair, but she was beginning to look chastened now. 'I wanted Marc to photograph me,' she mumbled, looking down at her feet.

'He doesn't do that kind of photography any more,' Angela snapped. 'He's been telling her that all afternoon! She's been stalking him. That's what it amounts to. And there are laws against that kind of thing now. I want her arrested!' Her voice had risen to a hysterical yowl by the time she'd finished.

Monica shot Jason an agonized look, and despite everything, he felt himself responding to her unspoken plea for help.

'Are you sure about that, Mrs, er, Linacre?' he inquired mildly.

'Yes.' Her eyes flashed in vindictive determination. Jason cast a quick glance at her husband, who looked as if he was praying, most diligently, for the ground to open and swallow him up.

'I see,' he said thoughtfully, and then he smiled, suddenly enjoying himself. 'That, of course, is your right,' he said smoothly to the irate photographer's wife. 'But I would have thought, myself, that you'd find the negative publicity attached to such a course of action a little hard to take,' he added craftily.

For the first time, Angela's spiteful face seemed to sag. 'I'm sorry?'

Jason shrugged. 'Well, it's the kind of thing the tabloids would find very funny, isn't it? They're bound to make both of you something of a laughing stock. And, of course, once other young hopeful models read about it . . . well, young girls being what they are,' and here he shot Carol-Ann another killer of a look, 'you'll probably find your husband being inundated with wannabe models. Still, you know best,' he said brightly, ignoring Angela's appalled face. 'Sergeant, take down the particulars, and arrest Miss Clancy.'

'No, wait!' Angela yelped, just as Monica got ready to let rip. Angela looked at her husband, and bit her lip. Visions of beautiful nymphets camping out on their doorstep day and night flashed before her eyes. 'Perhaps it might be better just to . . . overlook this incident. Just this once! But I want an apology from *her*!' she jabbed a pointing and imperious finger once more at Carol-Ann.

Carol-Ann bristled. 'Now wait just a min—'

'Carol-Ann,' Monica interrupted harshly. 'Apologize. At once.' She didn't raise her voice. She didn't scowl. She didn't even grit her teeth, but Carol-Ann took one look at her mother's face and ducked her head, and, blushing beetroot red, she muttered a painful apology.

Angela nodded grudgingly, then sniffed, grabbed her husband by the scruff of his neck, quite literally, and marched him away.

Another constable tittered.

Monica stared at her daughter. 'I want a word with you, young lady,' she said ominously, and took a step forward.

'And I want a word with you,' Jason growled, but under his breath. He supposed that the explanation for whatever she'd been doing in the flower show tent could wait.

Besides, it was high time that he had a word with the last of his primary suspects: Malvin Cook.

CHAPTER 17

Jason was still in an unsettled mood as Malvin Cook was led in. He'd deliberately saved interviewing the gardener until more or less last, in the hope of having received more information on his movements by now. Unfortunately, if anyone other than Pete Drummond had seen the old man in the tent when he shouldn't have been there, they weren't saying. Or at least, not yet.

The moment Jason saw the small, wizened man walk in and sit firmly down in the chair, he knew that he was going to get nothing out of him. He was, Jason realized at once, the kind of individual who would stick to his guns, come what may, with a stalwart pig-headedness that no amount of reasoning or threat could budge. Still, he had to try.

'Mr Cook. You're Sir Hugh's head gardener, I believe?' He began with the easy questions first.

'Yus.'

'And you were in the flower show tent for a while *after* Sir Hugh cleared it for judging?'

'Yus.'

'Why was that?'

191

Malvin shrugged. His face, the colour and texture of wal-
nuts, creased up in thought. 'Just wus,' he said flatly. 'I was
checking our glads,' he added, as an apparent afterthought.

Jason blinked for a moment, then nodded. 'Your gladiolus entry?'

'Yus. We wus gonna win it this year. The cup.'

Jason vaguely remembered seeing a monster of a silver
cup on the top table of the tent, and accurately surmised that
this was the prize in question. 'I see. Tell me, did you see Sir
Hugh sniff the display of Peace before you left?'

Malvin scratched his salt-and-pepper head and shrugged.
'Weren't paying him particular attention. I had my eye on
what the competition had entered, didn't I?'

Jason sighed. 'Who was judging the roses this year?'

Malvin's face solidified. There was no other word to
describe it. It was as if he had suddenly turned to stone.
'Ferris,' he said flatly.

'So were you surprised to hear that it was the Reverend
Davies who actually began to judge the roses this year?'

Malvin's small, deep-set eyes widened in evident surprise.
'Did he, then?' he said, but more to himself, softly, than as a
question for the policeman.

Jason shifted on his seat. He had a feeling that still waters
were definitely running very deep indeed with this old man,
and he was frustratingly aware that he had no idea how to
navigate them. Somewhat desperately, he tried to unsettle
him. 'I understand that you lost your son last year?' But if
he hoped for an expression of shock or outrage, he was to be
disappointed.

Malvin merely shrugged once more. 'Never know what life's
gonna throw at you, do you?' the old man said philosophically.

'But you blame Mr Ferris for your loss?' Jason, feeling
like a bully, was forced to persist.

'So did the courts,' Malvin snapped back quickly.

Jason nodded. At last — some sort of emotional response.
'You'd like to see Mr Ferris dead, I think,' he said softly.

'Yus.'

Jason saw Flora Glenn shift on her seat, caught off guard by the simplicity of the man's reply.

'If I told you that one of the scientists working at the lab had devised a perfect murder weapon, what would you say?' Jason was genuinely curious to see his reaction now.

Malvin shrugged. 'Don't have nothin' to do with anyone in that place,' he said flatly, and without any apparent curiosity. And Jason believed him. To a man like this, it would be the same as fraternizing with the enemy, he could see that at once. Besides, to a lifelong son of the soil, anything to do with science or modern technology would be anathema. So, how likely was it that Malvin would allow Dr Gordon Trenning to become an ally?

He couldn't imagine this stone-faced little man even letting Trenning so much as *talk* to him, let alone convince him that in Ross Ferris they had a common enemy and should join forces. But just suppose he had . . . Could Malvin then have killed Trenning afterwards, not just because he was an accomplice who had to be shut up, but also because he worked at the lab as well? And thus, he was one of *them* and therefore part of the company that was responsible for the loss of his boy — temporary ally or not?

It all sounded rather far-fetched and yet Jason couldn't altogether discount it. Malvin would certainly be strong enough to wield the mallet. Despite his stooped, small stature, this man had years of hard manual labour behind him to give him plenty of strength in his upper arms.

'You were also seen in the flower show tent after the judging had started, Mr Cook. What were you doing there?' he asked sharply.

Malvin stiffened, then shrugged. 'I wusn't there then,' he denied flatly. But his gaze refused to meet that of his interrogator.

'You were seen,' Jason contradicted him, his voice becoming hard.

'I wusn't there,' Malvin Cook repeated. He crossed his arms over his chest.

It was just as Jason had predicted. He knew that the old man would now never budge from that position, and if, in the end, it boiled down to Pete Drummond's word against Cook's, it wouldn't be enough for a jury. Not by a long shot. Hell, it wouldn't even be enough for his own bosses, let alone the Crown Prosecution Service. No, he was going to need much more than this.

He hid a defeated sigh. 'You're not planning on leaving the country any time soon, are you, Mr Cook?' Jason asked.

Malvin snorted in true scorn. 'Nope. Never been abroad before in my life, and don't intend to start now. Me and the wife are happy enough with Weymouth.'

'Good. We'll probably want to talk to you again,' Jason said ominously, but the little man barely acknowledged this sally with so much as a flicker of an eyelash. Instead he rose and trudged out as patiently as he'd trudged in, with that energy-saving lope that a lot of men of his generation had learned to cultivate.

Flora sighed. 'He had motive, sir,' she felt obliged to point out.

'Yes, but did he have the opportunity? Have we got a statement from anyone putting Malvin Cook and Gordon Trenning together?'

'No, sir. So far, the only people Dr Trenning seems to have talked to for any length of time are Melissa Ferris, a man with a beer crate beside the pavilion, and of course Sean Gregson during their little spat. But, if Carol-Ann Clancy is to be believed, he also had that secret meeting with Sir Hugh around the back of the tea tent.'

'Yes, and I think that it's high time we tackled Sir Hugh about that,' Jason mused. 'He's had enough time now to come forward and volunteer the information off his own bat, so it's obvious that he's not going to. Besides, it must have been worrying him all afternoon, wondering if we'd find out about it,

194

so he should be stewing nicely,' Jason smiled wolfishly. 'Yes. Let's have the squire back again.'

Flora smiled and left.

When she returned with Sir Hugh a few minutes later, he walked stiffly to the chair in front of Jason and sat down, careful to pull on the creases in his trousers to keep them straight. 'Chief Inspector?' he raised one white eyebrow courteously.

Jason, however, was not in the mood for social niceties. 'Sir Hugh. You were seen following Dr Gordon Trenning behind the tea tent at some time between 2:30 p.m. and 2:50 p.m. I want to know what that was all about,' Jason demanded briskly.

Sir Hugh went a little pale, then a little red, then coughed. He looked at Jason for a long time, then shrugged and reluctantly reached into his inside jacket pocket. From there, he pulled out a sheet of paper.

'I suppose there's no real harm in telling you. Though I wanted to keep it quiet in case *certain people* got to hear about it,' Sir Hugh began morosely.

'I can assure you I know the meaning of the word confidential, Sir Hugh,' Jason said, a shade sardonically.

Sir Hugh had the grace to look a little abashed. Then he took a deep breath. 'Yes, well. You know about my lawsuit against Ferris Labs, about the loss of my fish stock?' Jason nodded. 'What you may not know is that Gordon himself had had his troubles with that . . . man.'

Jason held up a hand. 'We know all about Dr Trenning's invention, Sir Hugh, and the fact that he believes it was stolen from him by his employer,' he said quickly. He wanted the old duffer to come straight to the point. He was tired of being given the runaround. It felt as if, all afternoon long, everyone, in some way or other, had been playing games with him. Perhaps he was becoming paranoid, he thought, forcing back a grim smile.

Sir Hugh coughed. 'Well, as you can imagine, when I approached Dr Trenning and asked him if he could keep an eye out for anything useful to me that he might discover, he was only too happy to act as my "spy" in the enemy camp, so to speak.' The squire cleared his throat uncomfortably, but ploughed on. 'Well, the thing is, he phoned me the day before the show, and told me that he'd managed to photocopy an incriminating memo that would help me in my lawsuit.' He tapped the folded piece of paper on his knee, then hesitated for a moment as Jason held out his hand for it.

Sir Hugh obliged and Jason quickly scanned it.

It was indeed a photocopied memo, and one that Sir Hugh's lawyers would no doubt be delighted to have, as it tacitly admitted that the financier had known about the industrial accident and seemed to be giving orders to cover it up. It would no doubt result in a hefty fine for Ferris — if Sir Hugh's legal team could get it admitted into evidence, that is. Jason shrugged the thought aside. Such legal wrangles didn't interest him.

'I take it that Dr Trenning arranged to meet you in secret behind the tent and hand this over in person?' Jason asked crisply.

'Exactly,' Sir Hugh confirmed. 'It's not as if he could have risked asking someone else to hand it over to me or trusting it to the post, is it? Not that there was anything in it for him, per se; he just wanted to make as much trouble for his boss as possible.'

Jason sighed. It sounded reasonable. And Sir Hugh had probably promised the good doctor a little monetary bonus, once his court claim had been settled and he'd won substantial compensation from Ross Ferris.

'I see. Tell me, Sir Hugh,' he said, fixing the old soldier with a gimlet eye, 'when you were both being so pally, did Dr Trenning happen to tell you about a clever little device that he'd just made? A tiny exploding capsule containing concentrated poisonous gas?' he added sharply.

Sir Hugh stiffened. 'Certainly not. If he had, I'd have told him he'd be crazy to use it,' the squire said firmly.

Jason stared at him for a few minutes, trying to read the real emotion behind the outraged expression.

Trenning *might* have handed the capsule over to Sir Hugh, along with the memo. If Sir Hugh had already suborned him into acting as his spy, why not also commission him to make a deadly weapon to get rid of the man that they both so bitterly hated and resented? Sir Hugh *might* have planted the capsule whilst sniffing his favourite rose. But the death of Ferris would only have held up the court case considerably, and Jason wasn't convinced Sir Hugh would want all that bother, no matter how much he hated the man. In any case, try as he might, there was still no way that Jason could place Sir Hugh both in the flower show tent *and* behind the tea tent murdering Gordon Trenning at the same time. Which meant that someone else must have killed the scientist. And the idea that there might be *three* people in on it was just too much to swallow. Conspiracies were dicey with only two to keep the secret. Three was just asking for disaster.

And yet — how else did it all make sense?

'Very well, Sir Hugh,' Jason said flatly. 'That'll be all. For the moment.'

The two police officers watched him go, then Flora said quietly, 'He's really got to be our prime suspect for James Davies, sir.'

Jason sighed. 'We still haven't eliminated Malvin Cook,' he reminded her. 'I suppose we'd better have Pete Drummond back and see if he'd be willing to swear to—' Yet again he was interrupted by a constable poking his head through the tent flap door.

'Sir. We've caught Mrs Ferris trying to sneak out of the field,' he said breathlessly. 'She pretended to be with a man in a car, and was guiding him through the gate, but Faraday was suspicious and challenged her. The man in the car confirmed that he doesn't know Mrs Ferris, except to nod to occasionally, and that she didn't come in with him.'

Jason turned to Flora with a grim smile. 'It never rains but it pours,' he muttered. 'Send her in,' he said wearily to the constable. After the time he was having of it, it would be interesting to see just what line the femme fatale in the case was going to take.

Flora felt her hackles rise the moment Melissa Ferris walked into the room. She was so aggressively *feminine*, and everything about her was so clearly designed to attract male attention that it was all the policewoman could do to hold back a snort of scorn.

Flora noticed, as she'd expected to, that Melissa's eyes zeroed in on the good-looking Jason Dury like a guided missile.

'Chief Inspector, is this really necessary?' Melissa asked softly, sinking down onto the wooden foldaway chair as if it were an armchair in a palace. 'I know nothing about anything, I do assure you.'

Join the club, Jason thought sourly. 'Then this shouldn't take long, should it?' he smiled wolfishly.

Melissa smiled dazzlingly back.

'Do you know what class of flower your husband was judging this year, Mrs Ferris?' he began briskly.

Melissa looked blank. 'Not the faintest. Sorry. Don't know, don't care,' she said airily, waving red-painted nails about in a one-handed gesture of exaggerated indifference.

'You're in the middle of a divorce, I understand?' he pressed.

'That's right.' She reached into her bag to light a cigarette. Filthy habit, thought Jason and Flora simultaneously, but Jason, at least, could enjoy the show. The genteel extraction of the cigarette, the single flick of the lighter, the long sultry look through the flame as she suggestively sucked on the cigarette and got it alight.

When she was finished, he said mildly, 'Is it an amicable divorce, Mrs Ferris?'

Melissa laughed harshly. 'Hardly. You obviously don't know my husband, Chief Inspector, or you wouldn't even ask that question. But my lawyers are more than holding their own,' she lied casually.

Jason said nothing for a moment. It was obvious that if Melissa had ever been in the flower show tent, everyone would have noticed her and commented ad infinitum. So she was out of it, at least as far as the planting of the capsule went. But what about as far as killing Trenning?

'You were seen talking to Dr Gordon Trenning fairly early on in the afternoon. Can you tell me what you talked about?' he asked mildly.

Melissa's smile faltered. 'Is it true he's the one who's dead?' she asked nervously.

'Reverend Davies is dead too,' Jason pointed out grimly, and had the satisfaction of making her blush. He'd surmised, quite rightly, that she'd hardly given the dead clergyman a second thought.

'Yes. Yes of course,' she said hastily. 'But I didn't really know him very well. But Gordon—'

'Yes?' Jason said sharply.

Melissa sighed. 'Well, I knew Gordon. And he was rather sweet, in an odd kind of way. He was a bit of a mummy's boy, you know. And then she died, and he came here and suddenly had all these village women chasing after him,' she laughed. 'It was really quite . . . touching in a way, to see the way he reacted to it all. Sort of bemused and pleased and terrified all at the same time. In fact, I rather teased him about it.'

'And this afternoon, what did you talk about then?' Jason persisted.

'Oh, this and that. Nothing specific.'

'Did you suspect that he had a deadly capsule filled with cyanide gas in his pocket?' he couldn't resist asking, and had the satisfaction of watching her jaw drop.

'You're kidding?' she gasped, with, for the first time, something approaching a genuine reaction apparent in her voice.

Jason sighed. 'No, I'm not. I believe he came here intending to kill your husband, Mrs Ferris.'

Melissa flushed a dark ugly colour. 'And he botched it,' she said bitterly and with very real angst. '*Damn*. What a fool. Still, that's just typical of Gordon, I'm afraid.'

Jason almost laughed, her frustration was so palpable. 'It's all very annoying for you, of course,' he murmured. She would have made such a very merry widow.

Melissa looked at him quickly, sensing his antagonism and amusement, and, for the first time, her eyes widened with fear. 'Hey! Look, I had nothing to do with any of this.' She waved her cigarette around jerkily. 'I don't know anything about capsules, and Gordon dying, or anything else. But if you want to ask someone who does, you should see that pompous twit Sir Hugh.'

Jason kept his face perfectly straight. 'Oh?'

'Yes. I saw him, Gordon that is, hand some sort of package over to Sir Hugh earlier on.' She wasn't about to admit that she'd been so intrigued by Gordon's manner that she'd been keeping a deliberate eye on him, even following him around at a discreet distance.

'I see. Was it a small, even tiny package?' He was interested to see if she'd lie.

'No. No, it was a sort of envelope size,' Melissa admitted reluctantly.

'I see. Well, thank you, Mrs Ferris,' Jason said smoothly. 'Oh, and please don't leave London without telling us, will you?' he added sweetly.

Melissa smiled enchantingly. 'Of course not, Chief Inspector,' she cooed.

The moment she stepped out of the tent, a wide, delighted smile crossed Melissa's face. She had him! 'Oh yes,' she muttered excitedly to herself, '*yes!*'

She quickly scanned the field. She had him now.

* * *

In the tea tent, Monica straightened her shoulders and stepped forward. It was high time that she spoke to Wendy Davies. She was aware that the new widow had had her closest friends with her all afternoon, and that Her Ladyship at least could be counted on to keep the well meaning but curious clear of her. But Monica knew that she would have a load of trouble with her conscience later if she put off expressing her condolences any longer.

Vera and another little woman were sitting next to Wendy, trying to keep her mind off things. Vera Gant spotted Monica first. 'Oh, hello, Mrs Noble.'

Wendy glanced up, her vague, watery eyes seeming to look right through her.

'Hello. Wendy, how are you doing? I'm so deeply sorry,' she ventured gently. It was such an inadequate thing to say, Monica knew, but Wendy Davies smiled vaguely.

'Oh, I'm all right,' she insisted automatically.

'Would you like another cup of tea, love?' the little woman said, jumping up and going to the vast tea urns at the back. Vera walked a little bit away from Wendy, beckoning Monica to follow her. Wendy didn't seem to notice, or mind. Monica suspected that by now she was probably used to being talked about as if she weren't even there.

'She's not doing all right at all, poor thing,' Vera whispered. 'And who can blame her? And she won't go home. She seems to think it's her duty to stay here. If you ask me, she's done too much of her duty already. Everyone and their grandmother comes to her with their problems, and her having enough of her own!' Vera said angrily. 'Even that chap who got murdered was pouring his woes into her ear earlier on. Well, you should know, you were there. And now they tell us . . .' she checked hastily to see if Wendy could hear, and lowered her voice even further, '. . . that he was the one who killed poor James. Wicked, I call it. Still, he got what *he* deserved,' she sniffed.

So, the favourite theory was that Gordon Trenning killed James, by mistake presumably, and then someone else, as yet unidentified, killed the scientist, Monica mused. As a theory, it seemed to be as good as any.

Just then, the magnificent figure of the countess came into the tent. She shot a sharp-eyed gaze at Monica, an admonishing one at Vera, then went tiredly over to Wendy.

'Won't you come home with me, Wendy, my dear?' Daphne said, obviously not for the first time, but the wilted blonde head shook restlessly from side to side.

The presence of the countess seemed to have an intimidating effect on the other two ladies, and Monica felt ashamed for leaving it all to them. Nevertheless she made murmuring noises to leave. As she stepped out of the tent, however, she found that the little woman had followed her. Monica wished she knew her name. Mrs Drinkwater, was it?

'I'm so glad you came, Mrs Noble,' the woman twittered. 'What Wendy needs is another vicar's wife to talk to. Her Ladyship tries hard, but . . . well.' She shrugged graphically.

Monica nodded. 'It seems to me that Wendy is still in shock. I don't know that I, or anyone else, can really help her until she's had a chance to get some rest.'

'Oh I know. The poor thing was shaking when we got her back in here. And, you know, she was sick as a dog too? Reaction, of course. Good thing the loos were back there,' the little woman nodded, her practicality and good sense bringing a much-needed bracing effect into the conversation. 'She only just made it in time, mind you, the poor thing. Can't you get that good-looking policeman to let her go home?'

Monica felt herself flush. Why did everyone seem to think she had some sort of influence over Jason Dury?

Suddenly, something started nibbling away at the back of her mind. It was a sensation that she'd only ever felt once before in her life — just before she'd realized the identity of the murderer amongst them back at Heyford Bassett last year, in fact.

She shook her head, but it couldn't be ignored. It was persistent and relentless. A sort of tingling sensation at the nape of her neck that told her she should know now who had killed James and Gordon. And why. She was sure she had all the necessary facts, but she just hadn't arranged them in the right way. It was aggravating, and the little woman beside her was still chatting on a mile a minute, which was not helping her to think any.

'Well, I'll see what I can do, of course,' Monica said, trying to stop the woman in mid-flow, 'but most people are leaving now anyway,' she said, gesturing around the now nearly empty field.

Her eyes narrowed for a minute as she noticed Ross and Melissa Ferris over by the swings, talking angrily. From their vivid gestures and rigid body language they seemed to be in the middle of a showdown.

'I'm sure Wendy will be allowed home shortly, if she wants to go,' she reassured her companion vaguely, and left the little woman sighing unhappily. For herself, she could quite understand why poor Wendy didn't want to return to her empty house.

* * *

Melissa put her hands on her hips and smiled up into her husband's furious face. 'But, Ross, you know that the newspapers pay huge sums for interviews these days. Especially when the scandal is such a big juicy one, as this one is sure to be.'

Ross swallowed back the bile in his throat. 'And it would be just like you to hawk your story around all the dirtiest rags you could find, wouldn't it?' he snarled bitterly.

Melissa smiled and shrugged. 'But, darling, what else can I do?' her eyes glittered. 'The divorce settlement you're proposing is so paltry that I can hardly turn down serious money for an exclusive, now can I? And just think what I can tell them about Gordon,' she carried on dreamily.

Melissa was enjoying herself enormously. The moment she'd stepped out of the tent after talking to that policeman, she knew that she had it made. It wasn't often that Ross Ferris was bested, and she intended to make the most of it.

Ross felt his hands itching to grab her throat. But he was in a bind, and he knew it. When the facts about the double murder here at Caulcott Green came out, it was going to be a PR nightmare. Putting on a brave front and presenting himself as the innocent victim was going to be vital.

But Melissa was a loose cannon. He shuddered, imagining the kind of tripe the newspapers would get out of her. Ross could almost see the humiliating headlines now.

Melissa watched her husband's face twitch and scowl, and knew that he was being eaten alive by anger and frustration. It made her want to laugh out loud. Revenge and victory was such a sweet combination.

'Come on, Ross,' she said softly. 'You know how you hate to be made a fool of in public. And all I want is a reasonable divorce settlement. Just tear up that pre-nup, and let's get together with my lawyers. I'm sure we can come up with a . . . mutually beneficial arrangement.'

And she laughed as he turned and stomped away, because she knew she'd won. The flat in Notting Hill would be hers, along with as big a lump of cash as she thought she could get away with!

Everything had come up roses after all.

And then she laughed again as the aptness of that phrase suddenly struck her.

* * *

Monica made her way from the tea tent to the pavilion, where she'd already spotted the tall, elegant figure of her husband. Suddenly, she desperately wanted to be near him. But as she walked, her mind was whirling like a kaleidoscope, flashing up images at her, nagging away at her for being such a dunce.

It must be obvious, if only she could sort out all the wheat from the chaff.

She could see it all in her mind. James and Ross Ferris, changing flower classes. Sir Hugh declaring loudly how much he loved Peace. Malvin's sneaky entrance into the tent. Daphne Cadge-Hampton and her secret long-ago love affair. Wendy, broken and shocked. James, crumpling to the ground. Gordon Trenning, and the fight with his girlfriend's angry father. Gordon Trenning, dead behind the tea tent, his head bashed in. The capsule. The capsule. Always it came down to what had become of the capsule . . .

By the pavilion, Graham saw his wife coming towards him, and as he watched her approach, he saw her suddenly frown. He noticed that her steps were slowing almost to a standstill, and, pushing away from the wooden wall, he went to meet her halfway. By the time he'd reached her, however, she'd stopped dead in the middle of the field, her expression grim and sad.

'Graham,' she said softly, when he took her cold hand in his. 'Oh, Graham!'

'What is it? What's the matter?' he asked, but in his heart, he already knew. He'd seen that expression on her face once before.

Monica looked at him with big, wide, tragic eyes. 'Oh, Graham,' she wailed, her throat clogged with unshed tears. 'I know who did it. And why. And . . . oh, Graham, I *wish* I didn't!' She leaned forward and rested her forehead against his shoulder, revelling in his strength. She felt his hands come around and press comfortingly between her shoulder blades. Their warmth seemed to seep into her, giving her courage, and at last she raised her face to his.

Tears were brimming in her eyes, threatening to overflow. He took a deep, fortifying breath. 'Let's go and see Jason, shall we?' Graham said simply.

Miserably, Monica nodded.

CHAPTER 18

'Sir, they're beginning to complain that they can't leave,' Brian Gilwiddy said, looking at Jason curiously. The Caulcott Green church clock had just struck seven. It was a good twenty minutes slow, and the remaining witnesses, understandably, all wanted to get off home.

Jason looked across the small fortune-teller's tent, noticing how the yellowing sun was creating the kind of light that made everything seem eerily underwater. It was time to—

'Sir, Mrs Noble and her husband are outside.' Another constable had stuck his head around the door, the same one that had announced Monica earlier. And, sure enough, once again his superior said unhesitatingly, 'Send them in.'

Monica came in nervously, a strangely abashed look on her face. Instantly, it triggered a memory in Jason, of another time and another place, when she'd come to him with just such a look on her face. He said, without heat and without mockery, 'You think you know who did it?'

The two constables and Flora Glenn boggled.

Monica merely nodded. 'I'm sorry,' she said, somewhat inanely. 'But yes, I think I do.'

Jason nodded, and glanced across at Graham, who looked steadily back at him, blank-faced. For a second the two men, so vastly different in so many ways, looked at each other in perfect accord. Then Jason stirred restlessly. 'Gilwiddy, tell the people on the gate that nobody's to go just yet — but that they'll be able to leave very soon now,' he commanded.

'Sir,' Gilwiddy said smartly, trying not to stare at Monica. At the tent flap, the other constable withdrew, correctly interpreting Jason's get-lost glance.

'Sit down, both of you,' Jason ordered wearily, indicating the two chairs. To Flora he said simply, 'Take every word down. I'll record it as well for a backup,' he added, and set his mini tape recorder going.

Flora, looking nettled, got out her notebook and pencil again, her lips held in a tight line of disapproval. It was clear that she didn't expect anything of earth-shattering importance to happen next, but also that she hadn't quite got the nerve to say so.

Jason looked at Monica. His level ice-blue eyes met her softer cornflower-blue gaze, and he took a slow, deep breath. 'You don't look happy,' he said quietly. He remembered that whilst he might have a heart hardened by years of dealing with criminals, this lovely young woman was still, in so many ways, worryingly innocent. And thus capable of being hurt. And here he was, once again, watching her being hurt.

Monica shook her head. 'No, I'm not happy. It's all so sad. So horribly sad,' she agreed dismally.

'Do you think we're dealing with just one killer or two?' he asked, wanting to get that out of the way first.

'Oh, one.'

He nodded. That seemed, on the face of it, almost impossible. And whilst he wasn't getting his hopes up too high yet, he nevertheless had the sneaking feeling that, just like last time, this woman had come up with the answer. Was it just a knack she had? Like some women could knit fantastically patterned jumpers, and others could paint pretty watercolours? Was Monica Noble just a natural detective? He was beginning to think so, but he'd reserve his final judgement until he'd heard her out. After all, her success last time could just have been a fluke.

By her side, Graham was looking more and more tense. She'd been totally silent on their walk over, and he had no idea what she was going to say, but a sick feeling, deep in the pit of his stomach, had him almost scared.

'All right,' Jason said, ignoring the you've-got-to-be-kidding looks his disbelieving sergeant was throwing at him. 'Who do you think is our killer?'

Monica took a deep, deep breath. Then she blurted miserably, 'I think it's Wendy Davies.'

Flora all but snorted. In his chair, Graham jerked further upright, opened his mouth, took one look at his wife's wretched face, then closed it again.

Jason blinked. *The widow!* Normally the first suspect in a killing was the spouse, of course. But this time he hadn't really given her much thought at all. In fact, in view of her precarious physical and mental state, he realized that he hadn't even got around to interviewing her yet. Perhaps if he had things would be different now.

'I see,' he said slowly. Then added simply, 'Why?'

Monica sighed. 'Look, it's all so . . . muddled. I've been hearing things here and there, putting bits and pieces together from what I've seen with my own eyes and should have connected, but didn't. Plus, with James being one of Graham's oldest friends, I'm aware of some of the background. Perhaps that's why I didn't see it at first — because I really, really didn't want to.' She gave another sigh, struggling to know where to start. 'Can I just tell it how I think it happened, and then leave it to you to . . . you know, pull my theory to pieces?'

And she really does want me to be able to do just that, Jason thought sympathetically, as once again their blue gazes met and held. She really wants to be wrong, and for me to prove it to her. But she doesn't really believe that I'll be able to.

'All right. You talk, we'll listen,' he said agreeably.

Monica nodded. 'It all begins, I think, with the death of little Tommy Davies. He was an only child, and his mother adored him. I mean, really *adored* him. He was her whole world. I think she and James had such a hard time having a baby that when Tommy came along . . . well.' Monica shrugged a shade helplessly. 'I don't know if you know all the circumstances of his death, but on the night that he was ill, we were all almost snowed in, the weather was that bad, and James was out in the Davies's only car, visiting a sick parishioner. I'm not sure who it was, but . . .' Here Monica waved a hand vaguely in the air. 'It doesn't really matter. The thing that *does* matter is that, in Wendy's mind, her husband wasn't there when they needed him so badly. He'd left them alone, taken their only means of transport and it was all up to Wendy to cope by herself. Of course, you and I and everybody else knows that it wasn't anybody's fault. Both James and Wendy thought at first that Tommy just had a touch of the flu. And James wasn't able to predict the future any more than anyone else can. If he'd known what was going to happen, of course he wouldn't have left. But he did, and Tommy died, and I don't think Wendy ever got over it. Or forgave James.'

Monica paused for a breath, then glanced across at Graham, knowing that what she had to say next would affect him the most, and wanting him to know that she wasn't getting at him personally. 'But it got steadily worse after that. Wendy was still "the vicar's wife." She was still expected to perform. To chair the meetings. To deal with everyone else's crises. To be the sturdy British oak who never wavers. I know it's not your fault,' here she reached across for Graham's hand, 'but I don't think you clergymen fully realize just how much pressure there is on your wives. We're not allowed to be like other wives. We're supposed to be perfect, all the time. And, of course, Wendy couldn't be.'

She was talking to him now, to her husband, and both Jason and Flora felt a shade uncomfortable to be listening in. Nevertheless, both of them were beginning to feel that she might be on to something. As police officers, they had already learned that motives arose not just out of the classic three — love, money, and revenge — but were also brought about as a result of many other kinds of human weaknesses and pain.

'What Wendy needed was to grieve,' Monica continued, her tear-bright eyes still on Graham, who was pale and thinking furiously. 'To get angry. To rant and rave and do all the other things that mothers who've lost their children are allowed and even encouraged to do. But she couldn't. And I think it all built up in her. I think she went . . . well . . . a little bit mad.'

Here she turned to Jason. 'Oh, I don't know whether you people would agree. I mean, I'm not a doctor, I don't really know what you or the law would call technically "insane." And I'm not trying to build up a defence for her. I'm just telling you what I feel myself. What others have been telling me. From Vera Gant to the milkman, everyone's been telling me that Wendy's been hit hard. And I think the Dowager Countess of Fulcome knows it more than most.'

Flora stirred restlessly on her seat. 'It's a long jump from harbouring a festering grudge against her husband to killing him,' she said, still with an edge of mockery in her voice. 'And especially in such a spectacular way.'

Monica nodded. 'I know,' she said, her voice a little wobbly as she tried to keep a hold of herself. 'And that's what's really so tragic about all this. I don't suppose for one moment that Wendy would ever have even *thought* about killing James if things hadn't happened the way they did. I think she would just eventually have had a complete breakdown, and would have been hospitalized for a while. With therapy, she would have been helped to grieve, and perhaps even feel some sort of happiness again. At worst, she and James might have ended up divorced. But — and this is what's really so hard to take — circumstances went so badly against her. A whole string of them. It's enough to make even sceptics believe in the Devil.'

By her side, Graham stirred. 'What do you mean?' She was getting into his territory now.

'Well, just look what happened,' Monica said, brushing away a single tear that had escaped and was running down her cheek. 'She's in the tea tent, minding her own business, when in walks Ross Ferris. As usual, he's cock-sure of himself and full of beans, and makes some remark about the flower show judging. Wendy, in all innocence, tells him that the real challenge this year is the dahlia class, and instantly Ross Ferris reacts.'

'Wait a minute,' it was Jason who interrupted. 'If you're telling me that Wendy Davies knew about the swap of roses for dahlias made between her husband and Ferris, you're on the wrong track. Ferris himself swears that nobody was around when he asked James to swap with him. James may well have had opportunity to mention it to his wife before the actual judging began, but surely not enough for some kind of plan to be enacted.'

Monica smiled. 'I daresay you're right. But how hard would it have been, do you think, for Wendy to have guessed what Ferris was going to do? You've interviewed the man — did he strike you as being subtle?'

Jason grimaced. 'No.'

'Exactly. Wendy tells him her husband's got the choice job, and instantly he gets this look on his face and walks off. Ask Vera Gant what she thought about it — she was there. I'll bet she confirms that it was as obvious as pie what Ross Ferris was going to do. And Wendy Davies knew it too.'

Jason slowly rubbed the side of his nose with a forefinger, a habit of his when he was thinking hard. He pictured the scene, and slowly nodded. 'OK. Let's just say, for argument's sake, that I concede that it wouldn't have been impossible for Wendy Davies to have guessed that Ferris would bully her husband into swapping his roses for the dahlias. But what does that prove?'

Monica smiled wearily. 'Nothing in itself. But who should come in a few minutes later, but Gordon Trenning.'

Jason and Flora both stiffened. Of course, Trenning had been seen in the tea tent several times, but so had everyone else there that day. It had been a scorcher of an afternoon, and everybody had been in and out seeking tea or cold drinks. Nothing in that to arouse *their* suspicions.

'So what are you saying?' Jason demanded.

Monica sighed. 'You should have another word with Vera to confirm what I'm about to say. But I was there myself and saw Gordon Trenning come in looking very woebegone and nervous, asking for James. Obviously, he had something on his mind. And now, I'm going to theorize a bit, but not, I think, beyond the realms of reasonable supposition,' Monica insisted. 'First, tell me what you know about Gordon Trenning,' she added.

Jason was willing to go along with her — up to a point. 'He's a man who'd been wronged by his employer; that was no great secret. Ross Ferris probably robbed him of millions. Stole his creation. Made him a laughing stock of the scientific community, or so he believed. But,' Jason was beginning to guess — or think he could guess — where she was going with all this, 'we've found no evidence so far to suggest that Trenning was a violent man.'

'Exactly,' Monica put in. 'Not the sort, you'd think, to simply get a gun and just shoot his boss?'

'No,' Jason concurred. 'From everything I've been hearing about him, he was a rather ineffectual sort of man. But a thwarted one, nevertheless. So what does he do? He makes a dastardly clever exploding cyanide gas capsule,' Jason finished, somewhat impatiently. 'Monica, we *have* already gone into all that.'

'I'm sure you have,' Monica agreed soothingly, 'but bear with me. Have you considered how he felt *once it was done?*' she urged.

Jason's eyes narrowed. With care, he attempted to put himself in Gordon Trenning's shoes. 'OK. Let me see. Here's a man who's probably enjoyed himself enormously building this little gadget. He's had a lovely time fantasizing about the moment of his boss's death.' Jason's eyes widened as he suddenly saw the point she was trying to make. 'But it's all been in his *head*,' he hissed, sitting up a little straighter. 'Making it was no doubt a wonderful catharsis. But, suddenly, he's left with an actual murder weapon, right in his hand. He takes it to the fete, but he's almost certainly already regretting doing so.' Jason wondered if he was getting carried away, but it had a very realistic feel to it. It simply *felt* right. Anyway, there was no harm in theorizing.

'And then he has the near miss with Sean Gregson,' Monica chipped in encouragingly.

'Right. And if the capsule had broken when he was grabbed by the lapels, they would both have been dead. Suddenly, it's all very real. And he was scared. Very scared,' Jason carried on.

Graham nodded. 'I see what you're both getting at. To him, the *making* of the capsule was all the release he needed.'

'Right. But the actual *killing*?' Monica shook her head. 'No. I don't think so. I think he was too much of a rabbit to want to go through with it.'

Jason, who wasn't as scared of using psychology as a tool as some of his fellow officers, was prepared to go along with this — again, up to a point. Just to see where it led. 'Fine. So, say the set-to with Sean Gregson brought him to his senses, what do you think happened next?' he demanded.

Monica began to look grim. 'Well, what do you think a mummy's boy would do when he's in trouble?'

'Run to mummy.' It was Flora Glenn who spoke, surprising everyone into looking at her for a moment. She flushed.

'Yes. But mummy's dead,' Monica said. 'So he had to find someone else. Someone who would make him feel better. Who'd take the capsule from him and destroy it and, most importantly of all, would never tell on him. Who does that sound like to you?'

'A vicar,' Graham said flatly. 'And he was right. If he'd gone to James, James would have counselled him. And he wouldn't have reported him unless he'd thought that there was any continuing danger to Ross Ferris.'

'Which, by now, there wouldn't have been,' Monica said firmly.

'But there's no evidence for all this, or that he even spoke to James,' Jason pointed out.

'No,' Monica agreed heavily. 'Because when he went to the tea tent, he found someone even better. Mrs Vicar. Another mummy. In other words, Wendy Davies.' Monica shook her head as she thought back to that scene in the tea tent. 'Poor Wendy. At the time, I could see that Trenning looked in need of help, and almost offered to step in, but Wendy beat me to it. James wasn't there, but she was. I even saw Wendy take him to one side to chat. I lost sight of them for a bit until Wendy came back a while later. But it's not hard to guess what they talked about, is it?'

All afternoon something had been nagging at her, insisting that she'd seen or heard something important. But it just hadn't occurred to her, until a few minutes ago, what it was.

Jason was leaning forward on his seat now. 'You think Trenning gave her the capsule?'

'Don't you?' Monica challenged. 'After that near miss with Sean Gregson he was probably desperate to get rid of it. And Wendy, being Wendy, would have listened to him, and soothed him, and told him that he was doing the right thing, and that of course she'd take the nasty, dangerous thing off him. And probably promised him that she'd talk to her husband about it, and not say a word to anyone else.'

'But would Trenning really just hand it over like that?' Flora said doubtfully. She too was beginning to get caught up in the tale, in spite of herself.

'Why not? Don't forget, Gordon was used to doing what a mother figure told him. And Wendy, in spite of everything, still had that aura of . . . kind competence about her,' Monica answered, her voice as tired as she was beginning to feel.

'All right, so she suddenly has this fantastic gizmo given to her,' Jason said briskly. 'But you're contending that she actually *used* it?'

Monica nibbled her lower lip. 'Yes. It's all those circumstances conspiring against her again. She had *time* to think

214

about it, you see. She knew what Ross Ferris must have been planning to do — swap flower classes with her husband. She knew, thanks to Trenning, how easy it was to kill someone. Just hold your breath, plant the capsule, remove the tiny covering from the little sponge so that human breath would set it off and . . . there you go. No more husband. Your son's death avenged. And no more life as a duty-bound vicar's wife. Like I said, I think she was a little mad by then. I think she was utterly desperate. I think, in her confused mind, she saw some kind of freedom for herself in killing James.'

For a moment the room was silent as everyone considered her words.

'So far I agree everything's *psychologically* sound,' Jason said. 'But what about the rest of it?'

'The rest of it was easy,' Monica said bitterly. 'Even there, fate was conspiring against her. Or with her. Or . . . whatever. She even shared a table with James. How easy it must have been for her to plant the capsule unseen and unsuspected. Dead easy, in fact,' she added sadly, then winced, the unintentional pun making her wish that she'd chosen her words with better care.

'But she wasn't the only one with motive and opportunity,' Flora pointed out stubbornly. 'What about Malvin Cook?'

Monica, to everyone's surprise, suddenly grinned. 'Oh, I know what old Malvin was up to,' she said. 'That's why I had to go back to the tent and check. When you caught me, I was counting the number of flowers on each of the gladiolus stems.'

Jason blinked. 'Huh?'

'Why, the clever old sod . . .' Graham said, understanding Monica's drift instantly.

Monica nodded. 'I know,' she grinned at her husband. Then, taking pity on Jason's puzzlement, she explained. 'Earlier on, we'd all heard Sir Hugh threaten to fire him if they didn't win the Cadge-Hampton Gladiola Cup that year. Oh, nobody took the threat seriously, but I'll bet Malvin was just as miffed as anyone to discover there was an entry that could upset their victory. Especially when the contender was Ross Ferris! You can imagine how *that* rankled. So Malvin sneaked back into the tent to simply snip off the bottom flower on each of Ferris's stems.'

'Why?' Flora asked, fascinated in spite of herself.

'Because the judges, amongst other things, think the perfect flower stem has to have so many flowers out in bloom on it. I can't remember now how many it is for gladioli. Five? Six? Anyway, when I counted the flowers up, *all* of Ross Ferris's entries had one less flower on them than the rest of the other entries. And you could even see the pale green scar on the stem where they'd been snipped off.'

Graham shook his head, almost in disbelief.

'So you see, Malvin Cook *did* go into the flower show tent sneakily, and for nefarious purposes,' Monica confirmed. 'Just not to plant a murder weapon, but to nobble his opponent!'

Flora, who'd momentarily stopped scribbling, suddenly set to on her shorthand again.

'For a while there, we were looking very strongly at Sir Hugh,' Jason mused. 'He was seen sniffing the Peace, giving him the perfect opportunity to plant the capsule. He hated Ross Ferris. And we know now that he and Gordon Trenning had a little arrangement of their own going on.' Briefly, he told them about their rendezvous behind the tea tent.

Monica shook her head firmly. 'No. If Sir Hugh was going to kill someone, he'd do it face to face. The soldier's way.'

Flora shifted on her seat. 'You've explained about the Reverend Davies. But what about the murder of Gordon Trenning?'

Monica's face paled. 'Yes. That was bad. I mean, I know James's death was bad but . . .' She faltered, shook her head, and took a deep breath. 'This is how I think it happened. Wendy knew, once James was dead, that Gordon Trenning would realize what she'd done and go to the police.'

'So he had to die too?' Jason said. 'A bit cold-blooded, wasn't it?'

Monica licked her dry lips and nodded. 'Yes, and I think that's going to haunt her for a long time to come. When she's back to being her normal self again.' She shook her head, forcing herself to carry on. To think logically and freeze out her emotions as best she could. If she stopped to think about what Wendy would have to go through . . .

'Has anyone told you about the lady falling over in the tea tent, and how Ernie came to get the mallet?' she asked.

Jason nodded and she rubbed a hand wearily across her forehead. She was feeling as wrung-out as a dishrag. Nevertheless, she ploughed on gamely.

'It was just after Ernie had fixed the tent peg that Sir Hugh called the judges to the tent again. At this point, we were all outside comforting the woman who'd taken the tumble, and Wendy said something about going back for her handbag. *When the tent was momentarily empty.* It was the only chance Wendy had to take the mallet from where she'd seen Ernie toss it and transport it to the back of the tent and hide it in the loos.'

'That's premeditation,' Jason said sharply.

'Yes. I know,' Monica said miserably. 'After, well, after James died, she was counting on the fact that someone would take her back to the tea tent. It was the obvious place after all — under cover, and with hot sweet tea for shock ready on hand. And, of course, that's just what happened.'

'And that's significant how?' Jason pressed.

Monica sighed. 'How long do you think it was before the rumours started to flow that someone had died in the flower tent?' she asked quietly.

'Not long,' it was Graham who spoke.

'No. And what do you think would have been Gordon Trenning's first reaction to it?' Monica turned to look at him.

Graham paled and nodded. 'Yes, I see. He'd already be nervous and highly strung. If he'd heard that someone had died, his own guilty conscience would immediately have him wondering if his capsule was somehow involved,' he predicted.

'And of course, he would have seen Wendy being helped into the tea tent,' Monica took up the tale once more. 'You can bet that he was keeping a worried eye out for her, if only to see that she brought her husband over to see him. And seeing her leaving the flower show tent so soon, he was bound to be worried. He'd want to know what was going on. And because he'd been around the back of the tea tent before, to talk to Sir Hugh—'

'He'd know there was a way in there without being seen to enter,' Jason interrupted. 'But wait a minute, none of the ladies who were with Wendy Davies mentioned seeing him in there. He could hardly have just walked in and demanded to know what was going on.'

'No,' Monica said grimly. 'It was more . . . horrible than that. The other woman who was with Wendy — I can't remember her name — said that Wendy was in shock, that she was shaking and ill.'

'Acting, no doubt,' Flora grunted.

'No, I don't think so,' Monica said, more inclined to be charitable. 'I think she probably *was* in shock. I wouldn't be surprised if she'd thought that in reality the capsule would never work. But it did, and suddenly her husband really *was* dead.'

'Let's get back to Trenning,' Jason said flatly. He'd had enough of speculation; what he wanted now were more solid leads. Facts that he could get his teeth into.

'All right,' Monica agreed. 'He sees Wendy being led to the tent, and hears the rumours. Someone's dead and he's worried. It's imperative that he find out what's happening, so he goes to the back of the tent and Wendy is waiting for him.'

'Wait a minute,' Jason said.

'How do you make that out?' Flora said, at the same time. Monica held up her hand. 'If you talk to that little woman again, she'll tell you that Wendy went to the loos to be sick. Very sick. Naturally, Wendy would have made sure that they didn't go with her, and they wouldn't have pushed it. It's one thing to offer tea and sympathy, but when somebody's being physically sick, the last thing they want is someone around to witness it. It's one of the most embarrassing and horrible things that can happen to someone in public, and no one wants anybody around to hear and smell and . . . well, you just don't. Especially if you're a lady,' Monica added, a shade primly.

Jason nodded. 'OK, I'll accept that. But they wouldn't have left her alone for long,' he pointed out.

'They wouldn't have needed to,' Monica pointed out sadly. 'Through the tea tent's open front, Wendy would easily have seen Gordon approach and veer off to go around to the back – he may even have signalled her, discreetly of course. She'd have known that he was after a private word with her, and that she was being given the perfect opportunity to deal with him. She wouldn't even have to come up with a plan on how to find him or engineer the use of the mallet without being seen. How long would it take her to feign sickness, nip out the back, reassure Gordon that her husband had died of a very natural heart attack, and then, when he'd turned around to leave, lift the mallet, bring it down on the back of his head, and then toss the mallet over the fence?'

'Not long.' It was Graham who finally spoke into the appalled silence, echoing what they'd all been thinking.

'No. Not long at all,' Monica agreed grimly. 'Then it's back to the tea tent and her friends to simply wait. Don't forget, everyone else was still in the flower show tent at that point. Wendy was the only one who'd been in both the flower show tent when James died, *and* in the tea tent when Gordon died.'

'And there she stayed,' Flora said softly. And shivered.

'Perhaps she wanted to stay in the tea tent so she could hear all the developments of the case, but it may just be that she didn't want to go home and have to face up to what she'd done,' Monica ventured.

Once again there was a long moment of silence.

'It all fits,' Jason admitted at last. 'All along we've had trouble connecting the two murders. Finding someone who could have done both. And had a reason for committing both.'

'I'm only surprised no one else suspected her,' Flora said flatly. Like her boss, she had no more doubts that Monica Noble had got it right.

'Oh, but someone did,' Monica contradicted softly. 'I think someone else was on to her right from the start.'

Jason stared at her for a moment, then his eyes narrowed, and he slowly nodded. 'The countess,' he said softly. 'And you weren't totally right when you said that Wendy was the only one in both the flower show tent and the tea tent. Her Ladyship was also in both.'

Monica nodded. 'Yes, exactly. And I think she's one smart and on-the-ball woman. I think she knew how close to breaking point Wendy really was. Whether she actually *saw* her do anything, or whether she just put it together, like I did,' Monica shrugged, 'I don't know.'

'And she'll certainly never tell us,' Jason predicted wryly.

'No. But all along she wanted to get Wendy away from here,' Monica pointed out. 'A woman like Daphne Cadge-Hampton feels a very strong sense of community. I think she'll probably get Wendy a top-notch lawyer and stick by her through thick and thin.'

Jason rubbed his eyes tiredly. 'She might get away with the manslaughter of her husband due to diminished responsibility, but the murder of Gordon Trenning . . .' he shook his head.

He turned to Flora. 'Right. Now we know where to look, it shouldn't be too hard. We'll already have fingerprints from the mallet, and I want Wendy Davies's clothes gone over by forensics too. And for pity's sake, get me some corroborative testimony.'

When he thought of all there was still to be done, he could only hope that they'd find enough evidence to convict.

'I think you know,' Monica interrupted diffidently, 'that if you tackle her with it straight out, she'll probably give you a full confession.'

* * *

Monica was to be proved right about the confession. Wendy Davies, when questioned, did indeed admit to both killings, breaking down thoroughly and being sent at once to a secure psychiatric facility.

She pleaded guilty in court four months later.

And, barely a week after that, as they were sitting in the living room of their flat back at Heyford Bassett, Monica and Graham's local news programme began to give out a short report on her sentencing.

Monica rose hastily and switched off the television. Graham, watching her, held out his arms, and when she'd snuggled up against him once more he held her close. He'd buried his old friend, taking the service in James's own parish church, and now it was time to let go.

'Do you think they'll hold another flower show next year?' Monica asked, her voice a little muffled, since her head was tucked under his chin and her ear was pressed to his chest, listening to the comforting rhythm of his beating heart.

'I imagine so,' Graham said quietly. 'Life goes on, after all. They've already appointed another vicar to Caulcott. And I don't think Sir Hugh or Her Ladyship will let the tradition die along with James. Which is just as it should be.'

'Yes,' Monica agreed stalwartly, then added more tentatively, 'but if they *do* have another flower show, let's not go.'

'No,' Graham agreed, his hand tightening on the top of her hand and squeezing gently. 'We won't go,' he promised.

And kissed her.

THE END

THE JOFFE BOOKS STORY

We began in 2014 when Jasper agreed to publish his mum's much-rejected romance novel and it became a bestseller.

Since then we've grown into the largest independent publisher in the UK. We're extremely proud to publish some of the very best writers in the world, including Joy Ellis, Faith Martin, Caro Ramsay, Helen Forrester, Simon Brett and Robert Goddard. Everyone at Joffe Books loves reading and we never forget that it all begins with the magic of an author telling a story.

We are proud to publish talented first-time authors, as well as established writers whose books we love introducing to a new generation of readers.

We won Trade Publisher of the Year at the Independent Publishing Awards in 2023. We have been shortlisted for Independent Publisher of the Year at the British Book Awards for the last four years, and were shortlisted for the Diversity and Inclusivity Award at the 2022 Independent Publishing Awards. In 2023 we were shortlisted for Publisher of the Year at the RNA Industry Awards.

We built this company with your help, and we love to hear from you, so please email us about absolutely anything bookish at feedback@joffebooks.com

If you want to receive free books every Friday and hear about all our new releases, join our mailing list: www.joffebooks.com/contact

And when you tell your friends about us, just remember: it's pronounced Joffe as in coffee or toffee!